DIRTY Business

RICHARD ALLEN

Richard Allen is a retired senior police officer who, in addition to uniform duties, saw service with the CID, the Vice Squad, the Drug Squad and Special Branch.
Richard is the author of two best selling works dealing with police management and leadership,
which were listed as recommended reading by both the US Department of Justice and the Police Staff College.

'DIRTY Business' is the first in the
Mark Faraday Collection.

By the same author

Non-fiction:

Effective Supervision in the Police Service

Leading from the Middle

Fiction:

DIE Back

Darker than DEATH

Published by MARS Associates

www.richard-allen-author.com

Member: Crime Writers Association (UK)
Member: International Thriller Writers (USA)

To Ann,
my wife and best friend

'There is no priority higher than the prevention of terrorism'

John Ashcroft

'All terrorism is theatre'

Raymond Kelly

Chapter 1

Wednesday 11th April.

County Wicklow, Republic of Ireland.

'WILL I be forgetting your birthday mother?' asked Tim Pat O'Brien. He was always charming, even now as he spoke on the phone.

'You will not,' was her assertive but warm reply.

'I'm a thinking I should be with you more mother,' he said, 'so I'll be after visiting you this evening for supper and staying the night.'

'You'll be staying for the 12th, you always have?' The sharpness had left her voice now.

'That I will and I shall be bringing some dancing girls from Machen Street.'

'You're a *jackeen* if ever there was one Tim Pat O'Brien, and I'm a fool for loving you all these years.'

'Bless you mother.'

'And bless you my son.' It was the way they always ended their conversations.

'Won't you be staying a while longer mother?' asked Mary, as she gently took the phone from the frail, old lady's hand.

'No,' she replied with resigned sadness. As always, her daughter and only grandson would take her home. It wasn't that it was far, about five and a half miles, from Ashford to the cottage near where the Vartry River tumbles down from the reservoir above. But although there was electric lighting and water now, it was also a lonely and dank place for a ninety-three year old.

She would not move of course. It had been her father's cottage before hers and she and her husband, Michael Pat, had lived there until he went up north as a member of the 3rd Western Division of the IRA in Sligo. That had been in the April of 1922. She thought of his beautiful tenor voice and, for a moment, could see him and hear his gaiety as he sang 'The Broad Black Brimmer' and 'The Boys of the Old Brigade'. It was a sad, bitter-sweet memory.

Michael had been a handsome, tall man, particularly in his fawn trench coat buttoned to his neck, and with his cloth cap worn jauntily over his left eye. He was killed, with four others of his division, in action against the British on the 17th May. Their second child, Tim, was born in the December.

Now, seventy-six years later, and four hours after their telephone conversation, Tim Pat drove alone from Dublin on the N11 to Bray and then on to Newtown Mount Kennedy, passing the beautiful Glen of the Downs on the right. It had rained earlier in the day but, unlike England, there were few April showers and it had dried quickly in the afternoon sun. The soft rain had come again now adding a blueness to the Wicklow Hills and a richness to nature's colours endlessly changing as the clouds drifted by.

At Roundwood, beside the Vartry Reservoir, O'Brien turned his Vauxhall towards Ashford. The detour would add miles to his journey but, by this route, he had ample opportunity to check if he was being followed. He was sure that he had not, but since that phone call two months before he had become more wary, more cautious.

It had been at precisely 7pm when the phone had rung at their headquarters. All five men had expected it but, when it rang, they tensed. The atmosphere had an embarrassed schoolboy jollity about it, as if they were engaged in truancy or defying the headmaster's latest rule. The telephone call instantly put an end to those thoughts. The atmosphere changed.

Daniel O'Callaghan looked at John Pearse through the upward swirls of grey cigarette smoke with a tight-lipped smile and raised one of his eyebrows. Both turned towards Tim Pat O'Brien at the head of the table, behind which was draped the green, white and orange tricolour of Ireland alongside the insignia of the New Irish Republican Brotherhood.

Across the worn, green baize table were the two junior members, Fuller and Dolan, their eyes darting over the other men's faces with expectation to see what action their three senior colleagues on the headquarters' staff would now take.

The telephone rang a third time. If O'Brien waited any longer the others would sense weakness, although they had already noticed the rigidity of his mouth and chin which was not disguised by his casual, 'Let's be seeing what the man has to say.'

He picked up the telephone. 'Yes?' he said.

'Nelson's Column, London,' the reply came in a cultured English voice. He had used the agreed code words.

'Nelson's Pillar, Dublin,' replied O'Brien firmly, his anxiety diluted by the ironic thought that republicans had blown up the 1808 O'Connell Street monument in 1966.

'St. Patrick will be pleased,' said the caller. It was confirmation. It was him. O'Brien had not bothered to disconnect the relay speaker. All could hear.

'I have now attended to the troublesome item as requested,' said the caller, 'all that now remains is for you to conclude the arrangements. My instructions are simple. They are clear. You will ... '

'Before you'll be going any further,' interrupted O'Brien, 'we have had to reconsider the value of the work you have done for us.' The caller allowed O'Brien to continue. 'We think the first instalment was generous. We are grateful, that we are, for you helping us out like you did and so we'll be paying you another £50,000.'

The caller's tone remained the same, cold and precise. 'You agreed to pay me £100,000 as a consultation fee and a further £100,000 upon completion. It is ... '

'Well, we'll be doing no such thing,' interrupted O'Brien and, seeing the strained grins of support, added, 'In fact, we won't.'

'You have interrupted me again,' replied the caller who continued in a cold, level tone. 'My business arrangements are always made on the basis of trust, reinforced by reputation. It is clear that I must make an example of those who welch upon agreements. Consequently, I shall kill you and then contact your colleagues again to finalise our business.'

Click. The line was silent, as was the room.

Now the silence was only broken by the monotonous and steady drone of his Vauxhall car. Just before Ashford he turned right and a mile later was in the thickly wooded scenic glen. O'Brien smiled to himself as he thought how aptly this glen was named.

He had to use the gears more as he passed through oak and conifer. This was hiker's country. O'Brien dropped to second gear and the small engine laboured in the dusk. These journeys, the distance travelled, had become more tiring recently; a reminder of his age, if that was really needed. He also realised that he needed to acquire a car with a larger engine and automatic transmission. Although tired he had not however failed to notice the Land Rover a few miles back. This would not be the first time he had been stopped by the Irish army or the Garda Siochana. If they searched his car they would certainly find his second pistol which he now carried since he had reneged on his deal with the Englishman. There was only one Land Rover. That would be six men at most he reasoned - but all in a confined space. That was good and evened the odd. He was not unduly alarmed. Lately he had used his long years of experience to confuse and mislead unwary opponents. As a result, he was still alive and they were all dead. O'Brien smiled again as he considered his advantage and muttered: 'The odds could be worse,' as he adjusted the pistol in his waist band.

A few minutes later, the smile faded from his face as the Land Rover moved even closer and began to overtake as the road ground up and around, O'Brien's tired eyes on the road in front yet flitting constantly to the right like a moth attracted to a flickering flame.

As the Land Rover passed O'Brien by the smell was intense. The trailer it pulled rattled and bounced about. As it did so, green-brown lumps of manure slithered down the sides, splattering on the road, some onto the Vauxhall's windscreen from the spinning trailer's wheels. There was a metallic clunking as the driver of the Land Rover clumsily attempted to engage a lower gear, losing for a few seconds the power to the axles, only a little but sufficient for the trailer to collide with the Vauxhall's front bumper and grill.

The Land Rover stopped on the narrow bend blocking the road. O'Brien slowed to a halt about ten yards behind, his right hand at the pistol's butt. He had good vision even in the early evening light and he could see the rustic, slightly stooping, limping figure clearly now. He began to relax his grip only to grasp the butt more firmly again at the movement in the rear of the Land Rover. There was no need. The man was alone, the movement in the rear just some empty sacks swaying from a hook.

'Oh, Holy Mother, will you see what we have here,' said the slightly stooping figure in the lilt of a native of Galway. 'I'm begging your pardon; it'll be the cow shit over me boots. Your front's done for.'

O'Brien stepped from the car. The stench was now even worse as he looked at his Vauxhall Astra and saw the damaged plastic bumper and grill. What he did not see until it was too late, was the left hand jab to his jugular; silent but sufficient to momentarily stop the blood flow to his brain. Unconsciousness flooded over O'Brien as his knees buckled and he slumped to the road.

The stooping man moved to the Vauxhall's boot and opened it. Leaving the boot lid up, he returned to the old Irishman, picked him up with ease and placed him in the boot. He looked casually about. No one was on the road. He felt into his inside pocket and drew out a clear plastic bag and placed it over O'Brien's head, sealed it at the neck and then shut the boot lid closed.

The stooping man was no longer stooping or limping. He briskly walked to the turbo-diesel Land Rover, started the engine again and effortlessly engaged the gears. He was able to turn a short distance after the bend, then drove down the hill, up on to the grass verge and passed the stationary Vauxhall, entering once more the conifers and oaks of The Devil's Glen. O'Brien would never smile at that name again.

On the outskirts of Ashford, the Land Rover was driven down a *bohreen* and parked against a long old stone wall. The driver got out and in the shadows of the dense beech tree and against its smooth silver grey bark; he removed the well-worn tweed jacket, pullover and dungarees he was wearing. These he placed neatly behind the passenger seat, he then strolled to the main road and crossed to the small car park behind the noisy public house. The hired Peugeot 604 was still there and more cars had now filled the car park. He unlocked the door and sat in the driver's seat, his feet still on the ground outside. He removed his Wellington boots and stood them up neatly as if to attention, then slipped on his Barker shoes and closed the door. The engine came to life immediately as he turned the key. He drove out of the car park and back towards Killiskey.

In Killiskey he pulled into the hotel's gravelled car park. It was a beautiful building in a beautiful setting, one hundred and twenty-four years old with large bay windows under pitched eves, the mellow stone illuminated in the glare of orange floodlights. He carefully alarmed his rental car then walked briskly through the hotel's twin glass doors. The receptionist glanced up, recognising 'Mr Stone' in his cavalry twills and highly polished brown shoes, the maroon and green handkerchief protruding from the top pocket of the well-cut Harris Tweed jacket. He smiled, smoothing his neatly groomed sandy-coloured hair over his right ear. It was an unnecessary gesture but one that he knew would have the desired effect upon Janet.

'Good evening, Mr Stone,' she beamed. Did you enjoy your day?'

'Janet, it was delightful,' Hadfield charmingly replied, holding her attention with his pale blue eyes, 'just as you said it would be.'

'Your key, sir,' she said brightly, 'and the coffee you asked for is in your room.'

'Ah. Kenya Peaberry. Thank you,' he said as he took the key. 'I shall have dinner at nine, if I may. All this exercise has made me quite hungry.'

'Of course, Mr Stone,' she said as he walked across the panelled hall and up the fine, wide wooden staircase.

He entered his suite on the second floor and went to the windows overlooking the stream, pushed open one of the leaded windows and breathed in the cool night air.

'Well,' Hadfield said to himself as he leaned out and pulled the window closed, 'I wonder how quickly they'll pay up now?'

Chapter 2

Friday 17th August.

Bristol, England.

MARK FARADAY stood at his second floor office window, immaculate in his uniform, the three silver Bath stars on his shoulder epaulettes bright against the black serge. He looked out across the Floating Harbour, so called because a system of lock gates ensured that the harbour was always full of water and ships would always remain afloat within it. To the left he could just see and admire the spire of St. Mary Redcliffe Church. In front of him was Redcliffe Parade, above Midland Wharf where the old *Pyronaut* fire-fighting boat used to be moored. The terraced houses of the Parade stood proud against the sky-line, confident and bright, the keenly sought after homes of the young executives. Immediately in front of him was Bathurst Lock leading to the basin itself.

For a moment, Faraday was pre-occupied with the little scene in the lock as a *Moody 425* made its way out into the Floating Harbour, pure white with furled sails and the two-man crew in pale blue foul-weather gear. The forecast of rain did not dampen their spirits as their boat moved to port, past the new town houses of Bathurst Wharf towards Prince Street Bridge.

Chief Inspector Faraday returned to his desk. His thoughts went back over a couple of years when he had served on this district as an inspector. The old station had been cramped and inadequate and known as a place to send difficult constables. His new district headquarters had only been open for a year and incorporated the old 1955 station which had been designed so as to accommodate two police launches. It occupied a prime position on the site of the old sand and gravel wharf, some would say more suited to a luxury hotel than for a district police headquarters.

Mark's office was well appointed with a large desk with a computer terminal and a comfortable executive-style chair situated in a corner at right-angles so that by looking to his right he could see out of his large, deep, full length window across the harbour. There were two bookcases against the wall above which were framed photographs, one of him as a recruit at Chantmarle in Dorset, the national training centre, some fifteen years before, another as a CID student at Hendon in London and a third of his father in uniform receiving the Stamford Efficiency Trophy from a Lord Mayor of Bristol. Immediately in front of his desk were a coffee table and four easy chairs. One door led to the secretary's office, another to his en-suite toilet and a third out into the corridor.

Although the accommodation and facilities for all were excellent and the views near perfect, the atmosphere in the station was wrong. There was no bounce or vibrancy about the place and this was due to Wynne-Thomas, the superintendent, who would mask his insecurity by surrounding himself with less able men and a continuous exercise of overbearing authority. The result was that the men and women carried out their duties superficially with no great enthusiasm or imagination. There was a dead hand on the tiller, and this morning there was little hope that the superintendent would weaken his restrictive grip. The buzzer sounded.

Chief Inspector Faraday rose from his desk with resigned acceptance and walked through the communicating door into the secretary's office and tapped on the superintendent's door. He walked in. The usual ritual would be observed. The superintendent, who resented what he viewed as the young chief inspector's privileged background, university degrees and future prospects, would carry on writing hunched over his desk and then silently wave a hand to the most uncomfortable chair in the office.

The office was virtually identical to Mark's except that it occupied a corner position so that two walls were glazed, giving a panoramic view of Redcliffe Bridge and the church to Bathurst Wharf.

'They're sending me to the Staff College for three months on the OCC,' referring to the Operational Commander's Course at the Police Staff College at Bramshill. 'They're going to tell me how to be a superintendent,' grunted Superintendent Wynne-Thomas from behind a cluttered and disorganised desk, his jacket unbuttoned and greying hair unkempt.

'Oh yes, in early September. I saw it in GOs, sir,' replied Faraday, his right hand fiddling with his jet black hair at his temple, a habit he realised was caused by frustration.

The superintendent ignored Mark's effort at conversation, peered through his owl-like glasses and ran his pencil over a desk calendar. 'I'm taking annual leave before I start on the 10th. Then I shall take annual leave when I get back. With Christmas, I'll be away until the 7th January.'

'Very good, sir.'

'I expect it is "very good, sir",' he said with a sneer. 'You can't wait to move in here and take over, can you?'

'I'm keen, of course, to have another opportunity to be in charge, but I'll keep to my own office and get the Acting CI to take over this one, if that's alright with you?'

Wynne-Thomas could not understand this logical reasoning and said aggressively, 'This chair not good enough for your arse then?'

'No, it's not that. It's simpler if I stay where I am. It saves me moving all my kit and bits and pieces about, thats all.' Wynne-Thomas hunched back over his papers as if to ignore Faraday, who nevertheless asked: 'Who will be my Acting CI, sir?'

'Passmore, I think,' he replied dismissively without looking up, although the appointment of Passmore would already have been known to him and sanctioned by the chief superintendent.

That decision suited Faraday well but clearly didn't suite the superintendent, who continued in a resentful tone. 'Just you remember that you are only the *acting* superintendent. That means you're just a caretaker. That means that you just look after *my* district for *me*. You don't make any alterations.'

'I shall take care of it for you, sir.'

'That remains to be seen,' then curtly added, 'There's nothing else.'

'But I understood that there were quite a few major operations in the pipeline?' queried the chief inspector.

'Did you,' said the Welshman. It wasn't a question. 'Then this should test you shouldn't it. *My* secretary and Sergeant Hodder will have all the details you require.' He paused and picked up the telephone. 'Now I've some private phone calls to make.'

There was no friendly or professional advice, no encouragement or support from the experienced superintendent for the young chief inspector. The superintendent merely suggested that one of the sergeants would be able to brief Faraday on forthcoming operational issues. It was nonsense; of course, a scenario so often acted out before to wrong-foot the younger man. Faraday turned and walked back to his office and shut his door quietly. He looked out across the harbour in silent reflection and utter contempt for Wynne-Thomas, a man so unlike his father. Mark thought of the comments made by his father when he was first promoted: 'Your mother and I are very proud of you, Mark, but one thing above all else you must remember, you must never let your men down. If you do, we won't be quiet so proud.' He missed them both. He stood there quietly for some minutes until distracted from his thoughts by the publican of the Ostrich Inn, adjacent to the lock, who was clearing his waterfront tables in preparation for the lunch-time custom. He thought of the forthcoming five months as superintendent in temporary command of the district. He would have to cancel any plans for a week's leave in October, but still he reasoned, at least it wasn't to be Stacey as his deputy. Passmore would be a very much more capable second-in-command. He was bright and lively, certainly the best inspector on the district, one who had introduced more workable initiatives than any of the other six uniformed inspectors. Faraday sat at his desk and keyed in Sergeant Hodder's extension. The call was taken immediately.

'Derek,' he said, 'I assume that you will have drafted the orders for any forthcoming operations, so I will need you to bring me up to speed. The superintendent will be off shortly for about five months, so, if there is anything outstanding I will need to run it past him. Are you able to come up and brief me now?' Sergeant Hodder replied in the affirmative. 'Excellent,' said Faraday, 'see you shortly,' as Faraday replaced the phone, Jane Hart, the superintendent's secretary knocked on the door.

'I thought you might like Mr Wynne-Thomas' diary.' Jane Hart was always the same; never ruffled or moody, as bright as a button and a competent secretary, petite and very pretty with dark brown hair.

'Has he finished with it, Jane?' said a bemused Faraday.

'He's gone, Mr Faraday,' she said hesitantly after a short pause.

'Gone!' said Faraday, looking at his watch. 'What do you mean gone, it's only ten past three?'

'He just said that there was no point in his hanging about and said "See you in the New Year".' She stood there, demure and embarrassed for him.

'OK,' he said, controlling his anger. 'Thanks, Jane. I'll look through and see what commitments he's pencilled in. Meanwhile, see if you can find Inspector Passmore for me and ask him to join me now, if he's free, and with all known commitments for the next seven days.'

Ten minutes later, Faraday was still thumbing through the diary as Martin Passmore knocked on the door and walked in.

'Martin,' said Faraday with a smile, 'I've just been told that the superintendent is away at Bramshill, absent altogether for about five months. I shall be acting and you, Martin; I'm pleased to say will be the Acting CI.' Martin was clearly pleased but confused as Faraday continued. 'I'm not getting into the ball game of criticising Mr Wynne-Thomas; but I have not been briefed at all and all I have to go on is his diary. I have asked Derek Hodder to join us.'

'This is bloody stupid, sir,' said Passmore. 'You had this last time. It's about time something was done.'

'Take a seat, Martin,' said Faraday gesturing towards the easy chairs near the window. As Passmore settled, Faraday continued. 'It isn't the way to do business, I agree, but neither would I be expected to criticise a more senior officer. Our task is to get on with it,' he said as he joined Passmore at the coffee table. 'I propose to have a morning conference at nine sharp with you, plus the duty inspector and the DCI to discuss operational matters. At 11 o'clock, we will all have coffee here for twenty minutes. During that time we can discuss anything you like, decorating, our cars, last night's TV or work. In that way we'll get to know each other and how each of us thinks. Little things will inevitably crop up for discussion which would otherwise be overlooked only to get out of hand later on. Are we agreed?'

'Seems good to me,' said Martin as Jane appeared in the doorway with three cups of tea, followed by Sergeant Hodder.

'I thought these might help,' she said brightly, wrinkling up her nose. Faraday and the secretary exchanged smiles. Women found Faraday attractive thought Hodder, yet he was still single, and he often wondered why.

Chapter 3

Sunday 2nd September

Dublin, Republic of Ireland.

IT WAS drizzling as the man knocked on the door of number 23. The off-white lace curtains in the front room window moved a little but were not pulled back. The occupants, satisfied at the identity of the caller, went into the hall and opened the front door. Light flooded out to illuminate John Pearse, the New Irish Republican Brotherhood's chief of intelligence.

'Will you be coming in John, and I hope you'll be having a bottle?' called the occupant convincingly. Pearse stepped in out of the rain and shook hands in the cramped hallway before entering the little front room. The heavy curtains were drawn across the small bay windows. Music began to play and laughter could be heard.

Fifty-two minutes later at 7.12 p.m., Sean Dolan, the NIRB's chief of plans and operations, tapped on the wet front room window of number 117 in the same gaunt terraced street. Sean was welcomed in, the curtains of a similar front room were drawn across and a television switched on.

At 7.30 p.m., both men had entered number 59 by the kitchen door and were shaking hands with the NIRB's chief of staff, Seamus Fuller. As their eyes became accustomed to the darkness, they could see the balaclava-clad figure armed with his pistol in the kitchen and another of Fuller's henchmen in the gloomy hall. In the darkness the three leaders made their way up the stairs to the back bedroom. The brown curtains were already pulled tightly closed. Fuller switched on the single, shadeless light.

The room was spartan and musty and some of the wallpaper had discoloured as a result of dampness. An ill-fitting pink-coloured carpet was on the floor and a large, bare, green painted kitchen table occupied the centre. There were three wooden chairs against the table and two brown and beige-coloured easy chairs each side of an electric fire in the grate. On the chimney breast was a crucifix and in the corner of the room, near the window, some cardboard boxes.

These three were odd bed fellows. Fuller and Dolan were taller than the nattily dressed Pearse. Pearse and Fuller were four years younger whilst Dolan was only thirty-seven. Fuller was carrying a little too much weight, his nervousness always apparent in smile and speech, whereas Pearse had a predatory glint in his eyes as he constantly played with his pointed chin and equally pointed but broken nose, evidence of his former prowess as a boxer. Dolan was more like a manager of a small supermarket in appearance, with dark and well-groomed hair and piggy eyes close together. He affected a cultured air that irritated Pearse.

'Well my friends,' said Fuller dispiritedly, brushing his greasy grey hair back behind his temples with both hands as the three men sat at the table. 'I'll tell you what I've been told by the Council.' He knew that to mention the *Council* would guarantee their attention and would emphasise his authority.

'They aren't pleased, that they're not,' said Fuller.

'Why in heaven's name not?' Dolan asked.

'We'll not be getting the Stinger missiles for a while yet', both men looked at him questioningly. 'Don't ask me why cause I'll not be knowing, least I'll not be telling now. The plan to sink the cruiser *Belfast* at London Bridge has been considered but it's like Fort

Knox since the Arabs have been more active, so that's out. Our reconnaissance unit was compromised at Tower Hamlets and with the Special Branch arrests at Preston; the Council were looking for something to cheer them up.'

'But we've been going bloody hard,' protested Pearse.

'They think they're side shows,' said Fuller dismissively shaking his head.

'Well that'll be cheering us up then,' said Dolan.

'Look, the Council,' said the chief of staff, 'are pleased with the laundry, restaurant and video levies and our provision of security services. C13's activities against us have been no more than an irritant. O'Grady's move into the gaming machines is going well, but all we're doing is collecting money. Our active operations have cost us some good boys and the mortars we got from Iran have been inaccurate, although it has discredited the Brits and upset the Prods. But,' he looked at both men for effect, 'there's a danger that war weariness is infecting the volunteers.' They nodded, and then Fuller continued in a matter of fact tone. 'Punishments have been meted out, but some are disillusioned with the Good Friday Agreement and our numbers are falling ... slightly falling,' he corrected himself for fear of his remarks being reported as disloyalty by the others.

'Volunteers came forward after the Harrogate Conference Centre and the pipe line jobs,' chided Pearse fingering the pointed end of his broken nose. He must be careful he thought not to show his resentment at Fuller's elevation to chief of staff.

'Very true,' agreed Fuller.

'But they fell again I'm thinking when those anti-tank missiles were seized by the Garda at Kilkeee,' cautioned Dolan.

'The Council,' said Fuller, bringing the attention back to himself, 'believes that the implementation of the Good Friday Agreement and everything that followed from it isn't worth toilet paper. What we've now got is no more than a devolved government of sorts for Ulster, a reduction of the number of British soldiers and some amnesties. Those treacherous Sinn Fein bastards are all smiles now but it is well short of the United Ireland that is our right.' The table was thumped in support as Fuller continued contemptuously. 'Sinn Fein, the IRA and the other weasels and traitors, have all cosied-up to the Brits with their pretty jobs in Stormont, the seats at Westminster and glad-handing with the Americans. We, the NIRB, are the only ones left in this fight but we have been side-lined. We'll be needing to remind the Brits, and our own people, that we are still to be reckoned with.' There were more vigorous nods of agreement as Fuller continued less emotionally. 'We must take action that makes the Brits, and the world, not just sit up, but sit back in shock. They must know that the NIRB must be listened to.'

'That will be needing something spectacular,' goaded Pearse respectfully. 'At the moment, the world is not looking to Ireland at all, so they're not, let alone the NIRB. The papers spend most of their time looking at the threats to European capitals, the Middle East or the fucking environment.'

Back in February, Pearse, O'Callaghan and O'Brien had been the top three and Fuller and Dolan the juniors. Now the pack had been shuffled. It had only been O'Callaghan's promotion to the Council and the headquarters' staff that had allowed him to keep his position as intelligence chief.

'Aye, it will require something that attracts world attention,' confirmed Fuller, 'and that is your task Sean.'

'Are you offering any suggestions, Seamus?'

'Maybe a hotel bomb, like the IRA,' Pearse suggested enthusiastically, forgetting his resentment.

'No,' replied the Chief of Staff firmly. 'It would take too long to set up. The Brighton Bomb took the IRA two years and that would upset the Americans. They will make comparisons with Oklahoma, their embassies and the World Trade Centre. But you're right you are that we need to do something that will make it clear to everyone that we are people to be reckoned with and feared.'

'Does the Council believe that this will help the cause?' Dolan asked. Pearse, still playing with his nose, looked at Fuller hoping for an indiscretion.

'The Council's view,' then added quickly, 'and mine, is that the Brits, and the Americans for that matter, are eager to be rid of Ireland once and for all, but we need to be pushing them harder. The more pressure we put on the Brits, the sooner they'll meet us over the table, and the sooner we'll be having a united Ireland.'

'Maybe so, but we'll have to be pushing them hard,' mused Pearse.

'Europe would not be standing in our way,' said Dolan. 'Brussels secretly discussed a united Ireland with the IRA a while ago.'

'But they left empty-handed, as before. And what happened, their volunteers drifted away right enough,' countered Pearse.

'We have had the prison releases, but they are just gestures,' said the Chief of Staff bitterly, 'and the momentum is falling away. What we need is something big, something that takes them by surprise and renews the pressure.'

'We could blow up Buckingham Palace,' sniggered Pearse.

'Shut up!' snapped Fuller, surprised at his own sharpness.

'No, that won't be doing at all,' said Dolan moderately, 'but we could blow up one of their power stations.'

'Oil refineries in the north-east have been targeted, but that has not be enough to be bringing the Brits to heal, why should a power station?' sneered Pearse, although the prospect did not seem unattractive to Fuller.

'But it would if it were a nuclear station,' replied Dolan, as if the thought had only just entered his mind, a thought that was key to his future plans.

'You might be having something there, Sean,' said Fuller, then asked: 'Who do we have to pull off that sort of job, Sean?'

'You won't be liking it,' replied Dolan as if he was reluctant to be drawn any further into the debate.

Fuller rose to the bait. 'I have full authority. They want, no, insist upon success Sean, and it's to you I'm looking as my chief of operations.'

'Well, you'll be wanting it to succeed then?' He looked at the other two men slowly in turn.

'Naturally,' replied Fuller, taking the lead. He had only been appointed three months before and had not been the immediate choice, but then there had been little alternative. After O'Brien's death, they had appointed Kelly, but he had been killed on active service at Newtown Hamilton. Fuller must not fail.

'Then should we not be using Johnson?' proposed Dolan cautiously.

'You must be fucking mad, Sean Dolan,' said Pearse angrily as he rose to his feet, rocking the table and toppling his chair into the grate.

'Well, you're the intelligence man, you bloody think of something?' challenged Dolan now also on his feet. 'All you could ever do was think of a fucking name for him.'

'Shut up both of you', whispered Fuller, glaring at them both. All three men froze their pistols out and cocked as they heard movements downstairs. Tense moments passed.

'Alright, alright,' said Fuller in a harsh whisper, 'it was our boys downstairs, obviously think we've woken up the whole street. Take a few tops of those bottles and let us all be sitting down.'

Pearse took a bottle from one of the cardboard boxes and petulantly removed the top. He put the bottle to his lips, some of the contents spilling onto his jumper. Dolan picked up two bottles and two glasses and returned to the table, placing one in front of Fuller. They all sat down.

'I'll just be wanting my protest recorded,' said Pearse, clearly still smarting at Dolan's suggestion. 'Tim Pat O'Brien was my friend and godfather to my eldest.'

'There are no records here, John. Please be sitting down again, you'll be knowing how we value your advice,' said Fuller. 'Now Sean, you were saying?'

'I said what I said. I hadn't given it a lot of thought,' although, of course, he had given it a great deal of thought.

'That's right enough,' said Pearse still seething with anger.

'Look,' said Dolan defensively, 'he did for General Dickson, that he did, and the pipe lines before that. He could do as much again for a power station.'

'He did for Tim with a plastic bag, the cowardly bastard,' snapped Pearse, 'for Christ's sake, Tim was an old man; he was seventy-six, seventy-six.'

'Come on, John,' said Fuller soothingly, 'can you be giving us an alternative?'

'Yes, we can have some more bombings,' replied Pearse unconvincingly. He was weighing the alternatives in his mind, but knew he was struggling, anger confusing his thoughts. Dolan remained silent and Fuller took the lead again.

'Do we have the active service units in place or could we? And do we have the explosives, John?'

'The ASUs are Sean's, and you know we haven't. The explosives will have to be got on the mainland and used there. The quarries here are as tight as a drum. In any event, the Special Branch and MI5 are everywhere and helped by those treacherous bastards in the CIA.'

'Sean?'

'We could activate an ASU over there, but if their past record is anything ….' He did not have to answer the question further.

'Have you not any more information for us Seamus about the missiles?'

'We can be forgetting a re-supply for a while,' he replied, then after a moment added, 'The Iranians are squabbling amongst themselves and couldn't organise a piss-up in a brewery, the Syrians blow hot and cold as you know. The Russian mafia have shipped some to us but they're missing, or so they say.'

'Missing?' queried Dolan.

Fuller looked at his chief of intelligence who obviously knew. 'They shipped some to us last month but they vanished.'

'Arms don't vanish,' said Dolan.

'They do all the time and these have. We think ours are in Sierra Leone or Chad.'

'So. What are we to do?' Dolan persisted.

'Were you being serious Sean, about a power station?' asked Fuller with ill-disguised desperation.

'As I said Seamus, it was just a remark, but it worked before with the pipe lines. If Johnson does the job well we can use the success as we think fit and to our advantage. If he cocks it up then we know nothing about it. He does all the work, we could just sit back, Seamus,' said Dolan, wondering whether he had overplayed his hand, but continued. 'It's going to be a devil of a problem if his price has gone up, that it will.'

'The Council will provide the funds. Are we agreed we approach this man?' There was no reply. He looked at Pearse. 'John?'

'OK,' he replied resentfully and took another gulp of larger from the bottle.

'Sean?'

'Yes,' agreed Dolan, adding, 'but I see money and our previous dealings with him being a problem. Many will feel as John does.'

'Right then, it's decided,' said Fuller with relief. 'The Council will give us up to one million sterling I know, and I'll be leaving you to make the arrangements, Sean.'

'I can,' he replied with pretence of reluctance, 'but, there's the question of whether this Johnson would do the job for us. Someone has to be making contact, agreeing the target and the terms. That's more for you, John.'

'There's no intelligence to do. I'm thinking we've decided it's an operational matter now,' he countered, distancing himself with any association with Johnson.

'Wait a minute,' said Dolan, 'this is intelligence work. Johnson might be dead, he might be abroad, and he might not read the papers. You wouldn't be having to meet him, John.'

'Sean,' said Fuller before Pearse could reply. 'I have decided that this is an operational matter and I shall be giving you the details of the advert tomorrow. We'll meet at Jimmy's at eleven. Then we can be getting on with it.'

'OK,' said Sean feigning reluctance again as he rose from his chair, 'as you say.'

The three men had more to drink around the electric fire before they left. The tension was still there, but the decision had been made, to the satisfaction of Fuller and Dolan, although for completely different reasons, and to the grudging acceptance of Pearse. The decision would alter all of their lives.

Sean Dolan made his way back through the driving rain to 117 and left the house by the front door, stepping out into the rain again, pulling the collar of his coat tighter about his neck, and, as he bowed his head into the weather he wondered if his devious plan would work.

Chapter 4

Monday 3rd September.

County Kildare, Republic of Ireland.

THE LAY-BY had once been part of the main road that wound its way through the soft green countryside, but now a wider road took the heavy traffic past. The lay-by was in a very slight depression and modern toilets had been provided which were in complete contrast to Jimmy's 'Bide-a-While', a drab off-white caravan that nevertheless served as a popular transport café. There were no seats but there was plenty of standing room under the faded red and white striped awning. However, Jimmy's mugs of tea and bacon sandwiches were legendary throughout Kildare and Meath and guaranteed him a regular flow of trade. Today was no exception and it provided the perfect confusing cover for terrorist liaisons where surveillance by the security services would always be difficult.

Dolan approached from the direction of Clane. As he entered the lay-by he could see Seamus Fuller's red Toyota four-wheel drive pick-up near the blue and white Scania articulated lorry. Fuller looked entirely natural in these surroundings, wearing his Wellington boots, green anorak and scruffy trilby hat, leaning up against the drop down counter of the caravan eating his thick sliced bacon sandwich. Sean Dolan paid for a mug of tea and a pack of 'No 6' cigarettes. To the casual observer, these were two strangers harmlessly talking and enjoying an unhurried morning tea break. The reality was quite different.

Fuller finished his sandwich, wiped the grease from his mouth with the back of his sleeve and took a cigarette from behind his ear. It was the signal. He picked up his mug of tea from the counter and walked a few steps away. Dolan approached him and unhurriedly offered his lighter. He lit his cigarette and spoke.

'Here are the details of the advert Sean,' he said, taking the piece of paper as he returned Fuller's lighter. 'It has to be put in word perfect for the second Friday of the month. If Johnson sees it he will contact us the following Tuesday, so it's got to be in for the 14th. Be sure that the advert says "7th" and "3rd", so he'll contact us at 7 o'clock on the third number we have given him.'

'That's the garage then?'

'So it is,' confirmed Fuller as he examined the smoking cigarette between his fingers. 'I'll be seeing you then, Sean.'

'Aye. That you will.'

Seamus Fuller walked to his pick-up, leaving Dolan behind to light another cigarette and order a second cup of tea.

Chapter 5

Wednesday 5th September.

Bristol, England.

ACTING SUPERINTENDENT Faraday drove from force headquarters at Portishead Down to The Grove, parked his Volvo T5 in his reserved bay and took the stairs to his office on the second floor. The meeting of all the twenty-seven chief superintendent and superintendents at Force HQ had been informative and interesting, particularly as normally he would not have been invited to attend and certainly Wynne-Thomas would never have briefed him on events. The size of the meeting reminded him of how easy it was to forget the size of the Severnside Constabulary with 6,384 police officer and nearly 3,000 civil staff, covering an area of over 120 miles in length, encompassing the counties of Somerset and Gloucestershire and the university cities of Bristol, Bath and Gloucester.

He was pleased that the chief constable, Sir Hastings Perry, had taken the trouble to spend a few minutes asking him questions and giving encouragement in a down-to-earth and practical way. The chief was a native of Northumberland and could be blunt to say the least. Sir Hastings had firstly joined the Metropolitan Police, transferring to the Liverpool City Police as an inspector, and then moved to the Lancashire Constabulary where he rose through the ranks to become their Assistant Chief Constable. It was at this time that Sir Hastings was seconded to the Foreign and Commonwealth Office and sent abroad for two years, although no one seemed to know where or why. Upon his return he was appointed Deputy Chief Constable of West Yorkshire Police and took command of the Severnside force seven years ago. He was about 5'9" with a canny manner and ready smile that belied his shrewdness and imagination. It was his foresight even as the docks were in rapid decline, to realise their inherent potential for their future development as the site for prestigious offices, expensive restaurants and luxury apartments. The result was the building of Mark's district headquarters.

The meeting had gone on longer than Faraday had anticipated and the city's traffic seemed determined to slow his return even more. When he did arrive in his secretary's office, numerous messages had accumulated. Martin Passmore appeared in the doorway.

'No real problems, sir. That small demo outside the Job Centre went off OK and it's covered in the Incident Log.' Both men walked into Mark's office as Martin continued. 'However, there's been a nasty rape as well.'

'This afternoon?'

'No. Yesterday afternoon unfortunately, but her parents didn't report it until 2.30 today.'

'How old?'

'15.'

'Where?'

'Castle Green.'

'Who's dealing?'

'DI Williams and Sally, sir.'

'Any progress?'

'Yes, but slowly. The girl was worried about what her parents would think so had a bath and washed her clothes before mum got home.'

'Suspects?'

'Could be anyone at the moment, but the MO is similar to Ronald Charles Baker, but it's early days yet. Task Force are up there now.'

'And the girl?'

'She could make a creditable witness,' then added, 'but her life is ruined and she'll never really recover will she?"

'No. No, not completely, if ever,' reflected Faraday, then said after what seemed a long pause: 'What about the support agencies?'

'Sally has that in hand, sir.'

'OK, thanks Martin.'

Mark Faraday thumbed through some messages. He made four calls before Jane brought in the final cup of the day. Another hour went by occupied with paperwork until he switched off his desk-top VDU, the lights and left the office.

On the way down to his car, he called into the general CID office. Detective Sergeant Gibbs was there.

'Derek, any joy yet with the rape?'

The sergeant was an intense, unsmiling man with an unfortunate Hitler-type moustache. He had a good brain and was well on his way to gaining his Open University degree, but he had difficulty in getting a team to respond. He was unlikely to reach inspector rank.

'We've got him, sir, but only just. Mr William's with him now. Chummy denied ever being on Castle Green but preliminary tests on his shoes and trousers picked up from his home indicate otherwise. The lab will confirm by 11 o'clock tomorrow at the latest.'

'Who is it?'

'Ronald Baker.'

'Who picked him up?'

'Norris, sir.'

'He's a good lad.'

'Yes. He asked all the right questions at the house and Baker gave all the wrong answers. And Norris grabbed all his clothes,' replied the sergeant.

'What about the girl's family?' continued Faraday.

'Elder sister's a nurse. Sensible girl. Mum's blaming herself, dad's blaming everyone else. Rape Crisis people should have called by now.'

'My compliments to Mr Williams, but I want Baker kept in overnight, court tomorrow and no bail under any circumstances at all.'

'Absolutely, sir,' said the sergeant as he nearly smiled but didn't.

'Thanks, Derek.'

Faraday called into the duty inspector's office. Inspector Stacey was sat at his desk.

'Good evening, sir,' the inspector said gushingly.

'Hullo, Roger. Everything OK?'

'Of course, sir. I've deployed some of the men regarding the car park incident and I've had a few sharp words with young Harper. I'm also keeping a weather eye on the rape job too.'

'PC Norris had him in, didn't he?'

'Lucky break,' he said quickly, and then added: 'I don't know but Norris sometimes thinks he's a law unto himself. Cocky. Needs to be screwed down a bit.'

'He's a good thief-taker, Roger.'

'Yes. He's had more than his fair share of luck, but I've put a stop to this nick-name business. They call him "Knock 'em off Norris" now. As far as I'm concerned, he's just another man on the group and not entitled to any special privileges.'

'He's certainly a personality, Roger. He was on my old group at Central when I was an inspector there. He's a bit of a loner, but he's really good and works best if you keep a very firm grip on a very loose rein with him.'

'I don't think the superintendent is too keen on him,' said the inspector, revealing the reason behind his remarks.

'Maybe,' said Faraday, then pointedly added, 'but I wouldn't like to think that initiative and flair were inhibited.'

'Of course not,' he replied enthusiastically. 'No, sir.'

'See you tomorrow afternoon, Roger. Good night.'

'Good night, sir.'

Faraday made his exit towards his car. He was glad he had not been lumbered with Stacey as the acting chief inspector as the superintendent had probably preferred. Stacey had nine years more service than Mark and resented Faraday's promotion. Stacey was always scrupulously correct but he was treacherous, giving no credit to others and uncomfortable with subordinates who exhibited any sort of talent or imagination. Sophisticated and extremely smart in appearance, he always spoke in a nasal, ponderous way, giving the impression that his comments were the result of great consideration. In fact, he didn't have an original thought in his arrogant head, and much of his limited ability was expended in ingratiating himself with the superintendent.

Faraday turned the ignition on and Gabrielle's 'Tell me what you dream' began to play on the CD. He moved out into The Grove and turned towards his apartment at Avon View Court.

Avon View Court was a modern and rather exclusive development with exceptional views over the Avon Gorge and towards the illuminated Clifton Suspension Bridge. The gardens, even at night, were a delight. The subdued lighting had been skilfully arranged so as to welcome and illuminate those arriving by car or on foot, yet highlighting the flowers, shrubs and trees that surrounded the three-storey block of apartments.

Faraday parked his car and walked towards the entrance foyer, past the *robinia frisia*, the vivid yellow foliage of which, like the crimson of the *atropurppureum*, was captured by the light. Mark inserted his plastic card into the security lock and the doors opened; the security camera constantly blinking, reminding those who entered of its presence. The lift took him to the third floor and the plush interior of number 16. He shut the door. For all of its comforts and lavish furnishings, the apartment was a lonely place.

Chapter 6

Friday 14th September.

Norfolk, England.

HADFIELD SEEMED to be far away as he looked out through the huge window across his lawn towards the River Glaven and Blakeney Point beyond. The tide had turned and some of the sailing boats and motor cruisers had started to rise from their listing slumbers on the banks of the twisting marshy inlet as if imitating the residents of this picturesque coastal town. Excitable herring gulls squawked and winged overhead as a small dinghy and some other shallower craft moved down the river to the North Sea.

'Your breakfast, Mr Miles,' said Mrs Fowler.

'I'm so sorry,' Hadfield said. 'I'm day dreaming. It's always so peaceful here, Mrs Fowler.' He looked at the plate of smoked bacon, sausages, eggs, tomatoes and mushrooms. 'That looks perfect. Thank you.'

Mrs Fowler, the housekeeper, smiled with pleasure. Mr Miles, as she knew him, was always so charming and considerate and the house seemed so empty when he was away.

Most would say that he was a handsome man with powerful blue eyes. His upper lip was thinner than the lower but it was a full mouth and his broken, although not unattractive, nose made him look a little older than his forty-eight years.

It was good to have him back, thought Mrs Fowler. The house seemed so much brighter and the Labradors, Lady and Sam, less restless. In any case, Mrs Fowler could do what she called 'proper cooking' now.

Debbie, the housekeeper's part-time assistant, dextrously balanced the tray on her left arm. 'I'll just move your paper, sir. Here's your coffee, Colombian Maragogype.' She put the pot and cup and saucer on the table and smiled, pleased that she had pronounced the name properly.

Hadfield savoured every mouthful. Maybe it was the sea air but the breakfast was just as he liked them, not too greasy and the uncooked Spanish tomatoes firm and just that little bit tangy.

Debbie waited patiently until he had put his knife and fork neatly on the plate before removing the plate and bringing fresh toast to the table. He rearranged his breakfast table so that he could open part of the paper to read, propping it up at an angle against the window ledge. Most of the river craft were riding serenely at their anchors on the gently water in contrast to the increased activity of the holiday makers about the quay. A dog's yapping broke the spell and Hadfield returned to his paper. After two slices to toast, he moved his chair back a little and used his napkin to brush off his cavalry twill trousers, flicked a crumb from the sleeve of his jumper and crossed his legs. He was still relaxed but the reading of his paper was no longer superficial as he searched the 'death' column, until he fixed his attention upon one entry:

'CARTER, John Frederik.
Funeral date should have read
7th, not 3rd . Deepest apologies.'

He put the paper down and poured himself another cup of coffee. He picked up the newspaper again, concentrating now, oblivious to the bustling scenes outside his window and the admiring glances of Debbie. He re-read the entry again, there was something wrong but he could not immediately see it.

'Stupid,' he said, after a few moments.

'Pardon, sir?' said Debbie.

'I'm so sorry. I wasn't meaning you, Debbie. You would have spotted it right away.'

'What, sir?'

'Only a silly spelling mistake in the paper. I've finished now.' He stood up and Debbie drew back. 'See you at lunch time Debbie, and my compliments to Mrs Fowler,' he said as he walked out of the dining room. Debbie did not see his charming smile fade away.

A serious and concerned Mr Hadfield stood in the pleasant sunshine at the front entrance porch to the fine Georgian red brick house, and then strode down his gravelled driveway past the crowded white-painted dovecote and through the open wrought-iron gates towards the waterfront.

He turned right and walked up the slight gradient towards the flint and brick-built houses, then along the South Passage. He was not so much troubled as irritated. He had returned to this tranquil corner of England to relax. Now this relaxation was disturbed. 'Frederick' had not been spelt with a 'c'.

Hadfield's rules were always the same. Any inaccuracies and he would never play ball. But, he was still intrigued.

Chapter 6

Tuesday 18th September.

Dublin, Republic of Ireland.

SEAMUS FULLER parked his Toyota pick-up in Clonliffe Road and crossed over the river on foot only to cross again at Ballybough Road into East Wall Road. As he approached the long railway arch he slowed his pace so as to mingle with a group of men as he entered. They did not emerge together. After five minutes, Fuller continued his journey convinced that he had not been followed.

Near the quay was a little side road. The terraced houses were bright and trendy and at its junction with the main road were now a small but expensive restaurant, across the road from which was an equally expensive boutique. Although the road consisted predominantly of terraced houses, there were varied styles and patterns and therefore Connor's Garage didn't look out of place at all. There were no windows to the front of the garage and the barley white double doors looked quite in-keeping. Seamus inserted the Yale key into the Judas gate lock and ducked into the dark interior as it opened. The neon lights flickered and the garage was gradually bathed in light. Seamus walked across the giant, oil-stained flag stones to the foot of the stairs where Sean Dolan was standing, his finger on the light switch.

'I have the glasses out, Seamus. It will be a long wait I'm thinking.'

Both men climbed the metal stairway noisily and entered the office. It was dusty but business-like and the office windows gave a panoramic view of the garage workshop below. A red Ford car was on the ramp; the other, a Mercedes-Benz had the bonnet raised and protective sheeting still draped over the silver-grey wings as if work had suddenly stopped and the mechanics spirited away. The whisky was welcome, not that it had been a cold day, on the contrary it had been a fine and sunny day, but the garage was cool and desolate. More whiskies followed.

'Well, if he'll be ringing it should be any time now,' said Dolan as he offered his chief of staff a cigarette. As if defying their scepticism, the old black and dusty telephone rang. Dolan looked at Fuller and gestured as if to indicate that Fuller should naturally be the one to answer it.

'Yes,' said Fuller.

'Nelson's Column, London,' came the reply.

'Nelson's Pillar, Dublin,' Fuller replied.

'St. Patrick will be pleased,' said the caller. As before, the exchange of code words appeared to confirm the genuineness of one to the other. Before Fuller could reply, the caller's crisp instructions began.

'You will now go to the Bank of Ireland. To its right is a telephone kiosk from which you will ring this number: 071-429-67452.'

'Now wait a minute ... where's a bloody pencil?' said a flustered Fuller.

'I shall only repeat the number once more. It is 071-429-67452. You will make the call at precisely 19:17 hours.'

'He's rung off!' Fuller exclaimed.

'Cheeky sod,' agreed Dolan.

'Come on, we'll have to shift ourselves to get there by "19:17 hours",' said Fuller, imitating the caller's cultured English accent.

Fuller was now agitated and clattered down the steps moving quickly to the gate. Dolan calmly switched off the lights as Fuller rattled open the little gate and sniggered quietly as Fuller hit his head as he stepped through out into the street. Both men walked hurriedly towards the bank, Fuller rubbing his head constantly and pessimistically speculating as to whether the phone box would be occupied or not. Dolan was, of course, pleased. Whilst he had only heard Fuller's telephone conversation, he was fully aware of the content of the conversation he did not hear. Dolan's accomplice clearly had so far performed his part well. All that remained was for the accomplice to continue to provide the voice of an ice-cold but cultured Englishman.

The phone booth was empty. Both men entered the booth and began fumbling about in their pockets for as much change as they could muster, at the same time Fuller counting off the remaining seconds until 7.17pm.

Fuller dialled the number that was immediately answered.

'Yes?' he asked abruptly.

'Nelson's Pillar, Dublin,' responded Fuller.

'Nelson's Column, London,' came the cultured reply.

'St. Patrick will be pleased,' confirmed a still breathless Fuller.

'Good. I am in a phone box as are you. As it is your money I shall be brief. Who or what is the target?'

'A British power station,' replied Fuller.

'Coal, gas, oil or nuclear?' came the cool demand.

'Nuclear,' was his hurried reply.

'I assume that it would be counter-productive to your endeavours to cause a massive loss of life, global contamination and international revulsion?'

'That will be true, so it will,' said Fuller, clearly having difficulty in keeping pace with the rapidity of the questions and grasping the consequence of his answers.

'Let me see if I can clarify the requirements,' the accomplice said feigning mild impatient. 'You require an attack upon a nuclear installation so as to cause the British government irreparable political embarrassment, at the same time making the security services and the police appear utterly incompetent and impotent, and thus, create sufficient international alarm so as to generate pressure upon the British government that will be hard for them to resist?'

'Exactly,' said Fuller, trying to regain the initiative, 'that will be exactly what we'll be wanting.'

'Can I further assume that, within these parameters, you will allow me to select the actual target?'

'Um, yes, yes,' replied Fuller, the control of the conversation firmly back in the hands of the accomplice.

'Finally, time-scale. By what date do you wish our business to be concluded?'

'By the end of February next at the latest.'

'My charges will be a half-million pounds sterling. £200,000 to be deposited by the 2nd October, the remainder payable upon completion. If you foresee any difficulties, say so now and we need not waste each other's time further.'

'No, no. We can manage that, so we can.'

'I will send to the third address tomorrow, a left luggage compartment key for a railway station, the location of which will be indicated in the letter. My instructions will be found in that locker which will be cleared by the 25th of this month. I remind you that if you fail to deposit the money by the 2nd, the deal is cancelled. Good night.'

Fuller replaced the handset onto its cradle.

'Come on, what did he say?' asked Dolan.

'He wants half a million.'

'Half a million!' said Dolan, apparently surprised. 'Euros or pounds?'

'English pounds and £200,000 by the 2nd. The rest when the job's done,' said Fuller, smiling and very pleased with himself. The deal was within the figure stipulated by the Council. Now he was sure of success and he would be part of it.

'Come on Sean. Don't look so surprised. I'll tell you what the man said.'

But of course, Sean Dolan was not at all surprised. He knew exactly what the man had said.

On the other hand, the Council would be surprised, and be vengeful. Dolan's accomplice would also be surprised and also totally unprepared for the reward that Dolan had prepared for him. This Irish teacher of English with mounting debts, who so often flawlessly performed the role of the English gentleman in school plays, would not be applauded nor financially rewarded for his performance tonight. He would die inside his garage as he parked his car, the explosion triggered as he pressed the little button that closed down his electric garage doors.

Chapter 7

Friday 21st September.

Dublin, Republic of Ireland.

THE KEY scraped in the well-worn lock. A slight turn to the right and the railway station locker door was open. The grey interior was empty save for a buff coloured envelope neatly placed squarely in the middle of the base of the locker. Fuller's podgy hand clasped the envelope and held it for a moment, his thoughts intriguingly suspended. In this little envelope contained the means by which he would secure his name and his future. He unzipped his green anorak and pushed the envelope clumsily into his inside breast pocket. He looked around. It was impossible to see if any one of the many hundreds of commuters were really interested in him. He left the locker door open and walked out of Connolly Railway Station to Amiens Street towards Custom House Quay and across the River Liffey. It was a pleasant walk past Trinity College to the car park next to the railway station and his Toyota. Fuller climbed in behind the steering wheel and drove off towards the old cattle market near Prussian Street and parked.

It would have been quicker to have walked to Connor's garage, but not so safe, and although the bus was late and the traffic still heavy, he was able to make the garage by 6.30pm as arranged.

'Well, Sean,' said Fuller, now clearly out of breath. 'Here it is,' patting his chest with his hand.

They both sat down at the office desk. Fuller removed the crumpled envelope from the inside pocket with his index finger and thumb like a magician performing at a children's party, and flattened it out upon the desk top with both hands. He was still fascinated and sat there grinning, just looking at the plain envelope. He picked it up with a flourish and rapidly slit it open with a pencil. Between the jagged opening he removed the typing paper upon which were clear and unequivocal instructions. In the folds of this single sheet of paper was also a blank bank deposit slip.

Both men craned forward over the paper, only Dolan's eyes flitted occasionally towards Fuller's flushed face and wrinkled brow. As before, the message was crisp and precise:

> *'The first deposit must be made at the Atlantic First Commercial Bank (Isle of Man) Ltd., Corn Street, Bristol by the 2nd between 10:30 and 15:30 hours. Your signature or other details will not be required. You will not require a receipt. Take the cash and endorsed deposit slip and present both to the bank.'*

Fuller picked up the deposit slip. It was similar to any other bank deposit slip that had been torn neatly from a deposit book. The amount, in words and figures, had been typed in: '£200,000'. There was a difference however. There was no signature or space for a signature, only what appeared to be a magnetic strip above which were two rows of uneven silver dots with a third thin golden strip.

'I've never seen a deposit slip like this before, Sean.'

'No, that's true enough. But how are we going to get the money to Bristol?'

Fuller forgot the bank slip and replaced it on the table. He sat back in the chair and said in a light air. I can go to a number of banks and get the money transferred to Bristol in one of our *convenient* accounts. We have a Central Counties account in Bristol I'm thinking and it can't be traced to our movement. But, you'll have to go to Bristol and take the money from Central Counties to this bank,' as he looked at the typed note now held in his hands.

'Just a moment,' said Dolan anxiously. 'I'm a marked man, Seamus.'

'You're not wanted, Sean,' said Fuller, irritated that his simple planning was being upset.

'Seamus. After Oxford.'

'You were acquitted,' snapped Fuller.

'Yes, but the Special Branch don't forgive and never forget. They'll pick me up at Fishguard just to be bloody-minded.' He sensed that Fuller was waning but was not yet convinced. Dolan masked his agitation, he wanted to go to the mainland of course, but not yet, he needed time to make the urgent arrangements necessary to ensure his future safety. He played his ace. 'If that happens we'll not be doing it by the 2nd. Seamus, John can safely do it.'

'I've been a thinking along the same lines,' lied Fuller. 'John might be spotted but he's safe. If he takes himself and no luggage, he'll be back in the wink of an eye. Yes. John will do it.'

Chapter 8

Friday 5th October.

Kinsale, County Cork, Republic of Ireland.

SEAMUS FULLER used his brother's blue Ford Mondeo for his 183 mile drive to Kinsale. The beauty of Carlow, Kilkenny and Waterford were lost upon him and although the traffic was kind and the weather fair, Fuller was apprehensive of his meeting with Daniel O'Callaghan of the headquarters staff. He could not keep it a secret a moment longer. Like the messengers of classical Greece, he was unlikely to escape retribution, his only hope was to minimise the damage. His greatest difficulty was to prove it was not him.

The afternoon sun was fading and the shadows lengthened as his scheduled meeting approached and a foreboding greyness settled upon the huge and ancient limestone fort that protected this vast harbour. Kinsale, now an attractive yachting haven should have appeared most inviting to Fuller as he made his way on foot towards the 17th century Charles Fort - but it didn't. Once inside the fortifications he was surrounded by the shell of the former garrison building, gaunt and lifeless. The roofs were missing now and the ivy had felt its way across the rough walls. Fuller shivered as he looked about him and blind, empty windows unsympathetically returned his looks.

He rested by a buttress beneath a sky pregnant with storm clouds and looked out past Black Head towards The Old Head of Kinsale nearly three miles away. It was off this point on the 7th May 1915, that the single torpedo of Kapitan-Leutnant Walter Schwieger's

U20 sank the *Lusitania*. Would he shortly join those 1,201 lonely souls, thought Fuller.

Two men approached him, both had cold, blank expressions. 'You are to come this way, Mr Fuller.'

Fuller helplessly followed them through an empty doorway but was barged aside as three burly louts bundled an unfortunate out, his facial appearance distorted by bruising and the painfully tight gag in his mouth. But it was the man's eyes that startled Fuller. The eyes were fixed and staring, contorted in fear as they seemed to plead for help. The man knew the cruel penalty for betrayal and the obscene ritual of torture that would proceed his death and those thoughts now held captive Fuller's mind and body. Fuller stared after the man then looked around himself. He was in a large bare roofless building, completely alone except for O'Callaghan.

'You have a problem, Seamus, that you'll be wishing to tell me about?'

O'Callaghan was short and dumpy with a round face and little hair. It was the eyes and the tight-lipped perpetual smile that were unforgettable. His eyes were small and dark, like those of a snake. They walked around the oblong room, over an uneven dirt floor. The arm around Fuller's shoulder did not reassure him as he explained that John Pearse had successfully arranged for the transfer of £200,000 which had then been withdrawn and deposited in the Atlantic First Commercial Bank but, the usual acknowledgement that should have appeared in *The Times* on the 4th had not materialised.

'Can we not be speaking … eh, sharply, to the bank manager?' said O'Callaghan, as he stopped and looked Fuller directly in the eye.

'No. I think that one of his girls typed in the amount being deposited, nothing else. The deposit slip had a sort of magnetic strip on it and silver dots and a golden strip, like you'll be having on a bank note, but the details are all scrambled up and known only to the bank's computer.'

'But the bank must have the deposit slip?' said O'Callaghan as they both walked on.

'That's just it. As soon as the deposit is made, the slips are shredded. It's a completely untraceable numbered bank account. Even the Swiss haven't got one like it.'

O'Callaghan was not deflected from his thoughts by Fuller's feeble attempt at humour.

'Whoever it is … Johnson you call him,' he paused looking at Fuller contemptuously, 'or another, then we can assume that he has the appropriate withdrawal slips with the magnetic strip and these little dots.'

'That's true enough.'

O'Callaghan ignored Fuller's comments, he had been thinking aloud, making a statement, not asking Fuller a question.

'We would have to be keeping an eye on that bank for months,' said O'Callaghan to himself, then stopped again, fixing Fuller with his stare. 'And there will be something else, Seamus, is there not?'

Fuller smiled weakly and swallowed hard before replying. 'Your chief of planning and operations has gone missing since Wednesday morning.'

O'Callaghan's icy stare froze Fuller. There was that smile but it did not hide a controlled contempt.

'No, Seamus. Not *my* chief of plans, he was *your* chief of plans. But that is for later. For the present we must concentrate on getting our money back.' His smile was almost a leer as he asked: 'Have you thought of a plan?'

'No. I was ... .'

'Then you'll be thinking of one tonight and telling me all about it tomorrow at St Mulrose Church.' They shook hands. 'Tomorrow, at eleven. At eleven, Seamus,' repeated O'Callaghan, the cold look never leaving his eyes and the pathetic grin never leaving Fuller's face.

Relieved, Fuller reflected gratefully upon the fifteen hours he had been granted to think and live. He walked towards then passed through the old doorway. He felt nothing. He did not hear the harsh croaking of the flapping ravens panicking above him, nor the dull *dumpt* as the .38 110 gram slug entered neatly the lower part of his occipital lobe, destroying his corpus callosum and thalamus before exiting a little over his left eye, and as it did so removing most of the frontal and all of the sphenoid bones. Fuller knew nothing of this of course because his death was instantaneous. Most of Seamus Fuller's victims had not been so fortunate.

John Pearse came through the doorway but did not waste his time to look upon the still twitching remains of Seamus Fuller in the dirt.

'I'll be thinking that your idea is our best chance,' said O'Callaghan. 'We'll try and make contact with this Johnson and offer him a further £50,000 for that traitor Dolan. And, if he can get the

£200,000 back he can keep it, plus the remaining £300,000 if he gets the power station job done.'

'But four days have passed, Dolan could have gone anywhere with the money.'

'He could but I'll be thinking that he'll lay low and make his plans,' said O'Callaghan thoughtfully. 'He'll have had his treacherous thoughts long ago, but he couldn't have started planning this until after the beginning of last month when the Council agreed to *his* foolish scheme.' He spat over the now still body of Fuller. 'Even then he would not be sure that the money would have been safely deposited until Tuesday. We'll have to be hoping that he'll have left the money safe and snug in the bank until he feels confident enough to move it.'

'That could be months, years even.'

'If you had £200,000 to spend, John,' said O'Callaghan slowly, fixing his cold eyes upon Pearse, 'how long would you be leaving it alone?'

There was a hint of a confident yet cruel smile as O'Callaghan reflected upon his comments. He could do no more just now to right the wrongs of the last few weeks or could he?

'John,' asked O'Callaghan thoughtfully, 'Dolan has a brother, has he not?'

'Aye, he does that. He's a coach driver, but not one of us.'

'Kill him. Kill him as a warning to others.'

Chapter 9

Monday 8th October.

Salisbury Plain, England.

THE MEMBERS had split into little groups of two or three after lunch and were walking along the Jacobean terrace to the north of the manor house. The urns that paraded along this terrace had brimmed over with scarlet, purple and white *lobelia* and *alyssum*, but were now past their best, even in this mild October. Towering over the terrace for its full length was a dense yew hedge behind which had once been an enclosed garden. What it now enclosed was an Army Air Corps Westland Lynx helicopter.

This Salisbury Plain estate had been the home of the powerful Stackpole family for nearly 600 years until forfeited to the Crown when Sir James Stackpole became one of the many victims of Judge Jeffrey's 'Bloody Assize' for sheltering a kinsman after the Battle of Sedgemoor and the Rebellion of 1685. The estate has remained the property of the Crown ever since.

Salisbury Plain is a place of space and loneliness. There are many ancient houses which skirt this vast expanse of undulating chalk down or nestle within it; Eastleigh Court and Sutton House, Heytesbury House and Elston House, Shrewton Lodge and Urchfont Manor, but this house, dating as it does from 1492 was inaccessible. It had the name of Lavington Court and also a reference number of '907' in the Ministry of Defence, Whitehall. According to Whitehall, Lavington Court is the home of the Inter-Service Technical Board, the Central Research Services Department and the Joint Field Services Branch. It is in fact home to none of these for none of these exists. On military maps it is marked, but on conventional tourists maps it is now forgotten. Even on civil air navigation maps, it is not included, the area being classified as 'D127/12', indicating it to be one of the many danger areas of this principal military training ground. It is fittingly situated in a zone designated as 'CMATZ' airspace as well as being a restricted area within the meaning of The Official Secrets Act. Movement to and from the house was therefore difficult to monitor by those with either casual or malevolent intent.

The members began to drift down the handsome stone stairway to the lower gardens, past the gold *achillea filipendulina*, and around to the front and warmer south side of the house. In the middle distance, the well manicured lawns met the harsher pines that surrounded the estate, and the absolute peace was not disturbed even as some trod upon the gravelled driveway lined with the well clipped yew bushes that thrive in the chalky soil.

To the untutored eye, the members, dressed in conservative suits, appeared as lecturers or senior students at a top management college.

Some began to make their way back towards the old entrance porch, others confirmed the unspoken command by their watches and then all began to hasten their step. Important as they may all be, the Co-ordinator was a stickler for punctuality.

They gradually resumed their seats in the Great Parlour around the long 'U' shaped ultra-modern conference table, behind the identical leather rimmed green blotters, upon which rested numerous files marked **'Secret'** and **'Top Secret'**.

It was a fine yet business-like room, over thirty-foot long, oak panelled with a plastered ceiling, which gave the impression of sombre richness. Against the mullion and leaded windows of the west bay was a much smaller table, upon which were banks of telephones, cream, black and red, as well as a CD recording machine. By dialling a three-figured number, any of Britain's embassies or high commissions could be reached from this room. In the corner was situated a large shredder under which was an already half-filled black plastic burn-bag. This corner was complete with a photocopier, to the right of which, at an angle against the north wall and facing towards the conference table, was a fifteen-foot wide map of the world at the top of which were mounted twelve identical clocks representing the twenty-four time-zones.

The Stackpole family looked down from their portraits at the assembled officials. In many respects the scene would have been familiar to them, particularly the Tudors, although not the present day scale, ingenuity and technical sophistication. These would have been beyond their comprehension, but not so the more clandestine and necessarily covert activities of government.

The Co-ordinator, General Sir Ian Noble, adjusted some of his papers. He was a large man, although carrying a little too much weight, but at sixty-two years of age he was still remarkably fit. He was framed by a grand fireplace of mellow soft white chalk-like Compton Bassett stone that did not diminish him. On the contrary, it accentuated his central and commanding position, as did the motto of the Stackpole armorials in the plastered overmantle of the fireplace: *'Safe, if you're a friend'.*

He looked around the room. He appeared like a very friendly uncle with bushy swept-up eyebrows and bulbous nose, complimented by a ready and mischievous smile.

'Thank you for joining us for this item, Commissioner,' he said.

Deputy Assistant Commissioner John Bennett, in overall command of Special Branch activities nodded in the affirmative to the Co-ordinator.

'Thank you for inviting us again, sir.'

'Can I suggest it might be helpful if we go back, say to April, so that our new permanent naval member can be completely in the picture.'

'Of course, sir,' replied the forty-seven year old Bennett. He didn't show his annoyance at being reminded of a course he had intended to take anyway, but looked over at the slim, dark-haired Captain Cleeve, who smiled in return. Chief Superintendent Packham handed Bennett the papers as the latter looked around the room.

'It will be easier and sequentially convenient if we deal with the item regarding Ireland in date order. Charles can take us through this. Please feel free to ask either of us for any explanation as we go along if not clear.'

Charles Packham stood up. He was short for a policeman, with a round, jovial clean-shaven face, not the sort of man you would think was the deputy head of SO13, the Yard's Anti-terrorist Branch. He had a very professional manner and what became clear, in addition to hailing from Perthshire, was that he knew what he was about. He positioned himself so that he stood to the right of the world map, between the map of the British Isles and a screen. He deftly pressed a number of switches on the small lectern, and as he did so, the lights dimmed gently to nothing whilst his reading lamp and those along the conference table gently grew in subdued green brightness.

'Thank you, ladies and gentlemen. We can commence our up-date at 11th April with the death of Tim Pat O'Brien, the New Irish Republican Brotherhood's chief of staff, although he wasn't found until the 12th, his mother's birthday.'

The police photograph of O'Brien was quickly followed on the screen by the picture of the open car boot of a Vauxhall, a dead body within.

'The PM indicated that he died between 5 p.m. on the 11th and 4 a.m. on the 12th.' As if in response to an unasked question, he continued. 'We cannot be more accurate with the time of death because as he was found in a car boot, this had a confusing effect upon the body temperature. He was found here,' a small but bright arrow was beamed directly onto the map screen by Packham, 'at the Devil's Glen, County Wicklow.'

'Most apt,' muttered Brigadier Midford of Military Intelligence.

'O'Brien's vehicle had clearly been involved in a minor road accident as a small amount of debris at the scene indicated, but this did not constitute the cause of death. The cause of death was asphyxiation by way of a plastic bag over his head.'

The grisly photograph still fascinated those gathered, although all had seen it before save the naval captain.

'He was incapacitated immediately before death by a chopping-type blow to the neck.' Packham imitated the type of blow that must have silenced O'Brien, but his gesture went unnoticed as a further slide showed bruises to the neck.

'Very cool,' commented the naval captain.

'Yes. Since my last presentation to you, I have had the opportunity to check further. The PSNI have no record of a similar type of killing, nor have the Garda Siochana. Robbery was not the motive. He was a cautious man clearly taken off guard. There was no sign of a struggle and the killing took place immediately before or on his mother's birthday. It was no coincidence. It was an execution and not an internal one by the NIRB itself. Nor, our intelligence indicates, was it by any other terrorist group.'

Packham looked across towards James Cleeve. 'You said "cool" captain. The manner of this killing was, in my view, intentionally chilling in a calculated way. Calculated to show others that, whoever the killer was he could strike at close quarters and had the ability to get that close to a key member of a terrorist organisation and kill him with ease and apparent impunity.'

The Co-ordinator sat in his chair, hands steepled at his chin, deep in thought.

'Surely your people have picked up something, Sarah?' questioned the Co-ordinator.

'Afraid not, sir,' replied the head of GCHQ.

'But you have a view?' he persisted.

'Only that I'm sure this made the NIRB feel rather uncomfortable. Can Charles tell us who the killer was?' she asked, deflecting attention away from her organisation.

'No,' said Chief Superintendent Packham.

'But surely you will continue to try and find out?' asked Roberts of the Foreign Office.

'Of course,' said the policeman, as if such future action was not in question. 'A considerable amount of intelligence has already been received, but we don't know *who* he is. We believe that the killer is not Irish, or so we are reliably informed by the RMP's Courts and Witness Section. As a result we have liaised with Naval Intelligence at Belfast regarding all small boat movements around the Irish coast. The Garda have also checked sea and air arrivals and departures for us again. The Garda are being extremely helpful but there are gaps in that helpfulness as you would expect when we ask an independent sovereign state to assist us.'

'Thank you, chief superintendent,' said the Co-ordinator unnecessarily, 'we are aware of the delicacy of the situation.'

'The problem is, of course,' interjected Bennett, 'that if we were asked to invent an island that was as easy to enter as well as to leave, we would probably have ended up with Ireland.' Mildly humorous comments flowed around the room.

The naval officer surveyed his colleagues, all reasonable people in their own way but possessing the full range of human frailties, naked ambition and self-interest, professional rivalries and greed. Sarah Davidson of GCHQ seemed relieved or bored, he knew not which, and Derek Roberts maintained a smug air. The iciness had now gone but self-interest lurked below the surface of most. Maybe not too much, maybe a great deal, but it was there, he could feel it.

'In June, it was the 6th,' continued Packham, 'we had the death of John Edward Kelly at Newtown Hamilton.' Pictures fluttered onto the screen. 'He was heir apparent, otherwise the incident was of no great importance. His death in a shoot-out was a direct result of poor planning by the NIRB and good planning by the PSNI.'

The members were now smiling with self congratulation.

'The new chief of staff was a character named Seamus Fuller.' The face appeared. 'I would not have put my money on him, I wouldn't have thought him to have been in the frame. Pearse appeared to have a better claim and Dolan was up and coming.'

Bennett caught the captain's eye and silently mouthed, 'It's photos four and seven.' The Co-ordinator raised his bushy eyebrows.

'Is it of any significance now that Fuller is dead?' asked Matt Brittan of the Home Office, as he pushed his thick glasses up his little nose with fat fingers.

'In this case it does in that nothing is done without a reason and every action creates a reaction. We know that Fuller was executed by his own. But why?' asked the policeman rhetorically. There was silence. He continued. 'Maybe the answer lies in the fact that Pearse is now chief of staff.'

'Well, that's it then,' offered the Home Office representative.

'No. I don't think so,' said that policemen. 'Pearse was always a contender for the job and a close ally of O'Callaghan, but there were others. Pearse could never assume that it was always automatically his.'

'That's true,' said Colonel Sullivan, 'confirmed by our DET people.'

'There has been other intelligence from the Garda,' continued the deputy assistant commissioner. 'We are pretty certain that a major meeting took place on a wet 2nd September in Dublin.'

'Where?' asked Brittan. A street map appeared on the screen and the bright little arrowhead moved about for a few seconds then stopped, identifying the road.

'We do not know the number of the house,' said Bennett, 'but we are certain.'

'Why?' asked the Co-ordinator. This was more promising. All reflected the Co-ordinator's interest. The policeman had their complete attention.

'We know that normally their meetings are held in a number of locations, but principally Connor's garage.' The chief superintendent's torch shone the arrowhead onto the map again. 'But, on the 2nd, Dolan entered number 117,' the arrowhead skitted over the map and stopped, 'at 7.12pm. and left at 10.42pm. Two streets away was Fuller's vehicle.' The arrowhead moved to that location. 'Nearby was Pearse's car.' The arrowhead moved and stopped again. 'But they both did not enter 117.'

'Could one not have got in through the back way?' asked the haughty Foreign Office man, Roberts.

'Yes, he could have, but I'm sure he didn't. You see, I don't think the meeting was held at 117.'

'Alright, why not?' asked Derek Roberts.

'Because Dolan's coat was wet when he left 117 at 10.42.'

'Of course it would be,' said Brittan, his glasses nearly falling off his nose, 'you said it was raining that night.'

'That's true,' replied the policeman, 'but not inside the house.' They all looked at the policeman. 'There was a little drizzle at 7.12 but a downpour for well over thirty minutes after 10 o'clock. Dolan had been out. 117 was a cover. For what address in that street we do not know – yet. The meeting could have been about anything. Since that meeting, if it was a meeting and I believe it was, a variety of NIRB activities have taken place but nothing would warrant a deviation of this type, particularly as Fuller and Dolan used Connor's garage later on the 18th September when they threw caution to the wind to such an extent that our friends in the Garda were able to follow them to a phone kiosk near the Bank of Ireland.'

'Just a moment,' interjected the Co-ordinator. 'I'm only thinking aloud. What benefits would accrue to the NIRB if the Garda Siochana knew they were making a phone call?'

'Maybe it was a come-on, to see if the Garda were following?' suggested Brittan. Reed of MI5 sighed loudly.

'Clumsy,' observed the Co-ordinator, then asked, 'Is the garage tapped?' He looked at the Commissioner.

'We know that they have no warrant to do so, but we think it is or at least has been, but the Garda will deny it. Any information they pass on to us is as a result of personal contacts and never official. However, they openly admit that they have had observations on 117 for some time.'

'They may have gone to the kiosk at short notice to receive a call. It wasn't that risky,' commented MI5.

'That seems a logical conclusion,' said Packham, 'but we have unofficially requested access to tapes, even limited access, but it would be foolish to press it further at the moment or our informal access will be closed to us. I am told that nothing of importance would be found on the tapes or they would have told us.'

'Alright,' said the Co-ordinator reluctantly, 'but as we all know, information is only considered to be of value if you know its value, and I suspect that our friends in the Garda would not automatically appreciate its value. It's a great pity we can't get our hands on those tapes. Please see if we can, John,' then turning to MI6. 'Your people, Colin, or those at Oswestry, have we nothing from them?'

'There is an ever increasing volume of traffic now, not just between Ireland and the UK, but also to Europe via the UK,' replied Colin Sutton of MI6. 'We thought we had something that's connected in February and then in September. Codes used by the NIRB matched up but voice prints didn't. Still working on it,' he added unhelpfully.

'Work harder,' countered a clearly frustrated Co-ordinator, then turned his attention back to Sarah Davidson. 'And what about GCHQ?'

'I think we can all agree that if something was cooking then we would have picked something up,' replied Davidson vaguely.

'I am well aware of the difficulties,' observed the Co-ordinator, 'but some of the contributions today lack the feel-good factor for me.'

'Maybe, sir, it would be appropriate if I moved on to the developments on the mainland', suggested Chief Superintendent Packham helpfully.

'Before you do,' said MI6, 'who lives at 117?'

'A NIRB sympathiser, a one time IRA man by the name of Michael James Cohalan. We believe he is no more than that.'

Bennett looked towards the Co-ordinator, then gestured approvingly towards Packham.

'A bank has recently opened,' said Packham, 'in Bristol; the Atlantic First Commercial (Isle of Man) Bank Limited.' Another photograph shone onto the screen showing an impressive, granite stone building in Corn Street. 'This bank provides a deposit and withdrawal service that is essentially secret. Let me explain.' He had their attention again as he explained in detail the bank's procedures. 'The Bank of England, however, is not impressed with the enterprise and have not issued a licence to what is a representative office of an off-shore bank. Such a licence is needed before deposits can be taken. However, the consequences of this breach of rules does not help us at the moment, in any case, the local Fraud Squad have been keeping observations on the comings and goings of customers for a number of weeks. We know that last Monday, a NIRB man, in fact it was John Pearse, entered the First Commercial carrying two Marks and Spencer shopping bags. He had come from the Central Counties Bank. The two Fraud Squad detectives only noticed him because the cheeky fellow walked to the First Commercial chatting to the local beat bobby. The constable has been interviewed and we have tried to estimate how much money could have been carried in those bags. Ladies and gentlemen, it could have been as much as three-quarters of a million pounds.'

'Could they be intending to buy arms?' inquired Naval Intelligence.

'They could,' interrupted the brigadier, 'but for what they normally get up to, they probably have arms and equipment enough. No, the significant thing must be *why* First Commercial? The NIRB and other terrorist groups can launder money through all manner of banks often without our knowledge nor the bank's.'

'What about missiles, that sort of thing?' asked Roberts.

'SAMS, Milans, Law 80s, Carl Gustavs, RPG-7s and Stingers are an ever-present possibility,' Reed of MI5 commented soberly.

'I believe the unanswered question,' observed Packham, 'is the one posed by the brigadier: Why this bank? Why now?'

'Have we anything from the bank?' asked MI6 seriously.

'Central Counties will defend client confidentiality and the courts have clipped our wings about the police and the Serious Fraud Office conducting fishing expeditions into people's accounts. What we want to know is where the cash is destined and First Commercial can't help us unless we have the seven-digit code number. The code number is confidentially selected by the client and he feeds it into the computer when he opens the account. The system is so fool-proof even the bank manager doesn't know the number, only the client and the bloody computer.'

'Can Technical Ops Branch help us?' asked the Co-ordinator, examining his fingernails.

'Charles and I have already discussed this, sir,' said the MI5 man. 'We can certainly get into the bank and, given time, could access the computer, but I don't see how that is going to help us. We don't know the number, nor does the bank, nor do we know the account name or the amount.'

'You've spoken to the bank?' asked the Co-ordinator, although already anticipating the negative answer.

'No, sir. We can, of course. If we do, we will possibly blow the Fraud Squad job. But I don't think it will help at the moment,' replied Bennett.

'We've come a long way from a wet overcoat,' said Sutton of MI6 dismissively. 'Are you sure we're not being over-imaginative and over-reacting?'

'No,' interrupted the brigadier briskly. 'If I can say, number 117 was basic police work, but jolly good police work. Even if we forget the Dublin telephone kiosk thing, which is curious but may not be connected, I don't like this Bristol bank business. The whole thing has an unpleasant odour about it. No,' he said as if reflecting, 'that deposit was made for a specific purpose and I suspect for a specific person or persons, and he, she or they must have the means to withdraw it. The question that should be occupying our minds, as always, is *why* and *for whom*? If we can answer these questions then we may be able to understand their intentions.'

'But all we've now got is extra pieces to a bloody big jig-saw puzzle and we don't even know what the picture looks like,' said Roberts of the Foreign Office.

'That's what intelligence work is all about, old boy,' replied MI5, more exasperated than ever.

'Gentlemen, gentlemen,' said the Co-ordinator. Heads lowered slightly in recognition of the chastisement as the general continued: 'Is there anything else, Commissioner?'

'No, sir. I can liaise with the local force and increase surveillance on the bank. I think that would be prudent.'

'Approved. Thank you,' he said as he stood up. 'Let's take a stroll after which we can see which way we should proceed. Ten minutes if you please, ladies and gentlemen.'

There was much shuffling of papers and scraping of chairs on the old, well-worn wooden floor. Some of the members walked to the bay windows and stretched, waiting for the Co-ordinator to leave before speaking amongst themselves, whilst others followed the Co-ordinator through the Great Parlour door. One of these was Lieutenant-Colonel Richard Sullivan.

The brigadier and the colonel met in the porchway and both instinctively moved to the right towards a small group of blue spruce.

'You've been a little quiet this afternoon, Richard. Is everything alright?' enquired Brigadier Midford.

'Bit of a problem, sir. Had a signal just before the meeting resumed.'

'Oh yes,' replied Midford as he stopped walking and looked directly at Sullivan, then continued quietly: 'Tell me.'

'I didn't think I should mention it in front of the others; it would have made the Army look a little foolish.'

'What is it man?' snapped the brigadier, but still in a hushed voice.

'A couple of experimental mines have been stolen, sir,' came the sheepish reply.

'Brief me,' he ordered as if giving battlefield commands via a radio link - short, crisp and to the point.

'They are new, sir. Type 851s; demolition mines designed primarily for bridges, reinforced buildings, dams and such like, a tremendous capacity for penetration into foundations, that sort of thing.'

'Get to the point, Richard.'

'It's slightly worse, sir. Two barometric detonators have gone as well.'

'Same time and place?'

'Yes, sir.'

'We've had barometric detonators for years, is there anything particularly special about these?' he asked calmly but anticipating the answer.

'They are, of course, electronic but these are computerised to such an extent that they are highly sensitive.'

'Extrapolate.'

'I've been trying to work it out since the signal came in. The detonators were originally designed for precision air-bursts, but more recently our SBS boys have been playing with them.'

'For what purpose?'

'Traditionally, SBS have mined vessels in ports or sunk ships in water where they have subsequently been salvaged. A mine used in conjunction with these detonators would provide the ability to sink a submarine at depths where recovery would be almost impossible.'

'Hhmm,' mused the brigadier. 'So, in addition to the loss of an expensive weapon system and crew, it could have a disabling effect upon the confidence of enemy naval chiefs to deploy simply because they would not know the reason for the original loss.' Midford gestured with his head for them both to walk on towards a quieter corner of the garden, then continued as if amused by a thought. 'However, I'm not sure that Her Majesty's government have any immediate intention to put the SBS's latest toy to use. More importantly, were the 851s intended to be compatible with the detonators?'

'No, not initially, I understand.'

'Would their use together be impossible or quite complicated to achieve?"

'No,' replied Sullivan as his brigadier stopped walking and turned to look disappointingly at the colonel.

'So, a half-baked terrorist could use one?'

Colonel Sullivan pulled a grimace. 'Certainly, it has that potential.'

'We must assume for the moment that they are compatible. The 851s. Size? Weight?'

'They would fit easily into a lady's handbag, sir.'

'So,' probed the brigadier, 'it could be used against an aircraft?'

'It could, but unlikely. The explosion created by an 851 is totally disproportionate to its size. A small amount of Semtex would do the job on an aircraft. This sort of mine was designed for use against reinforced structures.'

'When were the 851s taken?'

'Last evening.'

'From?'

'School of Infantry, sir.'

'Who's dealing?'

'MOD Police.'

The brigadier turned sharply on the colonel, 'I don't want that bunch cocking this up. You call them off. Gently, but call them off. Tell them what you like, provided it convinces them. I don't want them involved. Where's Lovell?'

'He's in the UK.'

'Then he's available. You and Lovell deal with this now. And don't tell anyone else.'

'Right, sir. On to it right away. Will you make my apologies?'

'Yes, yes,' he said impatiently, 'just get on with it.'

Colonel Sullivan turned and was about to make his way towards the flight quarters.

'Richard,' said the brigadier as he turned around, 'You did the right thing, but you have given us an intriguing problem.'

Sullivan was still thinking of that comment as he strapped himself into the helicopter's seat and the two Rolls-Royce Gnome turbo-shaft engines raised the Lynx above Salisbury Plain, turned westward and flew towards Warminster.

Chapter 11

Tuesday 16th October.

Bristol, England.

HADFIELD HAD occupied the third floor office since the 10th October. There was a kitchenette, toilet and, importantly, a little outer office that led into a communal corridor, with the main office overlooking Corn Street and the banks. The rental was high but it provided for ease of access and egress as well as near perfect observations. There was absolute privacy, other than the tenants of the other two identical offices on that floor, and it was close to his hotel, The Grand, which was only one hundred metres away around the corner in Broad Street. But, as Hadfield prepared himself again for another period of observation, he wondered if Dolan had eluded him.

Although the Atlantic First Commercial only opened between 10.30 a.m. and 3.30 p.m., it was impossible to maintain concentration throughout. He had to leave his window to use the toilet and to refill the percolator. He knew his love for coffee was a weakness but he convinced himself that it aided concentration. He poured another cup of Kenya Peaberry.

At 10.15 a.m. Hadfield positioned his chair and adjusted the lateral blinds. Staff had been working in the bank since 9.30 a.m., now they milled about behind their counters, the junior managers at their desks, and what Hadfield believed to be the branch manager in his first floor office. This manager was a large man, tall and overweight, with short curly brown hair. Hadfield checked his Canon camera and placed it carefully on the low table to his right, exchanging it for his Alderblick binoculars. He used them to look once more across the road, moving from ground floor counter to counter, then to the manager's office, adjusting the focus as he went. He could see that the manager was at his impressive executive desk equipped with angle-poised lamp, three telephones and a sleek computer terminal. The high resolution glasses were adjusted again more finely as the desk-top family photographs in silver frames came into sharp focus. One last scan of the building and he set the binoculars down and tasted the smooth, nut-flavoured coffee again. It started to rain.

***

Sean Dolan was still tired after his journey from Falmouth. He had been on his feet most of the previous day trudging around the port with his minders. Still, the cottage they found was just what he wanted. It was not too ostentatious, well place but not too prominent. He could lie low there until the job was done and they were ready to let him out of the British Isles once and for all.

He sat on the edge of the bed in the safe house. He smelt. The room smelt. But he was glad that his minders had moved the date forward so that the cottage purchase could go ahead early.

He looked out through his miserable bedroom window. It was raining and his new dark suit would get wet if he wasn't more careful, but at least he would be driven most of the way. He scrunched his Corn Flakes.

By 12.20pm., Dolan crossed over Bristol Bridge on foot and approached the bank and the old commercial heart of the city. His dress gave the appearance of a middle-grade manager amongst dozens of middle-grade managers who thronged the streets. Spots of rain fell again, a little heavier than before and he put up his black umbrella.

He knew they would be there of course, but somewhere unseen to Dolan. The two-man surveillance team also felt the rain and pulled up their coat collars against it.

***

As always Hadfield's concentration was making his eyes ache. Four men had entered the bank but he couldn't make out their faces because of an assorted collection of umbrellas.

As each man transacted his separate business and turned away from the counters towards the main doors, Hadfield could see that none matched the description of Dolan. Hadfield knew that this was always the most wearing part of an operation, but years of practice had curbed frustration. Then he saw him. A figure fumbling in the doorway trying to let down his unfamiliar black umbrella. His eyes narrowed. He had him now. There was no doubt. He checked against the full-face photograph sent to him by the NIRB. As Dolan stood at the counter looking to his left and right, the brunette attended to the customer in front of him. Hadfield kept him in sight a moment longer adjusting the Alderblicks, checking the profile against another photograph. It was definitely his man.

It took Hadfield less than four minutes to leave the office, cross the road to the Atlantic First Commercial and stand immediately behind Dolan who was already in the process of passing over a completed form to the stunning brunette. He sensed Dolan tense. The Irishman did not turn completely around but only slightly to his right, almost imperceptibly, but enough for him to see the well-polished brown Barker shoes and the brown hide attaché case at Hadfield's feet. It was enough to reassure him.

'There you are, sir. £5,000 in fifties and twenties and the Banker's Draft for £84,950 will be ready for collection on Thursday. I'm sorry if there has been some confusion,' said the brunette.

'It was nothing at all. It just put me out, so it did,' said Dolan as he put one bundle of notes in an outside coat pocket and the other inside.

'If it will help, we can send the draft by fax to Falmouth on Thursday; it would be about mid-day.'

'No, no, that will not be helpful at all,' replied Dolan, trying desperately to conceal his eagerness to leave.

'I am so sorry,' she persisted, 'maybe you would like to phone Falmouth now, you can use our complimentary phones in the clients' lounge over there,' she said, pointing to his left.

'No, that's kind of you, but no. I'm in no rush,' he said hurriedly buttoning his coat. 'I just forgot the procedure. Good day to you.'

'A confusing business,' said Hadfield to the young brunette as he moved forward to the counter. She had no difficulty in returning his charming smile, clearly finding this tall, sandy-haired, rugged customer a lot more interesting than the Irishman.

'When I bought my little place, nothing seemed to be straightforward,' she replied.

Hadfield had overheard enough; he posed no questions regarding Dolan or his account - that would come later. For now he continued to fascinate her as he knew he could most, if not all, women.

'I wish to open an account. Could you let me have some literature to take away?' he said, noting her name on the counter plate as Miss Clare Hopkins.

'Of course, sir,' she said, handing him an impressive glossy brochure but still holding his attention with her eyes. 'If there are any other services we can provide, sir, we would be only too happy to assist you.'

'That's always reassuring to know,' he said in a friendly but non-committal tone.

There was an opportunity here he thought. Miss Clare Hopkins was beautiful and seriously tempting, but he was too much of a professional to take advantage of that now. However, he would bear Miss Hopkins in mind – she could be the only key to Dolan's account.

Chapter 11

Wednesday 17th October.

Bristol and Falmouth, England.

HADFIELD PARKED the Ford Mondeo rental in the Fish Stand Quay overlooking the Inner Harbour and zipped up his anorak against the wet and cold, walked up the steep incline between the houses to Church Street and turned right against the approaching one-way traffic along Market Street towards the Prince of Wales Pier.

When he left the bank the day before, Hadfield drove immediately for Falmouth and checked in at the Greenbank Hotel. After dinner he had checked the internet and searched the Yellow Pages for listed estate agents in the town, he then spent the next two and a half hours peering through estate agents' windows. This morning he had already visited six; now, near Webber Street, he lingered outside the fishmonger's from where he could see Hagley's.

Hagley's was a long established local firm which had recently been taken over by Mr Hagley's two sons. They wasted little time in bringing the business up-to-date whilst still retaining the reliability and quality of service that had been the hallmark of Hagley's since 1946.

Hadfield crossed the road and scanned the photographs in the bright window display. There were many properties ranging from the large detached houses in their own grounds occupying prestigious positions overlooking the River Fal to small terraced cottages. A number of photographs bore red 'Sold' tickets and others blue 'Under Offer'. It was these that occupied his attention: £180,400, £99,950, £122,750, £78,895. But what caught his eye was '£84,950' moving around on an electric mobile display; a very small two bedroom semi-detached cottage. He noted other similar properties, then entered the well organised offices and walked up to the receptionist sat at a modern desk in the middle of the floor.

'Good morning, sir, can I help you?' she said brightly.

'I was just looking at some of your cottages in the window. I'm really after a little quiet place for weekends, something that's not too much of a fuss to look after.'

'We have some very attractive properties, what price range were you thinking of?'

'I suppose between seventy and ninety. I can't really go above that.'

She stepped out from behind the desk, a little shorter that he had at first thought but very pretty and very trim in beige blazer and black trousers.

'We have some nice ones here,' she said pointing to a display. 'This one is in Stratton Terrace with glimpses of the hills.' She handed him a leaflet.

'But only one bedroom.'

'Yes, that's right. You were looking for more?'

'I would prefer two.'

'We have these here. This one at Barracks Ope at £79,950 which would need quite a good deal of up-dating and there is this one in

Grove Place at £78,500. Oh, I'm sorry, Grove Place only has one bedroom and it's a little run-down. Ah, but there is this one,' she said pulling a leaflet from the stand. 'Very pleasant and at £91,500. I'm sure that the price is negotiable.'

'That's alright. If it was absolutely what I was after, I could probably find the money.'

He read through the details as the young lady stood there, hands clasped in front of her, smiling patiently.

'These are interesting. Can I take them with me please?'

'Of course you can, sir. This one is empty and we have the keys. The others, well, just knock on the door.'

'I see.'

'Would you like to view the empty one?'

'I think I'll drive around and get the feel of the area first, then if I like what I see we could arrange an internal inspection of a few.'

'Let me give you a little map and I'll mark where all of these properties are.'

'That is thoughtful of you,' he said with an engaging smile, 'and it will save me such a great deal of time. You are being most helpful.'

'Could I have your name for my index?'

'Of course,' said Hadfield, 'It's Stotesbury, 37 Harley Court, Clifton, Bristol.'

'Thank you, sir,' she said and walked to the door and opened it.

'There was one in the window,' he said as if an afterthought, 'for £84,950.'

'Oh yes. An Irish gentleman is buying that one. He only rang this morning to say he would be bringing the money down tomorrow.'

'He's from the North then?' he asked. He needed to be sure.

'Not really, from Bristol, like yourself.'

'But you say he hasn't paid for it yet?' he said, not aggressively, but with mild authority.

'Yes,' she said hesitantly, 'I mean … no, he hasn't yet,' the smile leaving her face.

'You will let me have the details then,' the authority still clear in his mild voice, adding more softy, 'You never know, he might change his mind, and it did look rather nice.'

'Just a moment, sir,' and she went to the revolving display. As it turned she deftly removed a leaflet. 'I'll mark on your map where it is.' He handed her his map and she penned a small cross. 'There it is, sir, 3 Beacon Cottages. It's unoccupied but furnished. The owner has gone away and it's available for immediate occupation. If you want the keys … '

'I know, I must come to you,' he said with a disarming smile.

He left the shop and walked back through Market Street to the quay-side car park. In the car he studied the map. The Greenbank Hotel was more convenient than he had realised.

The hotel was directly on the bank of the River Fal and the Nightingale Restaurant looked out across the grey, ruffled waters of the river towards the pretty white cottages of Flushing in the distance. Between the hotel and the little village of Flushing, yachts, dinghies and cabin cruisers faced the oncoming tide, straining upon their moorings, sheets beating upon the masts. To the left, further up this inlet was Penryn and to the right, the jetties and derricks of the busy deep-water harbour overshadowed by the granite mass of Pendennis Castle which, together with its smaller sister St Mawes, guarded the mile-wide entrance to the Fal Estuary and the Carrick Roads. It was there in 1588 that many of Sir Francis Drake's ships assembled before engaging the invasion Armada of Philip II of Spain.

Greenbank Terrace continued up the hill behind the hotel and joined Bassett Street which ascended further to a small 'Y' junction of Polwheveral and Longdon Terrace in the middle of which could be found Beacon Cottages. It was here many centuries ago, as elsewhere in Falmouth, that beacons were built and lit, relaying their fiery message from headland to headland along the south coast and inland from hill-top to hill-top, warning of attack and calling the militia to arms.

The cottage had been easy to enter. He had stood on the pavement and made a pretence of studying the brochure, then opened the little white painted wooden front garden gate and walked confidently up the uneven path, stepping onto the grass so as to avoid the wet hydrangea bush growing near the wall that ran alongside the path. No one noticed that he opened the door with a plastic bank card and not a key.

It was a neat and attractive cottage. Off the little hallway was the main living room - two original rooms knocked into one. Both fireplaces remained, one of natural stone, the other of brick.

Double glass doors opened into an 'L' shaped kitchen that still contained the original Victorian, iron kitchen range. All along the opposite wall were the latest kitchen units with cooker, fridge/freezer and washing machine. A window looked out onto a long, narrow but unkempt garden. An extension had been built here with the original kitchen door leading into a small back corridor. He stepped through this door. Immediately to the left was a shower and to the right, down a little corridor past a newer back door, was a toilet and bathroom.

Hadfield concluded his reconnaissance up the stairs where there was a medium sized front bedroom and a smaller one to the rear. Altogether there was little room for a large family, although under the stairs was an enclosed storage area and, at the back of the hallway, a large storage cupboard. The reconnaissance had confirmed Hadfield's plan. The cottage, its lay-out and location would suit what he had in mind admirably.

Back at the hotel, his thoughts were interrupted by the waiter.

'Would you care to have your coffee now, sir, or would you prefer to take it in the lounge?'

'I'll take it in the lounge,' replied Hadfield. 'Do you have Kenya Peaberry by any chance?'

Chapter 12

Tuesday 23rd October.

Bristol, England.

IT HAD been twelve days since Hadfield had commenced his observations on the Atlantic First Commercial Bank. He had now adopted a realistic pattern with sleep that provided the best opportunity for establishing the routine of the manager, as well as to ensure that Dolan did not withdraw the remaining cash without his knowledge.

The bank opened at 10.30am. and closed at 3.30pm.; the manager arrived between 8.15 and 8.25, the remainder of the staff at about nine. In the afternoon, the staff left between 4 and 4.30, the manager and one other leaving a little after 6pm.

The manager was of course the principal target, but not the only target. One morning, the manager's routine had changed and he had boarded the 7.22am. train to London, Paddington and was away from his office for two days. As a result, Hadfield had seized the opportunity on the first day, once the bank had closed, to tail the lovely Miss Hopkins' car to her address in apartments at Cornwallis Crescent, Clifton. On the second day, Hadfield had been able to follow the not so lovely older woman, whom Hadfield believed to be the manager's secretary, as she took a bus to what appeared to be her home address at Clouds Hill, St George.

The manager's home address had been a little more difficult to ascertain, simply because the manager left the bank later in the day when commuter traffic was heavier. Because of the manager's absences, it had not been until the previous Tuesday that Hadfield had been able to follow him to the nearby multi-storey car park and had seen him drive off in his metallic granite-green Porsche 911. Early the next morning, Hadfield had parked his Mondeo rental near the car park exit on the first floor and was then able that evening to tag the Porsche to its owner's home at 3 The Cedars in Flax Bourton, south of the city.

Constant observations on the manager's house would have potentially attracted attention, but a clear pattern had emerged and Hadfield was able to observe the bank during opening hours as well as tail the manager to and from his home.

Today, as yesterday, Hadfield had been awakened at 5.45 by the early morning call from the hotel reception and made coffee in his bedroom. He laid out his clothes for the office on the bed and checked his briefcase, empty except for his cellular phone, then dressed in an unobtrusive dark green tracksuit under which he wore his thermal underwear.

At 6.20am. Janet and Carol at the reception desk smiled as Hadfield jogged past through the foyer.

'Good morning, ladies.'

'Good morning, Mr Blane,' Janet said.

'See you later.'

Both young ladies watched him as he opened the smoky-brown glass doors. The tracksuit was of a loose fitting design although not as loose across his broad back, chest and shoulders, and much closer fitting about the waist and butt. He knew, with complete certainty, where the ladies would be looking as he also knew he could charm any woman, young or old, naïve or sophisticated.

He turned left on the pavement and jogged gently into Wine Street and then towards Newgate and his car. Driving out of the city, he passed the cathedral and followed the river onto the Long Ashton by-pass. Just five miles later he parked the grey, two-litre Mondeo neatly in one of the bays in front of a rank of five shops which stood back but parallel to the Bristol to Congresbury A370.

Hadfield locked the car and began to jog again away from the main road. It was less than a quarter of a mile to the path that skirted the field that took him to the rear of the building site. Only six houses were being built in this walled cul-de-sac that faced onto the A370. Hadfield avoided, as best he could in the dull dawn, the clay mud, still wet concrete and the inevitable puddles, moving behind to the second house on the right. The roof was on but window frames and doorways still empty.

From the first floor second bedroom, Hadfield had a clear view across the main road to The Cedars. It was a recent development of sixteen exclusive detached houses set in five and a half acres. The manager of the Atlantic First Commercial was already at breakfast in number 3.

It was a little chillier this morning and Hadfield hoped that the previous day's routine would continue. If the manager kept to schedule he would leave his house at 7.30 and drive to the multi-storey car park, to walk the short distance up Newgate to his bank. If this routine was followed this morning, then Hadfield could return to the hotel for his usual bath and a late breakfast and be able to be in his temporary office overlooking the bank for his 10.30am. to 3.30pm. vigil. Today he would miss breakfast.

The front door of number 3 opened and Hadfield instinctively checked his watch: 7.26. The manager opened the door of the double garage to reveal the 911 Turbo and green Honda CR-V four-track. The manager started the 911 and the engine responded to the gentle touches on the accelerator pedal with a series of throaty growls. Apparently satisfied, the manager edged the Porche onto the drive, the garage door was shut and the manager returned to the front porch as usual. Hadfield's eyes narrowed and his heart rate perceptibly increased. This morning was different. The wife handed the bank manager his briefcase but he then leant back inside the hallway to produce a black *Napa* leather suitcase. This morning their embrace was longer and two young children appeared at the bay windows so as to wave their father good-bye.

A few years ago he would have had a team of twenty to watch one target, but nowadays he worked alone. Consequently, the odds were more in favour of the target. The Porsche could go anywhere. He had pinned his hopes on the manager as his only realistic and logical access to the account and contact with Dolan, but he realised that he could not maintain his lone observations indefinitely. He had to have some luck. The routine had now changed. Would this change of routine provide the luck he needed?

Hadfield remained in the shadows of the empty bedroom long enough to see the Porsche turn right towards the city. He jumped down the stairs, one hand on the unfinished wall, the other on the unpainted banister and carefully made his way back across the field, jogging the short distance to his car. Initially, he drove carefully along the A370 but once past the Jubilee public house he accelerated, taking maximum advantage of the dual-carriageway section to make up time, then descending down the Long Ashton bye-pass towards the light grey-coloured early morning haze ahead that appeared to shroud the city.

At 8.11am., Hadfield drew into the kerb adjacent to the Bank of England. If the manager kept to his routine of using the multi-storey car park and walking to his bank, then he must walk up Newgate and along Wine Street, past the Prudential Building.

Hadfield had only to wait a few minutes until the manager appeared – without the suitcase. Hadfield smiled with relief and professional satisfaction - he was beginning to understand his target.

His judgement had paid off. If he was right, he could not return to the hotel yet. He parked his car at a meter bay in High Street and jogged through the glass-covered market to Exchange Avenue and his office.

He knew who he would be looking for. Her daily conduct in the manager's office was not intimate but it was far more familiar than their relative positions would normally have permitted. He hadn't long to wait, the rich brunette hair and overnight case gave her away. Miss Clare Hopkins was walking, with a slight spring in her step, up Small Street from the direction of Colston Avenue and towards the bank.

Hadfield had seen enough. He left the office, jogged to the meter bay in the High Street and drove the car back to the car park, then returned to the hotel. Janet and Carol had gone off duty to be replaced by Sandra and Margaret. They had been told all about Mr Blane's early morning jogs and butt. Now they could see what the night staff meant.

As soon as he was in his room, he quickly checked the telephone directory and dialled out.

'Thank you for calling Atlantic First Commercial. How can we help you?'

'May I speak to the manager please?' Hadfield asked.

'May I ask in what connection, sir?'

'To open an extremely large account.'

'I'll put you through to Mr Peckham's secretary now, sir. Can I have your name please?'

'Yes, of course. Hancock, John Hancock,' said Hadfield.

There was a pause.

'Miss MacDonald. May I help you Mr Hancock? Mr Peckham is engaged with a client for the moment.'

'Yes, I'm sure you can. I wish to deposit £2.7 million within the next three days. It is a matter of some expediency and urgency. I am sure you will understand. Can you tell me, is Mr Peckham free today. I could make it at 11.30?'

'His only free appointments are at 2pm. and then again at 3.30pm. Would these be too late?'

'Oh, I'm afraid so. What about tomorrow?'

'Tomorrow is out of the question,' she said defensively, but then more accommodatingly, 'What about Thursday?'

'Thursday would be fine. How about at 11am.?'

'No, Mr Peckham has another client at 11 o'clock, but he would be free at 12 noon.'

'Yes, I could make it for 12 noon,' he replied.

'We look forward to seeing you then, Mr Hancock. Good day to you, sir.'

Hadfield was now confident that Peckham would be at his bank until at least 4 o'clock this afternoon. If his hunch was correct, he and Miss Hopkins would be staying the night together out of town. He rang the car rental company and then reception.

'Reception, can I help you?'

I appreciate it is rather late but can I have toast and coffee in 43?'

'Of course, sir.'

'Colombian Maragogype.'

'Of course, sir, it will be with you directly.'

'And I shall need an alarm call at 1.30pm. and a tuna salad and coffee at 1.40pm., in my room please.'

'Right sir. We'll call you at 1.30pm.'

***

The alarm call had woken Hadfield from a deep sleep at precisely 1.30pm. He dressed in the towelling robe and slipped the latch on his bedroom door. When room service tapped on the door, he didn't open it but called her in. He sat in the easy chair next to the bed, near the crumpled pillows, as the maid entered alone.

'Did you want me to take the "Do not disturb" notice off now, sir?' she asked as she put the tray on the table.

'No,' he smiled. 'That is thoughtful of you but you can leave it there for a little while. I hope it hasn't inconvenienced the maids too much?'

'Oh no, sir,' she said as she finished placing the tray on the table, then turned and left his room closing the door behind her.

Hadfield removed his SIG Sauer P220 semi-automatic 9mm pistol from under his pillow and slipped it into his towelling robe pocket. He moved to the door and locked it. It was not that he was overly anxious, but, years of experience had resulted in naturally cautious habits. He ate his snack unhurriedly and read *The Times*.

At a little after 3pm., Hadfield was at the hotel's reception again, wearing a beautifully cut hacking jacket, roll-neck sweater and light brown trousers.

'I have some business in Manchester tonight so I may not be back until late,' he said.

'Well, have a good trip, Mr Blane,' said Margaret 'but I think we're in for some showers.'

'You're probably right,' he replied, 'but I shall be OK,' patting the Burberry raincoat over his arm. He picked up his overnight bag and left the hotel.

Margaret looked admiringly after him as he left the hotel, casual and comfortable, but always smart.

Hadfield exchanged the grey Mondeo for a two-door 2 litre Golf GTi. The Golf would provide greater performance, but his real reason for the change of vehicle was that he had used the Ford rental continuously for over two weeks to observe his target. A change of model and colour would be a prudent move. He drove for a while - he had time. He quickly became accustomed to the vehicle and was satisfied with the Golf's comfort and performance. The VW Golf had an acceptable top speed of 128mph, but with a 0-60mph performance of only 8.9 seconds, Hadfield could not outpace a 300 bhp Porsche from a standing start. Nevertheless, he was sure that he would be able to out-drive the bank manager.

By 3.15pm., a little later than he had planned, he had parked in the High Street on a single yellow line outside the Rummer Restaurant. Soon a bay was free and he parked further up the road outside the Kard Kabin newsagency. From here he was confident that he would be able to see Peckham as he walked to the car park.

At 4.12pm. he saw her. If it hadn't have been for her luxuriant brunette hair be may have missed her. He should have realised that she would go to his car first, but he had been looking for him. He didn't follow Miss Clare Hopkins.

At 4.34pm. he moved off and edged into the traffic when Peckham crossed from Corn Street into Wine Street on foot. Hadfield drove along Wine Street, down Newgate passing the car park on his left and into Broadweir and stopped. From here he could see any vehicle leaving the car park. A few minutes passed, then the Porsche emerged and turned left.

Hadfield was only three cars behind the Porsche as they moved to the offside lane of the Bond Street ring road and halted in the traffic. Hadfield could now clearly see the Porsche's off-side rear tyre on its 19" rim, the exhaust's twin tail pipes and the massive rear spoiler. The traffic lights changed and both cars turned into Newfoundland Street and headed towards the M32, skirting the St Pauls area of the city and onto the elevated section of the motorway leading to the long gradient overlooked by the castle-like Stoke Park and the telecommunications relay tower.

Peckham moved effortlessly away. Hadfield pressed his right foot to the floor and the Golf responded smoothly, but in comparison to the Porsche the VW seemed impotent. Peckham, whilst impressing Miss Hopkins, unwittingly reminded his pursuer of the huge reserves of power and unparalleled performance of 3.3- litre turbo. This understandable exhibition however was short-lived and the Porsche slowed to a more modest speed as it approached the Hambrook Interchange and the junction with the M4. Whether this indicated a pre-occupation with his passenger or a lack of driving ability, Hadfield did not know, but speculated that it was probably a mixture of both.

At the junction with the M4, the Porsche turned towards London and Hadfield adjusted his posture for a long journey, switching to intermediate wipe as spots of rain began to fall. By using other vehicles as cover and alternating the light configuration from headlamps to foglamps, he was sure he would be able to follow Peckham to his destination undetected. But he knew there would never be room for complacency. At junction 18, the Porsche unexpectedly turned left along the A46 into the twilight of the Gloucestershire countryside, then branched right towards Tetbury, past the Westonbirt Arboretum to join the old Roman Fosseway four miles west of Cirencester.

Hadfield had difficulty matching the Porsche speed. Although his driving skill was well in excess of Peckham's, the acceleration of the Porsche was a phenomenal 0-60 in five seconds and he had to punish the Golf at the junctions which regularly dissected the Fosseway so as to keep close to his quarry. He, of course, would have noticed if he was being tailed. A less able driver in a less powerful car would have drawn attention to himself in a clumsy effort to keep pace with the Porche, but Peckham was oblivious to the Golf's presence, his whole thoughts were concentrated upon the lithe brunette at his side, her perfume that excited his thoughts and the ecstasy that he hoped lay ahead.

They passed through Stow-on-the-Wold and on a further nine miles to the beauty of honey-coloured old stone houses of picturesque Broadway, the village once known as the 'Painted Lady of the Cotswolds'. As the Porsche parked outside the 16th century Lygon Arms, Hadfield momentarily wondered if the more recent connotation of such a title was lost upon Miss Clare Hopkins.

Both the bank manager and his lovely lady companion entered the hotel with their overnight cases.

Hadfield consulted his watch – a little after six. There was nothing to be gained by waiting outside the hotel merely to contemplate what he knew was to take place. He looked at his watch again, then studied the Ordnance Survey map, gauging distance and time. He laid the map open on the front passenger seat and engaged first gear. He had made up his mind, he would take this opportunity to reconnoitre the tunnel approach and entrance before he returned to the Grand Hotel.

Chapter 13

Thursday 25th October.

Bristol, England.

ALISTAIR PECKHAM walked from his en-suite toilet and approached his executive desk, now clear of paper, to wait the few minutes before his next client. He wondered absent-mindedly why Mr John Hancock wanted to deposit £2.7 million. The thought of his bonuses and what could be achieved with such large sums of money still excited him, the vast sums involved still fascinated him and his clients still intrigued him.

Mr John Hancock would not intrigue him - he would shock him. The red pulsating light interrupted his thoughts. 'Yes, Freda?' said the manager of the Atlantic First Commercial.

'It's John Hancock, Mr Peckham, he's on line two. He has an appointment with you in five minutes. He does not wish to cancel but wishes to talk to you urgently.'

'OK, Freda, I'll take it,' he said, pausing only slightly and continued brightly, 'Hullo, Mr Hancock, this is Alistair Peckham, is there a problem, sir?'

'There's not really a problem Mr Peckham, but I though it would be so much more discreet if I discussed this extremely personal and delicate matter with you over the telephone.' Mr Peckham was not yet wary as Hadfield continued. 'The situation is quite simple. A relatively large sum of money has been deposited in your bank that belongs to associates of mine. They have asked me to restore to them what is rightfully theirs.'

This type of call was not unique.

'Mr Hancock, or whoever you are,' said the manager in an assured air, 'I am sure that you have done your homework and will know that the cash cannot be given to anyone other than he who has the computerised withdrawal slip and uses his personal seven-digit code which, of course, is unknown to anyone else.'

'I understand how extremely efficient your organisation is Mr Peckham,' said Hadfield, 'but, even your bank has to keep records and there is a means by which you can assist me.'

'Look, I'm going to have to cut you short here, I'm not prepared to discuss this further with you.' Then added unnecessarily and pompously, 'Our reputation rests upon discretion.'

'Then may I speak to you,' Hadfield said tersely, 'about *your* reputation and *your* indiscretion, particularly in respect of,' he paused, ' ... the Lygon Arms?'

'What are you talking about?' said an indignant Peckham.

'You know perfectly well, Mr Peckham. I do not wish to become unpleasant.'

'I don't know what you are talking about,' persisted Peckham not wishing to terminate the call but desperately keen to know what his caller knew.

'Then if you don't know what I'm talking about, your attractive wife and two delightful children soon will.'

'What are you after?' asked a now agitated Peckham.

'I do not wish to take money from you or from your bank,' he said disarmingly, then added more sharply, 'What you will do is simply telephone me when a certain individual makes any withdrawal from your bank.'

'Do you know his account number?' asked the manager grasping at straws.

'No, but … '

'Then, how do you expect me to know?' he said haughtily.

'Let me help you Mr Peckham,' Hadfield said calmly. 'I know that £200,000 was deposited at your bank on the 1st October and that £5,000 in cash was withdrawn on the 16th, as was a banker's draft drawn in the sum of £84,950. I am sure that if you search through your computerised records you will be able to make a cross-reference which will reveal the account number.'

'And what's in this for me?' he said as he finished scribbling down the dates and figures, personal anxiety overcome for a moment by personal greed.

'My silence, Mr Peckham,' Hadfield replied softly.

'But the account number won't help you,' he persisted.

The caller ignored the manager's comment and continued. 'All I require you to do is telephone me with details of the amount when a withdrawal is to be made from that account.'

'I have this conversation on tape,' he said defiantly.

'Mr Peckham, it makes not the slightest difference to me if you have this conversation embroidered on your underpants. I shall give you a number whereby you can contact me.'

Peckham recorded the number on his green blotter and said rashly, 'That's a Birmingham number.'

'It is Mr Peckham, of a cellular phone group. However, the mobile is not registered in my name and is therefore, for all practical purposes, untraceable by you.' Hadfield allowed this information to be absorbed by an extremely uncomfortable bank manager before continuing. 'It could be that a withdrawal from this account will not be made for a week or six months and consequently, as time passes, the significance for you and your family of your indiscretion with Miss Clare Hopkins of Cornwallis Crescent, will become less apparent. I shall therefore, from time to time, remind you, Mr Peckham. I sincerely hope that it will not be necessary to distress your family, nor inform your superiors. I understand that the penalty for such an indiscretion is instant dismissal from the bank.'

The phone buzzed in Peckham's ear. The conversation was at an end. He thought of the strict company rule regarding managers' affairs with staff and the consequences of discovery. He picked up the silver framed photograph of his family on his desk and knew that he had few alternatives but to comply, consoling himself with the thought that no one in the bank would be any the wiser and his career and his family would be safe.

Hadfield, from his third floor office across the road, also looked with the aid of his binoculars at the pin sharp image of both Peckham and the family portrait he clutched. He lowered his 10x50 glasses and, still peering out across Corn Street, savoured the slightly acidic taste of the smooth, nut-flavoured Kenyan coffee.

Chapter 14

Monday 5th November.

Salisbury Plain and London, England.

CAPTAIN JAMES Cleeve had worked with British Special Forces in many joint training exercises including a Royal Marine Raiding Squadron in Norway and with the SBS and SAS in connection with the protection of North Sea oil rigs. As a young lieutenant during the Falklands War, he had seen the SBS go into action from his ship in San Carlos Water, but even this had not prepared him fully for working with his colleagues gathered around the conference table in the oak panelled Great Parlour of '907'. It was a different type of exercise, a different type of war, unclear with ill-defined rules against indistinct and shadowy enemies, a war of uncertainties and distortions, operating in what one chief of the CIA's Counterespionage Department had referred to as a 'wilderness of mirrors'.

At his second meeting on the 22nd October, Cleeve had been able to assess his colleagues more accurately during the evening at dinner and later in the bar when, as so often in the case, their real character and personality had been revealed. His initial assessment of some had been confirmed whilst in the case of others he had found that appearances were deceptive. He warmed towards and was beginning to respect both policemen whilst disliking the arrogance of Roberts from the Foreign Office who was enjoying the luxury of being a spectator without responsibilities to the drama that was unfolding. Brittan was clearly a clown whom the Co-ordinator, General Sir Ian Noble, would soon get rid of. Brigadier Midford and the policeman Bennett were probably the best, although he liked the quiet Reed from MI5. He was unsure of the competence and metal of the MI6 man and there was a coldness between the two organisations. Reed seemed more dogged, patient and down-to-earth, whilst Sutton was blasé and outgoing, casual even. Maybe it was the individuals themselves or maybe it said something about their respective organisations and roles.

These opinions would be confirmed or otherwise today. However, he was sure he wouldn't change his mind about Colonel Sullivan. He didn't like him at all and during the next twenty minutes he would like him even less.

The meeting commenced at 8.45am. sharp.

'Let's get underway ladies and gentlemen if you please,' said the Co-ordinator, and everyone looked up. The room was quiet, except for the slight hum of the copier.

'Richard, to get all our thoughts together, bring us up to date regarding the thefts and bring in Major Lovell as and when.'

Colonel Sullivan smiled at the Co-ordinator, then glanced at the major, then bobbed about smiling at the Co-ordinator again as if in a state of perpetual gratitude. He stood at the small lectern near the map and screen looking like a slightly more intelligent version of the imbecilic French detective Clouseau. Having said that, he was exceptionally smart in appearance, clipped and precise in speech, clearly a loyal and willing subordinate although not possessing a great brain. Ambitious men with little brain are usually unattractive individuals.

'Thank you, general,' said Sullivan as the lights began to dim, shrouding in darkness Major Lovell, who was standing behind the colonel. 'Of necessity, I shall cover some old ground but we now have much greater detail to add.'

Sullivan spoke for a short while then introduced Lovell of the army's Special Investigation Branch in such a manner that everyone was left with the impression that any failure to be revealed would be the responsibility of the poor major.

'Thank you, colonel,' said the major. 'Ladies and gentlemen, it is as well for me to start by saying that as is inevitably the case, problems do not arise because of an isolated incident but because of a series of incidents that, by themselves would be insignificant, but together cause a headache.' He paused and looked around those seated before him. 'And we have a big headache.'

All those assembled, other than the Co-ordinator and Sullivan, were attracted to the major's no-nonsense and reassuring style and began to make themselves more comfortable for what was clearly going to be an informative presentation.

The major outlined the history of the development of the Type 851 demolition mine, his easy explanation being punctuated by appropriate graphics on the screen. The weapon looked very much like another but, when the significance of the changes in design, particularly its light, synthetic construction were explained, and its capacity for devastation detailed, the military's loss and the thief's gain were starkly apparent.

'Its compactness,' continued the major, comparing the 851s with conventional mines, 'is partially due to the explosives used.'

Major Lovell pressed his hand-held control with his thumb, the diagram vanished and all that remained was the blank, black screen. He moved unnoticed in front of it and pressed the button again. Now he was silhouetted against a glaring whiteness.

'Not only is its power,' he said, 'totally out of all proportion to its size, there is no limit placed upon its usage either by altitude or depth. Equally, if not more important, is the loss of the barometric detonators.' He extended his left arm, holding the detonator between his index finger and thumb. The screen went blank again and those around the table each reflected upon the significance of what this meant. The major touched the switch again and another picture filled the screen.

'Barometric and aneroid detonators are not new but this particular system,' he said, pointing to the screen, 'also incorporates the benefits of gallium-arsenide technology – *super-chip* technology. Again, as with the 851s, there is no limit as to its use, either in respect of altitude or depth.'

'There is a further point, is there not, major?' Sullivan said, as if Lovell had forgotten all about it.

'Absolutely, sir,' replied the major anticipating the interruption, 'these detonators can operate at an accuracy hitherto unattainable, the mechanism so sensitive yet the system so robust that it essentially operates for practical purposes at pico-seconds.'

'I'm sorry to interrupt,' Brigadier Midford said, 'but where these systems not designed to work together?'

'No sir, but they are utterly compatible.'

'Can the detonator be overridden manually, electronically?' continued Midford.

'They can be.'

'Thank you,' said the brigadier, scribbling notes without taking his eyes off the major.

'If there are no further questions, we should now proceed to the thefts themselves,' suggested Colonel Sullivan.

'One question, if I may,' Chief Superintendent Packham said. 'You say that the whole system is extremely sensitive. Help me with an example if you would then I can grasp the significance. If I put the mine and detonator in a lift and sent it up the Empire State Building, would that be sufficient to activate the mine?'

'Certainly.'

'On which floor?' Packham asked succinctly.

'The second or above,' came the reply. Then there was utter silence.

'And down into the basement?'

'The lower basement,' came the blunt and matter of fact response, 'but the system is so sensitive that you could set it for any floor above the second.'

'Humour me for a little longer, major,' said Packham. 'If I hear what you are saying, the system can be effectively set up operationally irrespective of where you are. You could for example be in the Grand Canyon, or in the rarefied atmosphere of the Andes, or down a mine shaft, is that so?'

'That is correct, sir.'

'I'm sorry to persist but let me make sure I understand you,' continued the policeman. 'All of these factors can be taken into account and accommodated virtually automatically so that detonation takes place precisely when the operator requires it so to do?'

'Exactly.'

The chief superintendent nodded, then smiled towards Lovell, who began to describe the circumstances surrounding the thefts.

'Ladies and gentlemen, initially you may have thought it odd that the mines and detonators were stolen from the School of Infantry, but I shall explain the series of events that lead to this blunder. The truth is that they were being temporarily stored at Warminster and had been there for a little under two months prior to the theft. You will recall that Major M.F.J. Harper of the Royal Marines, who was military head of the 851 project, was killed during Exercise Troubadour and the project put on hold for a while. Unfortunately, vague reference was made to this in his *Daily Telegraph* obituary and expanded upon rather extravagantly by some of the tabloids. It was no doubt this publicity that drew attention to their location.' He turned to the screen again.

'The school itself,' he continued, drawing their attention to a plan which now appeared. 'May I point out three buildings, this one here, the armoury. And this one, the wireless depot,' his billiard cue-like pointer moved across the screen, 'and here, the detention block.' Photographs on the computer screen replaced the plan in quick succession as the major provided more relevant detail.

'Both the armoury and wireless depot, as you can see, are in the process of refurbishment, in fact, a completely new system of heating and air-conditioning is being installed. Consequently, in the absence of recruits on exercise in Yorkshire, the detention block was chosen to store the new mines and detonators. With hindsight, one fact was overlooked. Detention cells are primarily designed to keep thieves in, not keep thieves out. Other than personal attack alarms, the block is not equipped with burglary-type alarms at all.'

'What about perimeter fences, capacitance fields, volumetric systems, those sorts of things?' questioned MI6.

'Only weld mesh I'm afraid.'

'Isn't that a bit poor?' scoffed Roberts.

'Yes, it was,' he replied as if the obvious had been stated, then continued to describe the thorough examination of the route from the A350 to the detention block which the thief was believed to have taken, and his short route away with the mines and detonators.

At appropriate times, photographs appeared to show a cluster of silver limes, the spot where a prone figure had rested; cut wires and a drain culvert; a simple door lock and loose keys on hooks; the grey interior of a cell and broken boxes. It was a depressing tale.

'In normal circumstances,' continued the major, 'items of this importance should be kept in a purpose-built bunker with seismic and video detection plus restricted access, something really secure. This wasn't the case. The facts are that they should never have been kept at Warminster whilst renovations were taking place.'

'But they were, major,' Sullivan said as if rebuking him. He turned towards the Co-ordinator and asked, 'If you wish, sir, I shall continue?'

'Please do, Richard.'

'I think,' said Deputy Assistant Commissioner Bennett, 'that you will find it more helpful if I take up the story now as it essentially, if not wholly, involves the activities of the civil police from now on. I think it may be simpler if I do, there may be the odd point that Richard would not be aware of.'

'Very logical, thank you,' said the Co-ordinator as if the exchange was of no importance. He didn't look towards the colonel until Bennett had started to speak. He need not have worried, Bennett's political antenna was quite refined, he would not embarrass the army. The exchange of glances however had not gone unnoticed by Captain Cleeve. His opinion of Colonel Richard Sullivan had not changed. Major Lovell had been brought along to give the bad news, whilst the colonel had hoped to be associated with the good. How petty thought the naval captain, it was neither the colonel's nor the major's fault, but Sullivan could not resist grasping every opportunity to ingratiate himself with the general.

'As you can imagine,' continued Bennett, 'there were many avenues of enquiry that were pursued, one of which was to check the guest lists of local hotels and guest houses for the two months prior to the theft. These checks threw up many individuals; one chap wanted on a matrimonial warrant from Bradford, another for failing to appear at Maidstone Crown Court. Yet another had traffic convictions whilst another a series of previous convictions for factory breaks. He was brought in, came from Solihull, I believe, but this job is out of his league and in any event he could not be connected. Many similar cases were checked equally thoroughly. All other persons have been checked by visits to their home addresses, checked and then re-checked. We have caused a few men to worry who were at locations unknown to their wives.' A few members fiddled with pens and paper and others lowered their eyes as if the policeman had struck a familiar chord. 'But, again, none could be connected.'

'So, we don't know who it was then Commissioner?' said the Co-ordinator moving back in his seat and raising his eyebrows questioningly.

'I believe I know who he is but I don't know his identity.'

The Co-ordinator's eyebrows remained raised, his face expressionless.

'We have checked every house, cottage and farm which offers holiday or bed and breakfast accommodation within a six mile radius. One farm, near Longbridge Deverill,' Bennett said, tapping at the map, 'just here, had a guest, a charming gentleman apparently, who had some sort of skin complaint. He wore cheese cloth-type gloves all the time.'

'Who was he?' asked Roberts. They were all looking at the policeman, Sutton of MI6 more intently than the others.

'He told the people at the farm that he was a Michael Beazley of Northampton. The address he gave does not exist, but as he paid cash the farmer and his wife had no reason to question him. I gather he was handsome and charming and the farmer is able to give us a description. This is him.'

It was in many respects eerie. The face of the man that had occupied much of their thoughts since the 22nd October grew in clarity on the screen as the lights dimmed. It was a portrait sketch of a handsome man, about forty-five years of age, sandy coloured hair, a rascally charming smile and a slightly broken nose.

Bennett continued to speak as those assembled examined the face as if hoping to detect what thoughts lurked in the head, what intentions were hidden behind those blue eyes. 'He stayed at the farm between the 22nd September and the 6th October.'

'Are you suggesting that the theft occurred before the Sunday?' probed David Reed.

'No, the theft undoubtedly occurred in the early hours of Sunday, but he left the farm on the Saturday as would be normal for a holidaymaker. To have done otherwise could have attracted suspicion. It also allowed him to leave the area immediately after the theft, well before the possibility of road blocks, without the danger of having to return to the farm and explain his nocturnal activities,' the policeman explained.

'Risky,' Roberts said.

'Such an enterprise is not without risk. He had prudently reduced his risks to the minimum,' commented the brigadier, then added more earnestly, 'and the 29th was Open Day at the School of Infantry.'

'Precisely, and one of the locations that is a must for the public to visit is Battlesbury Hill,' added the policeman as a map of Warminster appeared on the screen and the hill was indicated.

The brigadier sighed, 'Where they assemble to watch displays, which also gives a clear view of the ranges, the detention block, every ruddy thing.'

The colonel remained silent.

'There was another matter of significance,' continued Bennett. 'On the 1st, a man using the name of David Miller, asked for and was granted temporary membership of the Arnhill Golf Club. As you see, Battlesbury Hill provides a vantage point to the east and the Arnhill course does so to the west. We cannot be one hundred per cent sure, but the temporary member was distinctive because of a purple-check golfing cap he wore with a yellow bobble and also a large ornate ring on his right hand.'

'Why do you think they are one and the same person?' asked Sutton, whilst Brittan looked at the MI6 man, then the policeman, utterly confused.

'Because it is often the way of confidence tricksters and others to wear something, maybe quite small, which attracts attention away from the whole. If this was the case with this temporary member, then it nearly succeeded. Staff and members think he was tallish but can clearly recollect that he wore this purple cap and some can remember the ring. However, the club secretary rang one of my detectives three days after their initial visit to say that he now remembers that when the man with the purple cap was signing his temporary membership form, he held the form steady with his knuckles. At the time the possible significance had not been apparent.'

'Only conjecture,' suggested Roberts.

'True, but Miss Zoë Appleby, the receptionist at the club does remember him. She only saw him once, but she remembers his handsome, smiling face. She says that this artist's impression,' he turned again to the picture on the screen, 'is the same man.'

They all concentrated in their own way upon the face. Some looked at it expressionlessly, chins on hands. Others sat back frowning, whilst the others sat forward, arms folded on their blotters, searching the face.

Bennett broke the silence.

'None of the facts surrounding this man are incriminating. By themselves they are insignificant. Together they may mean that this is our man.'

'Circumstantial,' said Roberts.

'But as any good judge or defence barrister knows,' replied Bennett, 'circumstantial evidence is very often more reliable, compelling and damning that one or even two first-hand witnesses. Such evidence comes from so many independent sources that it is unrealistic and illogical to assume that it is coincidence. In any case ladies and gentlemen,' he stopped and deliberately looked slowly at each member in turn before continuing in a quieter tone, 'we have nothing else.' He sat down.

'Surely you have something more?' said Brittan. 'What about a car, fingerprints, DNA or something?'

'Our report, Mr Brittan, deals with those possibilities and others at paragraphs 42 to 83. The car was grey, either a Vauxhall, Ford or maybe Japanese. Not that helpful. And there are no prints. The forensic team has been over the room and the farm. We do have some DNA. We are pretty certain it is his, but this alone does not help us, certainly not at this stage.'

'Why not?' enquired a confused Brittan.

'Because,' offered the brigadier, 'in this case such a DNA sample is rather like having a fingerprint of someone who has never been fingerprinted before.'

'That is absolutely right,' continued the policeman. 'Colonel Sullivan and Major Lovell have been through the police part of our joint report and Charles and I have been through theirs. The brigadier has kindly gone through the lot.'

Brigadier Midford waved his hand and gently shook his head as if to say that it was no trouble at all for him to be of help.

'I'm as sure as I can be,' said the policeman, 'that we haven't missed anything.' There was silence again.

The Co-ordinator spoke, 'Does MI6 have anything to add to this report?' he said, waving the buff coloured folder.

'No sir,' replied Sutton.

'And what about you, Sarah?'

'There's speculation of course, we can't keep this sort of thing quiet for long. Middle and Far East dealers have got the scent,' said Davidson of GCHQ. 'CIA are jumpy, Langley knows something is up, so I think we can anticipate being asked more questions by them shortly.'

'How much do they know?' asked the Co-ordinator.

'My summary is at paragraph 13,' she said as she passed copies of her report around the table. 'What we pick up from Cyprus, they pick up from Majorca.'

'Your assessment, Derek?'

'They have been asking probing questions,' replied the Foreign Office man. 'They know we've had a loss, not the detail, but they know it's important.'

'And their people?'

'Increasingly active but discreet.'

'I think quite frankly that it would be better to put them completely in the picture, they could be of help, sir,' observed Roberts.

'On that depressing note,' said the Co-ordinator, 'does the Foreign Office have anything *else* to contribute?'

There was no response.

'Right,' said the Co-ordinator deflating his lungs. 'I'll brief the Secretaries, then the Americans. Thank you for your reports. Let us now move on. It's you again for the next item, Commissioner. The Bristol bank business.'

'Charles will take this one, sir,' said the policeman as he handed over to the deputy head of SO13.

'Taps have been put on the bank,' said Chief Superintendent Packham, 'the bank manager's home and that of the chief cashier by Field Services. At this stage the fifth floor reports nothing. Observations are being maintained by the Fraud Squad. The two local detectives have been supplemented by another man, and we have boosted that team with three SB men from the Met.' He smiled as he added, 'that gives us 24 hour cover on the bank should anyone wish to transact business outside of office hours.'

'And what about you MI5?' said the Co-ordinator.

'I checked this morning at eight' said Reed. 'There are no updates, sir. None of their active service units are out, there are rumours that the NIRB have put out a contract for a special job but the NIRB themselves are not in a position to mount anything themselves yet. They will of course recover but at the moment they are inactive.'

'Something is active,' said the Co-ordinator tersely. 'We have mines and detonators stolen. We haven't a clue where they are and we have a cocky Irishman wandering about the city of Bristol with shopping bags brimming over with bank notes.'

Colonel Sullivan mumbled as if to speak but the Co-ordinator silence him with a raised finger.

The Co-ordinator was uncomfortable but didn't reveal it. MI6's report gave no update on the NIRB's calls in February and September, yet he knew from GCHQ that British Telecom's computer at Oswestry could analyse speech, was capable of voice recognition and keyword targeting, and had identified the calls on the 6th February and 10th October as having been made by the same person, but, although the call on the 18th September had used the same codes, the voice pattern was different.

Sutton and MI6 may not have known, they couldn't know everything, and MI6 staff at BT may not have realised the significance particularly as the September call had not been that clear. Fortunately, GCHQ had identified *The Times* obituary notice pattern. Davidson had passed this to the Co-ordinator and

Sullivan's staff had done the rest, including activating sleeper agents and implanting additional military and MI5 agents in all nuclear installations throughout the UK.

'There are a number of measures we are going to take now before the momentum of the enquiry is lost,' concluded the Co-ordinator. He looked towards the policeman and continued, 'John, remind me, who is the local police commander in your report?'

'Chief Inspector Faraday. He's the Acting Superintendent.'

'That's him. David, get onto "B" Branch. I want someone selected to be attached to our young Acting Superintendent just to make sure everything is being covered. I'll speak to Sir Hastings direct.'

Other measures were ordered before they broke for coffee. All those assembled were tasked. Directives would go to the Landline Interception Centre in Belfast; 'F' Branch would re-double their surveillance on the left wing; Section 'K' of MI5 would join with 'J' Division of GCHQ and MI6 would now link with the Americans at Fort Meade.

Captain Cleeve left the Great Parlour and walked through the Inner Hall to the Drawing Room, an even larger room, forty-foot long and nearly twenty-foot wide with deep moulded beams and hung with 17th century Flemish tapestries. It was a bright, airy room and the views towards Chapperton and Chitterne Downs were superb. The naval officer poured coffee for himself and then for the brigadier who had joined him.

'Brigadier,' said the captain.

'Please call me, Peter. We're all off parade here, old boy.'

'Are all chief constables as helpful as Sir Hastings Perry?'

'Not all. They are an independently-minded lot generally, but Sir Hastings has been in this game before, he knows what the requirements are.'

'I can see the point in all the measures that Sir Ian has got underway, but why attach MI5 to this chief inspector? I'm sure he's a good man, but isn't the rank a bit low?'

'Oh, good God no,' smiled the brigadier. 'The Co-ordinator has just taken out part of his insurance package.' He sipped his coffee and had another ginger biscuit. 'They don't make coffee like this in Whitehall. One of the perks of coming down here.' He smiled again, looked around the great room and then led the naval captain to an empty bay of tall, leaded windows. 'If it all goes wrong, then the poor chief inspector is just the right rank. In fact, *acting superintendent* is even better. Any failure would confirm the prudence of not appointing young Faraday to the substantive rank of superintendent.' He popped the remainder of the biscuit into his mouth. 'The rank of chief inspector is not too high so as to cause public disquiet and a lack of confidence in the police, but,' he continued with a wry smile, 'not too low. You see, you can't blame a sergeant if there's a major cock-up can you?' He stooped to put his empty cup on the coromandel wood table. 'Like the Falklands, The Gulf, Bosnia or any other operation for that matter, keep everything in perspective, James. We're in a dirty business. I try to keep my end of it as clean as I can.'

***

'Good evening sir,' said the doorman, proud and tall in his grey double-buttoned coat and top hat, but Colin Sutton of MI6 made not the slightest acknowledgement as he strode through the portals of Blacketts, the London gentlemen's club, just as The Cambo Clock struck a rather squeaky 8 o'clock. He crossed the black and white marbled entrance salon and draped his coat across the mahogany cloakroom counter. Unknown hands spirited the coat away as Sutton mounted the staircase, the walls of which were adorned with portraits of old Lancers who had risen to become Whitehall warriors.

'Mr Flores has arrived, sir,' said a familiar voice. 'I took the liberty of asking him to wait in your usual place,' the footman continued to say but the sounds trailed away as Sutton advanced towards The Colours, the drawing room containing the pale, threadbare colours presented to the now disbanded Rothbury Light Horse so many years ago.

Sutton knew whom he was to meet. His name wasn't Flores of course, that would have been most careless, but it was a name that would do as well as any so as to conceal the true identity of Robert Hausman, formerly Head of Clandestine Services under the CIA's Deputy Director (Plans) and now security chief of Vesco-Schuck Dynamics. VSD was huge by any standards, employing 437,000 people world-wide in 27 different countries, and specialising in nuclear generated electricity. More recently, VSD had obtained contracts for the decommissioning of Russian 'VVER' reactors in the Urals and significantly two of the former USSR's 76 nuclear-powered submarines. These major and prestigious contracts had been gained on the basis of VSD's outstanding reputation for decommissioning expertise as well as the quality of design and the reliability of engineering and construction of nuclear power stations, two of which had been recently built in the UK.

Sutton approached his usual place, a corner filled with shadows created by the great glass-fronted bookcases, the brown marble

Doric pillars and table lamps. He couldn't see Hausman's face but he knew he was there; his bulk largely concealed in the high-backed leather Chesterfield chair, swirling cigar smoke trapped in the light above.

Hausman rose through the smoke, turning to display a chiselled, granite-like clean-shaven face with a powerful smile.

'Colin, it's good to see you,' he said clutching Sutton's extended hand, 'the staff here have looked after me very well. Take my seat.'

Sutton found himself seated and dwarfed in the Chesterfield whilst Robert Hausman occupied another Chesterfield, his back to the wall so as to provide him with a commanding view of all who now moved in Blacketts, able to raise and lower his voice as prudence and confidentiality dictated.

'How can we help you Colin?' he asked, concealing his contempt for a man easily persuaded to assist VSD for a handsome retainer and now becoming agitated at the prospects of detection.

'I don't like how this is developing,' Sutton said nervously, 'I thought my role was going to be limited to providing a little information here and there.'

'That was the original intention, but time moves on Colin. Unexpected problems arose with the power station. The important issue now is to consider how we are able to close down one of your power stations before it causes your Government and my company a lot of embarrassment. All we need is a small incident to justify a temporary shut down that will allow some minor modifications to be made. Fortunately, disloyalty amongst the NIRB provided us with Dolan. He will do a job for us and as a result the station's capacity can be reduced, a hardened terrorist will be killed, your security services triumph and no nuclear catastrophe,' he concluded with a smile and raised both hands as if he were a magician who had just completed a remarkable illusion on stage before a packed audience.

'Passing information was one thing, this has gone too far,' said Sutton through clenched teeth.

'We're in the big boys' park now, Colin, and it's not a one-way street. You and your Dti people had been helped by us even before the "super gun" affair, and continue to be helped in many, many ways. Now your people will receive information from us regarding the Russian nuclear electric capacity and requirements. Your intelligence services and industries will benefit,' he said, then pointing his finger added, 'as you have.'

Sutton said nothing, he began to rationalise his conduct. The power station's defect existed. If he didn't do something about it there would be a disaster. Thousands of people would be killed instantly, tens of thousands over the years that followed. He had an opportunity to prevent that and keep his bank manager happy. Winners all round, he thought.

Chapter 15

Tuesday, 6th November.

Bristol, England.

THE CHIEF officers' suite was in a self-contained wing on the fourth floor of police headquarters, separated from the orderly bustle of the rest of the building by large polished redwood doors. Immediately behind these was the secretariat, to the left the staff officers' office and immediately across the wide corridor the office of the chief constable's secretary, Suzanne. Behind a further set of doors were the three assistant chief constables' offices, the plush corridor finally leading to a comfortable lounge-like vestibule. The furnishings were substantial yet relaxed and inviting with copies of *The Times*, the *Daily Telegraph* and the *Independent* on one coffee table whilst on another lay a copy of the annual report and a souvenir brochure of the Severnside Police.

Acting Superintendent Faraday was nearly fifteen minutes early for his 11am. appointment and so sat down. He could not relax. He looked around the room. Three doors led off from this vestibule. The first door on the left was to the deputy chief's office, the second opened into the conference room. Immediately in front of Mark were the double doors to the chief constable's suite itself. To the right was a wall of windows giving a spectacular view across the peaceful flat meadows of Clapton Moor towards Tickenham Hill and the old Iron Age hill fort of Cadbury Camp. The weather was slightly overcast but this did not detract from the view, in fact, it was clear today. Often in the summer months on bright, sunny days, the haze from the wetlands served to obscure the beautiful view – but not today.

The doors opened. 'The chief constable will see you now,' said Superintendent Caine, his principal staff officer.

Mark reached for his cap and gloves.

'No need for those, Mr Faraday. Please go straight in,' said the staff officer.

Mark adjusted his uniform jacket and walked smartly towards the doors, one of which was ajar. He tapped on the door, more as a respectful gesture and walked straight in followed by Superintendent Caine.

'Come in, Mark.' The chief smiled and gestured to an easy comfortable chair a little to the side of a wide desk. 'I shall only be a moment.' Mark sat down as the attentive staff officer remained near the chief.

Mark looked around the office. It was impressive. It was business-like as well as comfortable; uncluttered yet containing items both personal and professional spanning a life-time of service. On the panelled wall immediately behind the chief was a portrait of Her Majesty the Queen and to the left were plaques and shields from a variety of sources including the FBI and the Gare Republicaine, HMS Bristol and the police departments of the American cities of Bristol in Pennsylvania, Rhode Island and Tennessee. On a low occasional table were photographs of the chief and Lady Perry at Buckingham Palace as well as his two sons, one in the uniform of a RAF flight lieutenant and the other in the mortarboard and gown on graduation day at Oxford Brookes University. Arranged on the wall immediately above this polished table were the shields of the Metropolitan and Liverpool City Police, the Lancashire Constabulary and the West Yorkshire Police, neatly surrounding a shield of the Federation of Malaya Police with the emblem of the crossed Malay daggers, the traditional *kris*, in a wreath of laurel leaves above the force motto: '*Bersedia Berkhidmat*' – 'Ready to Serve'.

Behind Mark to his right near the windows was more lounge furniture, a low coffee table and television. He hadn't been invited to sit there, not that he had expected to, so he guessed that the meeting was not going to be that informal.

'This bundle can go now, Peter,' the chief said to Superintendent Caine, as he handed up folders to the waiting staff officer. 'Arrange for Mr Dorrington to see me this afternoon at three regarding the Princess Royal's visit and I think that is all. Leave us now, thank you.'

The staff officer gathered up his files and glanced at the acting superintendent as he dutifully left the office. The chief constable waited until the doors were closed and then looked at an expectant Mark Faraday.

'Well, Mark, I'll get straight to the point. I shan't ask you how you are getting on as an acting superintendent, I know. You are doing well, as I anticipated. No one has a complaint, in fact, we are more than pleased.'

Sir Hastings said he would get straight to the point but he didn't immediately. He spoke in brief statements, punctuating each with short but distinct pauses; pauses not so much for breath or effect, but for time as if he was reflecting and confirming in his own mind what he should tell the young policeman, or, more accurately, what he should not tell him.

'As you know Fraud Squad detectives, Pitman and Charlton I believe, have been keeping observations on the Atlantic First

Commercial and you have supplemented them with one of your men.'

'Yes, Norris, sir.'

'Yes, that's him, Norris. And three Met Special Branch men have joined the team?'

'So I understand.'

'Further information has been forthcoming, as a result the security services want one of their people in *loco parentis*, so I intend to attach her to you.'

'I see,' said Faraday, but he clearly did not thought the chief. 'Are you in a position to tell me what the new information is?'

'Merely precautionary,' replied Sir Hastings, neatly side-stepping the question. 'The security services are on to something but don't know what that something is. Consequently, they would like one of their own people on the ground.'

'Her name, sir?'

'Helen Cave and she will be living in room 219 at the Marriott Hotel.' He smiled, thinking of Mark's apparent reputation, then added, 'I don't suppose you have any objections to her sharing your office, Mark?'

'Of course not, but I assume she has a cover?'

'Yes. As far as everyone is concerned, she is a researcher with the Audit Commission studying police efficiency and cost-effectiveness.' Mark looked surprised. 'There is no need to worry, she has a BA or MA or something in Business Studies so her cover will be quite sound. You will also find that they will be installing a computer and VDU plus a secure line in your office today.' He didn't have to explain who 'they' were.

'What is her actual position, sir, her authority?'

'All you need to know is that, how do they put it, she is *about Her Majesty's business*,' and looking directly at Mark added, 'as we all are.'

'Who else knows?'

'Only my deputy and the ACC Ops. As far as you are concerned you can forget them both. You and Cave will be like Siamese twins. You will work closely together and only together. SB don't know about her, nor does the Fraud Squad.'

'But she'll have to be officially explained away. Can I assume that there will be a GO entry announcing her temporary secondment to the force?'

'Your assumption is correct. A general order entry will appear this Friday, that should do.'

'Is Miss Cave the only MI5 agent involved?'

'Officially, yes, but I think it would be naïve of you or I to assume that to be the case.'

'I see, sir.'

'I suspect that you don't, Mark,' he said gently shaking his head. 'Let me help you get your mind in focus. Miss Cave will have already arranged for your private car to be fitted with a multi-channelled radio this afternoon. She will also issue you with an untraceable 9mm.'

Mark was silent.

'You are a level-headed and sharp officer, Mark. I have complete faith in your ability and judgement. Help the security services all you can but do not meddle and don't get in their way. Only act in consultation with them, but, remember, they are faceless people with no identities. They are, for all practical purposes, like the 9mm, untraceable.' He paused. '*You* are not.' He opened the top right-hand desk drawer and picked out a matchbox-sized blank card and wrote three numbers upon it and handed it to Mark who stood to take it. 'If you have any doubts then ring me. The first number is this private line here,' he said pointing to an ivory coloured telephone. 'The second is my home number and the third my mobile phone. Always feel free to phone me, I know you won't waste my time. Are there any other questions, Mark?'

'I don't think so, sir.'

'Then you had better be on your way,' then added wryly, 'Miss Cave is waiting for your car.'

Mark Faraday didn't drive straight to his office but detoured around Westbury-on-Trym and the Stoke Bishop suburbs of the city. It gave him time to think of what the chief had said and what brief he had really been given. Maybe he should have asked more questions but he hadn't, and he was still not sure what was expected of him in the days to come.

His detour gave him time to think and by the time Faraday had parked his Volvo in his parking bay he had resolved that his relationship with Cave would be on his terms. He could not dictate to MI5, neither would he be used by them - if he could avoid it. He was prepared to assist them but he had no intention of being Cave's assistant. It was not a matter of semantics, or of pettiness or pride – well maybe a little pride he conceded - but the calibre of Cave was unknown to him.

Following his normal routine, Mark checked with the Custody Officer then took the stairs to the second floor and entered his office via the corridor. He peered at his in-tray and his forehead wrinkled into a frustrated frown. More paperwork. He walked to the window and gathered his thoughts, at first taking little notice of the *Ann-Maria*, an *Atlantic 37* cabin cruiser, turning slowly and expertly to a mooring against Bathurst Wharf opposite. One of the crew remained at the wheel as the other nimbly climbed onto the quay wall and secured for'ard. The engine was cut as the helmsman threw the coiled rope to his bearded companion and secured aft.

He thought how smoothly the two-man team had worked, without shouts of command or arguments, to berth the craft. He wondered if he and Cave would work so well. He went to the telephone and pressed a button.

'Jane, I'm back. Pop in would you,' he said as he inserted his security code into his desk-top computer and brought up the latest district information. He quickly absorbed the detail as his secretary breezed into the office, bright and unruffled, but made a point of closing the door.

'I'm expecting a Miss Cave, Jane. When she arrives I propose to keep her waiting just two or three minutes. I shall also want some tea. When you bring it in, put my cup on my desk and put hers on the coffee table. OK?' he winked.

'Of course. By the way, a British Telecom man is here to fit another phone and a Mr Cartwright from the Scientific Research and Development Branch about another computer for your office. Did you know?'

'Found out half an hour ago,' he said, and raised his finger, 'but let them wait.'

Miss Hart left the office with the slightest trace of a conspiratorial smile on her face - she liked more interesting days. Faraday, still reading the screen, picked up the phone and tapped in some numbers and spoke for a while. As Mark replaced the receiver it rang. 'Miss Cave has arrived.' said Jane Hart.

'Thanks, Jane. I shall only be a moment.' Normally, whilst in his office Faraday would have removed his tunic and worked in short-sleeve order. Today he would keep his tunic on. He adjusted a few items on his blotter and opened his briefcase, purposely heaping some papers on the chair to the side of his desk. Four minutes went by. He pressed a button again and when Jane answered he replied. 'Please ask Miss Cave to step in.'

Jane knocked on the door, walked in and announced the visitor: 'Miss Helen Cave.'

It was impossible not to immediately notice her jet-black hair, beautiful brown eyes and radiant smile. Helen Cave of MI5's 'B' Branch was confident and alert. About 5'4" and lithe. He guessed her age to be between thirty and thirty-three. She carried a slim Samsonite briefcase and wore a smart, single-breasted dark grey suit with a white blouse, more like a solicitor or banker ready for business than a spook. The fit of her expensive jacket and skirt left little to the imagination, accentuating her natural assets. As Faraday rose from his chair and stepped around his desk towards her, it wasn't difficult to conclude that Miss Cave would always appear extremely attractive, irrespective of what she wore, and whilst her dress would allow her to blend into the city's banking world, there was, he thought, more. Today, at this first meeting with the policeman, Helen Cave was making statement - a woman not to be ignored or forgotten.

They approached each other, hands extended. 'I'm Helen Cave,' she said confidently.

'Mark Faraday,' replied the policeman gesturing to the coffee table. 'Please take a seat, Helen. We could start with some tea I think.'

Helen Cave did not answer as Mark looked at Jane. 'Nearly ready,' she said as she returned to her office.

Mark sat on the edge of his desk, one foot on the floor but the MI5 agent remained standing.

'I was thinking,' said Cave with a slightly dismissive air, 'that before we have tea I can get the wheels in motion. I think that you have been told that we require your car for a few hours and that a telephone engineer and computer man are waiting outside now.' The opening rounds of the trial of strength had begun.

'Before you have my *private* car, Helen,' he said in a level cool voice, 'I would be interested to know what your brief is?'

'But you have been briefed by your chief constable,' she countered as if concluding the subject.

'That is true,' Mark said lightly, 'but even chief constables are not gifted with clairvoyancy. I am interested to know what *you* propose to do.'

'That naturally remains to be seen,' she said with a slight smile, then added in justification. 'This is, of course, a very fluid situation. It will depend on how things develop.'

'Let us assume that the situation remains as it is now, what do you propose to do?' Mark persisted.

'Nothing is ever static, chief inspector,' she countered, although it was impossible for her to speak without smiling. Her smile was captivating and disarming. Faraday would need to be cautious.

The secretary entered with the tea and placed a cup on Mark's desk, then the second cup on the coffee table. 'Do you take sugar, Miss Cave?' she asked. Cave ignored her and remained standing.

'Please sit down, Helen. Enjoy your tea,' then turned and thanked his secretary.

Cave did not sit but strode to the window.

'Just a moment,' said Mark sharply. 'Do not just wander around my office as if it's a hotel lobby. Sit down or I shall have you escorted from this building.'

There was no smile on Helen Cave's face. For a fleeting moment there was surprise in those dark eyes, not at the remarks but at the man.

'Your chief constable would not be pleased.'

'Nor would your superiors,' said Mark and, not giving her time to reflect added immediately, 'If I am removed and you remain, which I very much doubt, this whole district will black ball you.'

'I am keen, chief inspector, to get things going. I am sure you must appreciate that I am dealing with a rather delicate situation', she said, more annoyed with herself than Mark.

'And I am keen to establish the appropriate ground rules. The facts are that the security services have got themselves stuck up a lot of blind alleys and need our help. I am naturally prepared to help and you may find that I can be extremely useful, as can the three hundred and eighty-six officers under my command.' The point was not lost on Helen Cave as the policeman kept up the pressure. 'In the short time available this force has been quite open and accommodating to your people,' he said not revealing how little he really knew. 'I expect openness in return. I shall not put my life and career nor the lives and careers of my own people in jeopardy without it. Therefore, my request is quite simple. I shall require unlimited access at all times to your computer terminal.' Before Cave could respond Mark continued. 'If the security services are anything like the police service, you will have plenty of enemies to contend with.' Mark only paused for a second. 'There is, however, a difference between us, Helen. We, by and large, know our enemies. Together, we may discover yours.'

Cave smiled in unexpected admiration. She had anticipated meeting an arrogant young officer or a rather slow-witted one. Mark was neither, nor was he smiling.

'You have it, chief inspector,' she said as she sat down, placed her case besides her chair and reached for her cup of tea. 'I haven't started this meeting too well, have I?' she said.

'Can ... can I suggest,' said Mark, struggling to ignore his naturally sympathetic instincts, 'that once you've finished your tea we see to my car first, then lunch. That should give your people an opportunity to start on the telephone and computer link.'

'Agreed,' said Cave, subtly making the point that it was an agreement between partners. The point was not lost on the policeman.

Mark picked up the telephone and dialled out. 'Sarah, Mark Faraday. Is table seven available for the next hour or so?'

There was an affirmative pause.

'Excellent. Just for two, a colleague and myself, but give us fifteen minutes,' said Mark looking at Cave. She nodded and smiled.
Mark led the MI5 agent through the secretary's office where he introduced Helen Cave from the Audit Commission to Jane. Clearance was given to the two engineers and they discussed the sighting of the computer terminal which would be against the window, the operator facing out towards the harbour, the secure phone on the extreme right hand side of Mark's desk so that both could reach it, although Mark realised that it would not be he that would use it most. As they talked, Mark took off his uniform jacket and black tie, exchanging them for a double-breasted blazer and the white, yellow and red striped tie of the Indonesian Police, a gift as a result of his involvement with the Overseas Command Courses at the police staff college.

Mark initialled one report that would be dispatched with the two o'clock orderly and returned it to Jane Hart. She was too good a secretary to query why there should be the need for another telephone and a computer, but she knew that the activities today were not routine. The meeting with the chief constable was hurried and unscheduled and the delicacy of the situation was confirmed when Faraday had cheerily told her that he and Cave were going to The Hole in the Wall restaurant. She knew him too well; he never went to The Hole in the Wall unless it was with a colleague who was involved in a confidential operation or engaged in a tough internal disciplinary enquiry and so she knew that something special was going on.

Outside the police station's main entrance, Faraday and Cave were joined by two men wearing garage overalls. They walked to the policeman's car and made a pretence of examining the engine. One of the men remained outside peering into the engine compartment whilst Mark revved the engine and spoke to the other, now seated in the front passenger seat. They discussed the positioning of the tracker system, the radio and mobile data system as well as a more secure alarm. Clearly they already knew precisely what was to be done. They diplomatically reassured Mark that his car would not be damaged and that, although the radio would be removed after the operation, the alarm would be left for his own use.

The policeman's car was soon driven off towards Prince Street followed by an innocent looking Ford Transit van equipped with yellow roof light and 'Bowtell's Garage' logos on the sides and doors.

It was only a short walk to the restaurant, an old historic quayside building dating from 1602 and once frequented by Admiral Benbow who famously captured the notorious pirate Captain Kidd and brought him back to England in chains. At the top of the creaking stairs they turned to their left and towards a discreet alcove. Sarah was there. She always seemed so genuinely pleased to see her visitors. Friendly and dependable, always charming, nothing appeared too much trouble for her and she had the knack of being unobtrusive but appearing always just at the right time.

Their table was in a remote little alcove which looked out over the harbour, but, also gave those seated at the table a commanding view of the remainder of the restaurant.

'Quiet today, Sarah?'

'Oh no, Mr Faraday, rush over now, but you're always welcome. We'll just clear the other table over there and then we can leave you in peace.'

She handed each a menu, her movements quick without being fussy and irritating. Her staff expertly and quietly cleared the nearby table, then they slipped away. Mark need not have glanced around, Sarah would be there, out of hearing, but just in view, waiting.

'It's very pleasant here,' Helen Cave said as she looked around the restaurant. 'A strange name, The Hole in the Wall?'

'Ah, it was all about spy-holes in the wall which gave sailors a good view of the quayside.'

'So that they could keep an eye on their ships?'

'Oh no, certainly not,' Faraday replied with a chuckle. 'It was so that they could keep watch for the approaching naval press gangs.'

'Oh, I see,' she said. 'So, nothing about my trade?'

'No. Any connection with your trade was merely coincidental,' he smiled. 'This restaurant is convenient, it allows me a clear view towards my station. It is discreet; the food is good and I like the history of the place.'

'Anything in particular?'

'There are lots of things, I suppose. The first American consul to Britain had his offices in Queen Square and he came here regularly to dine. It amuses me,' he continued with a smile, 'that we may now be sitting in the very spot occupied by Robert Louis Stevenson when he was inspired to write his novel *Treasure Island*. He based the novel's Spyglass Inn on this building and one of his characters, Long John Silver, on its one-legged landlord.'

Sarah moved into view and they ordered sandwiches and two halves of lager but neither ate a lot. Helen Cave talked and held Mark's attention. She described the deaths of Tim Pat O'Brien and Seamus Fuller; John Pearse's visit to the Bristol banks and the joint Fraud Squad and Special Branch operation. As she talked they examined together the photographs from her case.

Much later Sarah moved nearer their table but still some distance away and stopped. Mark looked up and nodded, then quite openly but inoffensively covered the photographs with a paper napkin as Sarah approached as if in response to this gesture.

'I have another pot of coffee on now, Mr Faraday. I can set the hot plate up just here. I shan't disturb you and you can come and go as you please.'

'Oh Christ. It's 3.15,' said Mark looking at his watch. 'I'm sorry Sarah, I got completely engrossed.'

'It's quite alright. Let me take away these dirty plates, and here are your cups. It's quite private here as you know.'

The plates were silently whisked away but not the slightest inquisitive effort was made to move the napkin. The coffee cups and saucers arrived just as quickly as did a little side table and hot plate.

'That's very thoughtful, Sarah. We haven't really finished yet,' said Mark.

'I didn't think you had. And here's some more sugar. Thank you,' she said as if it was a pleasure to be helpful.

Over coffee, Helen Cave outlined the details surrounding the thefts of the mines and detonators, their capabilities and importance. They examined more photographs, some of the mines, some of Warminster, a farmhouse and broken boxes. What engrossed them the most was the artist's impression of the unknown man, a deadly and dangerous man.

It was ten to four when they rose from their table. Mark unplugged the hot plate as Sarah appeared. He paid their bill and Sarah protested at the extravagant staff tip.

'Thank you, Sarah,' said Miss Cave, 'a very pleasant lunch, maybe Mr Faraday will bring me here again soon.'

'Well I hope you'll both come again, you're always welcome,' she replied with a knowing look.

It took only a brisk few minutes and Faraday and Cave were back at the district headquarters. Jane had fended off most of the callers and there were only two messages to deal with. One was dealt with quickly over the phone, the other would have to wait.

'Have the engineers finished?' he asked his secretary.

'Oh yes,' replied Jane. 'I hope you don't mind but the computer looked silly on that low table so I've had a proper small desk brought up from the basement and also a typist's chair with comfy arms and little wheels for Miss Cave. A lot more business-like.'

Mark walked into his office. 'Perfect, Jane. As you say, very business-like.'

'Will you be requiring me to do any work on it?' she enquired.

'No, not much,' said Faraday. 'Helen will be using it mostly.'

'Will there be anything else?'

'No thanks, Jane, but we'll be staying for a while. We'll see you tomorrow. Thanks for holding the fort this afternoon.'

'Good night, Mr Faraday. Miss Cave.'

She quietly closed the door and for a few minutes she could be heard tidying her desk and moving about. Her outer door was opened, then closed. Faraday and Cave were alone.

Helen Cave checked the secure phone. She tapped six digits and was almost immediately answered.

'Delta 17,' she said, there was a further pause then, 'Clear as a bell. OK.' Then she replaced the receiver.

'The phone gives us a direct link to some of my colleagues in the Bristol area and also with London. Some of the numbers I use will be unacceptable on the normal subscribers lines, some won't. There is no purpose in giving you the numbers because the people at the other end are faceless,' she said without offence, then picked up the complete phone unit. 'If it's on my desk it will be less suspicious. We can tell the curious that it's a direct line to a computer bank or the offices of the Audit Commission. Are you happy with that?' That smile again, thought Faraday.

'Seems sensible,' Mark replied as she occupied the little chair. He was still wary that Helen Cave might try and take over, and it would be very, very easy to allow that to happen, yet, everything seemed to be working along the appropriate lines but added: 'But what about the computer?'

Helen Cave smiled as she picked up a computer disk and inserted it into the side of the machine.

'What we have here,' she said, 'is a micro-computer, virtually identical to your in-force facility, with a range of CDs and also linked to a main-frame at MI5's HQ at Millbank. As a suitable cover,' she said, 'this disk gives costings by the hour and by calendar month of various activities that could be operating on a basic command unit. They are national averages.' She pressed the keys. 'And here are other national averages regarding time spent on patrol, dealing with specific crimes, vehicle usage, overtime, that sort of thing.'

Faraday noticed, not for the first time, Helen's beautiful hands and exquisitely manicured fingers as they glided over the computer keys. An orange matrix of figures and letters appeared. Other keys were pressed and impressive graphs, pie charts and histograms were displayed depicting resource information and crime patterns.

'It's authentic, but not for this force,' Cave said, 'however, a layman wouldn't know and if Miss Hart feeds in some local stuff tomorrow it will serve to satisfy her and your superintendent when he returns. If you could arrange for me to have hard copy section sheets daily, then heaps of those alongside the screen should convince everyone of my role.'

She looked at Mark with a very self-satisfied smile, which then faded quickly.

'This disk,' she said more seriously, picking up another marked '439', 'is the intelligence disk. It not only stores information it also acts as a trigger to the main-frame computer miles away at the end of the secure telephone link.' She pointed at the cable leading from the smaller secure phone. 'You merely insert it, then tap in my user's code: "D17-96281".' She looked at Mark and said nothing, then entered her code. The blank screen came alive with text. She looked at Mark again as if to say: 'I've just demonstrated my faith in you, I hope I'm not wrong.' The orange words 'accepted – select service' appeared quickly followed by a menu of subjects.

'If we tap in "E4 – Mines",' she paused as the details rapidly filled the screen line by line. 'There we are.'

Mark moved closer to Helen Cave and craned over so as to read the details of the stolen mines, their ability to create a crater in reinforced concrete six metres deep by four metres in diameter or penetrate a half metre of steel. He also noticed Helen's perfume, *Opium*.

'Let's try another,' she said. '"B9 – Update" for example and we get an update.' Details flashed onto the screen. 'If you tap in "C2 – Suspects" you get as much detail as we currently have.'

Mark read the four pages under 'C2' and then asked for an update. 'Let me clear the screen and you start from scratch.'

Cave pressed 'clear' and the screen became blank. Mark and Cave changed places, as they did so they brushed against each other. He would have to be on his guard, he thought.

'Just tap in my code letter and numbers and the menu code word.'

Mark tapped in 'D17 – 96281' and the cursor winked: 'accept – select service', then 'B9' and the update appeared, three-quarters of a page as before. They talked for another forty minutes and were just making a second coffee in the secretary's office when the phone rang. It was Constable Phipps at the enquiry desk.

'The garage has returned your car, sir. It's out the front.'

'I'll be down and have a word with them. Thank you, officer.'

'Sorry, sir. I've got the keys. They've gone.'

'OK, I'll be down shortly,' said Mark as he replaced the receiver and turned to Cave.

'Your guys have returned my car and cleared off,' he said shrugging his shoulders.

Cave looked at her watch. It was 6.52.

'A good time to call it a day, Mr Faraday. Is that OK?' Those eyes again.

'I think you're right,' he replied as they both walked back into his office.

'One thing,' said Helen Cave, 'if you're reviewing information from "439" and someone, your secretary or the superintendent, or anyone, comes in unexpectedly, just press "O" and "P" together. She leant over and depressed the key and the screen was filled with statistical details of police basic command units. 'If you keep pressing "P", more innocent information will appear, twenty pages in all. It may be a good idea to look at the first few pages of this dummy information in the unlikely event of anyone asking a question. If the questions get too heavy, refer them to me and I'll confuse them.'

'Yes,' thought Faraday, he was sure Helen Cave could but nevertheless asked, 'Wouldn't it be easier for your computer to interface with ours?' pointing to his own desk-top VDU.

'No. I'm not sufficiently familiar with the information it contains. It could interface, but I think it is better to leave both systems quite separate.'

'OK,' said the policeman as they both stood up. 'Do you want a lift?'

'Could you drop me at the Marriott and I could explain the radio and alarm systems on the way.'

'Good idea,' agreed Faraday, 'We'd better tidy up here, the cleaners will be in first thing in the morning.'

Helen Cave turned the computer off and placed '439' in her pocket, the others she left in the wire in-tray on top of some loose papers on her little desk. Both left the office and walked downstairs. The chief inspector checked with the custody sergeant and then picked up his keys from the enquiry desk. On both occasions Faraday took the opportunity to introduce Miss Cave 'from the Audit Commission'.

As they approached the Volvo, Helen spoke.

'You'll see that the key is a little different. The key has a pressure pad built-in each side, just press and the alarm is on, press and it is off.'

The policeman opened his door and sat in the driver's seat, the MI5 agent sitting in the front passenger seat.

'The interior lights haven't come on,' observed Faraday.

'I know. If we drive into Queen Square for a few minutes, I can quickly explain the system to you,' said Cave.

'Now's as good a time as any.'

As Mark switched the engine on, the day-drive lights did not automatically come on either.

'No lights,' said Mark, 'they should come on automatically.'

'They would have taken out the day-drive fuse. If we are stationary with the engine running, we won't always want to draw attention to ourselves unnecessarily. Likewise with the interior lights when we opened the doors.'

They moved off and then parked in the shadow of two great oaks, equidistant from ornate but ineffective street lighting, facing towards the centre of the square and the equestrian statue of Prince William of Orange.

'As you see,' said Cave pointing to the Volvo graphic sound equaliser fitted in the aperture below the standard car radio and CD player, 'it looks like a graphic equaliser and indeed the front panel is. You switch it on just by talking. There are mikes in the door pillars.'

She pulled up the lid of the storage compartment between the front seats to reveal a key pad.

'If I can have absolute silence for a moment,' said Cave pleasantly, but with the authority of a pilot in a cockpit, 'I will tell you when you can speak again.'

She pressed a sequence of keys then simply said, 'Delta One Seven,' then pressed the "enter" button.

'There you are. My voice print is now logged into the system. I'll call up my people,' she said and raised her finger to maintain his silence. 'Delta One Seven to Lima November. Testing, over.'

The response was reassuring but surprisingly instant.

'Delta One Seven, this is Lima November, I have you five and nine, over.'

'Roger, Delta One Seven, out.'

Mark peered at the extreme end of the bank of warning lights below the rev counter. The blue light that had glowed as Cave spoke now vanished.

'As you know,' said Cave, 'there are sixteen warning lights along there but two and sixteen are not connected on this model, so we put a warning light into the last one. If the light is on you know that anything and everything that is being said inside this car,' she said raising her eyebrows, 'is being monitored by my colleagues at Lima November.' Then continued more formally, 'If we adopt the same procedure for your voice print, I'll tap in the code and when I nod just say clearly "Delta One Seven Alpha", OK?'

'OK.'

Cave tapped in the code and then nodded.

'Delta One Seven Alpha,' said Faraday, and Cave depressed the 'enter' button.

'Call them up now,' invited Cave.

'Delta One Seven Alpha to Lima November. Testing. Over.'

The blue light glowed and the same metallic expressionless voice replied from the door mounted speakers.

'I have you five and nine, Delta One Seven Alpha. Over.'

'Roger. Delta One Seven Alpha. Out.'

Mark sat back and looked at the new radio.

'Incorporated into your door pillars are your voice-activated mikes and behind the roof lining another aerial. There's also a GPS tracking and information system installed in the glove compartment. It's standard stuff, I can go over those another time.'

'OK,' said Mark, 'I'm impressed and it indicates how important all of this is.'

'It is *very* important, Mark,' said Cave as if speaking with a trusted friend she had known for years. 'We want to get this man, whoever he is, but what I really need is to have a feel of this city and the surrounding area so that if he's here I can understand more of how the bastard's thinking and how he's likely to respond. It could get hairy and that is why in the boot we've put some other kit for you. You'll find it in a metal box welded to the floor on the left.' Mark frowned as Helen Cave added reassuringly, 'Don't worry, we haven't damaged your car.'

'What's in it?'

'Nothing at the moment. It's all in your boot in an overnight bag we've supplied. This will allow you to take the contents into your home tonight without attracting too much attention. Then you can examine it all at your leisure.'

'And what will I be examining?'

'Well, there's a small personal encrypted radio, an ear piece without wire and a lapel mike. All very small. You can use them virtually anywhere provided you're within two miles of your car; the radio unit in the boot acts as a relay station, so unlike your mobile you will never be out of contact and the reception will be perfect, even along the Portway where reception can sometimes be temperamental. We have also included a PTT for the click system. You're familiar with the click system?'

'Yes. Three clicks means "yes", two is "no" and five means "standby, standby" - I think,' replied Mark pulling a slightly confused face. 'But I've never used the system operationally.'

'That's OK. Full details are in the boot. There is also a pager, looks like a Seiko digital watch, and it is, but it's also a pager.'

'Sounds a bit over the top.'

'Not really, everything is getting smaller and a watch is something men and women always have with them. Digital watches are always bleeping and this one has a vibrator mode as well so it shouldn't arouse any attention. There are two other smaller items, both tracking devices. I doubt whether we will ever use them but they are there and might come in handy. I said that part of the glove compartment's kit is a tracker that is always live, but the two little gems in the boot are for personal use. Usual routine, two per vehicle, one for the driver and one for your partner. Like the bleeper, they will operate using the car as a base station, but have a radius of twenty miles of this car. If we get split up then whoever is with or can get back to the base car can track their colleague. Also,' she continued more soberly, 'you'll find the bag contains your Glock 17 and ammunition. I understand that you are an AFO and will be very familiar with this weapon?'

'I am,' he replied as he visualised the Austrian made semi-automatic, 'and you've concentrated my mind very well, Helen. Are you carrying?'

'Oh, yes,' she replied slowly, as if experience dictated that for the remainder of her life her firearm would always be within easy reach, 'but I favour the SIG P225 9mm.'

'Well, I think,' said Mark, 'that this is as good a time as any to take you to your hotel.'

'Before you do, just one last thing. The switch there, alongside your heated rear window switch marked "1", activates the blue strobe-lights now fitted behind the radiator grill. The switch is a little obscured,' said Cave peering over - *Opium* again – 'It's just there by the gear shift, but it should be OK and at least you are unlikely to activate them unintentionally. And, press the next button to the right marked "2" and you activate the two-tones.'

They were silent as they drove to the hotel, only to speak as they arrived to confirm arrangements for the next day. It was agreed that Helen Cave would leave her Rover in the police car park and walk the relatively short distance from the hotel to the police station every morning and would be there punctually at nine.

As she began to open the door she turned to face Faraday, 'I didn't start today very well, Mark, but I think we can pull this off.' She smiled again. 'I do hope so. I shall rely on you … completely.' And, without waiting for a reply, she stepped from the car.

He watched her as she walked up to the main entrance of her hotel. A doorman open the door for her and, just for a moment, she seemed to paused as if about to look back, but she didn't and continued to walk towards the reception desk. Mark selected his gear then drove away to slowly cruise around the city. He thought of all that had happened and of Helen Cave. He drove down Park Street on to College Green, past the imposing Council House and the stately cathedral into the vibrant City Centre. The restaurants and bars were busy, courting couples and groups of youths walked the streets and dodged the traffic. There was already a queue at the taxi rank and two policemen patrolled near the telephone kiosks. Street lighting illuminated the main roads in an orange glow and the multi-coloured neon signs flashed and pulsated whilst the traffic lights maintained their monotonous cycle.

It was all so normal, but Chief Inspector Mark Faraday knew that nothing would be normal again.

At Avon View Court he stepped out of the lift and turned to his left along the plush hallway carpet of the third floor. The ivory and pearl grey panelling was soft to the eye, its fine vertical ribbing creating warm, gentle shadows complimenting the luxuriant carpet and pale purple drapes. He walked slowly past number 14. He could hear the sounds of a party, but the door was closed, partially blotting out the music and laughter from within. He turned the key in the lock of number 16 and entered his empty home.

Of course, it was immaculately furnished as was to be expected of one of the ex-show apartments of this exclusive development overlooking the Avon Gorge. The fact that it was fully furnished to a high standard made Avon View particularly attractive after the break-up of his marriage. He had brought nothing with him from his previous home and wanted to start anew, but never seemed to have the time to search for furniture or decide on wallpapers and colour schemes. He realised that number 16 lacked a female's touch; it was more a base station than a home.

He went into the master bedroom and put the flight bag on the bed, his tunic on the valet stand and slipped off his tie. In the kitchen he flipped through yesterday's *Telegraph* as the percolator spluttered, then took his coffee onto the balcony. It was coo! and crisp evening, very clear. On the river below, the sand dredger *Harry Brown* negotiated Horseshoe Bend, its navigation and deck lights twinkling red, green and white, the only sound the muted music and laughter from next door. Mark Faraday thought of Helen Cave, her elegant walk and beautiful hands, her dark eyes and bewitching smile. He stepped back into the lounge and closed the French doors, returned to the kitchen, poured another coffee and thought again of those eyes and that smile, her walk as she mounted the stairs in the restaurant, her beautiful profile as they had sat at the computer together – and the lingering scent of *Opium*. This assignment was taking on a dimension he had not anticipated at all and which he knew could be damaging, both personally and professionally.

Chapter 16

Monday 12th November & Tuesday 13th November.

Bristol, England.

WHEN THE two Fraud Squad detectives, Pitman and Charlton, had been supplemented by Norris and the three Special Branch men from the Metropolitan Police Service, their shift patterns had been changed from the comfortable 8am. to 6pm. to continuous surveillance 8 to 8, 8 to 8 around the clock. There were three men to both shifts which would allow a reasonable degree of accurate observations whilst the other two could undertake the 'follows' – if that ever proved necessary. It wasn't ideal, but it was adequate.

Norris was now working 8pm. to 8am. with Charlton and a SB man. This left Pitman and the other two SB men with mobile surveillance expertise for the daylight watch. For many reasons these arrangements made logical sense.

The officers occupied office number two. There were two similar suites on the top floor, three on the second and a further three on the first floor of this old but refurbished building. On the ground floor was an open-plan office with large windows looking directly on to Corn Street and down towards Small Street. This floor had previously been occupied by an insurance company but was now vacant, whereas all the other floors seemed to be in permanent occupation, at least according to the door plates. The entrance to all the upper floors was by way of a large bronzed aluminium-framed side door in the cobbled Exchange Avenue which gave access up the stairs to identical corridors which ran the length of each floor behind each office suite.

All the suites offered similar accommodation, a main office overlooking Corn Street, a toilet, kitchenette and outer office for secretarial or reception purposes.

It was ideally suited for observations. There was the relatively discreet side entrance giving access to numerous offices with people coming and going a great deal of the time, and none of the offices had windows that overlooked the corridors. The toilet and kitchenette catered for human needs and the arrangements of the suites with windowless toilets and kitchens abutting onto the corridor and the outer office at the side of the main office, allowed for the problems of unwittingly illuminating those keeping observations being reduced to a minimum.

It was in this environment that Detective Sergeant David Charlton, SB Detective Sergeant Craig Howard and Temporary Detective Constable Carl Norris had lived since the 29th October.

Norris was in the kitchenette washing up when the day-shift SB men arrived early, followed shortly by Robert Pitman. They all talked boringly of the uneventful night, Norris leaving last at about ten past eight.

Like many modern office suites, this group was stuffy and the chill morning air hit Norris as he stepped into the cobbled avenue and walked into Corn Street, hardly noticing the handsome, sandy-haired man who passed him and turned into Exchange Avenue. But it was that familiar clang of the heavy aluminium door that he had heard so often during the last fourteen days that made the young detective turn round and back into a nearby doorway. He only had to wait a few moments to see the lights in office number three on the top floor shine through the blinds.

Other lights were already on in other buildings and businessmen and women clad in thick winter coats and scarves, carrying brief cases and newspapers, were already hurrying about the streets. Carl Norris went home.

***

'Yes, Freda?' said Alistar Peckham.

'It's John Hancock, sir, on line four. He only wishes to have a few words with you regarding his special account,' said the bank manager's secretary.

'Thank you, Freda. Put him through.' There was a hollow sound for a few seconds then the manager said cheerfully. 'Good morning, Mr Hancock. Good to hear from you again.' Then, as he realised that only he and the caller were on the line, spluttered angrily: 'What are you calling me here for? I agreed to ring you, you'll bloody ruin everything.'

'Calm down, Peckham,' Hadfield said in a cold and level tone. 'I said that I would ring you from time to time and *that* is what *I* propose to do,' then added more lightly, 'You have not heard from our client?'

'No,' he said painfully.

'Your bank closes for the Christmas holiday on the 21st and re-opens on Wednesday, the 2nd,' he said, and not waiting for a reply, 'I shall assume that you will be at your desk on the 21st and again on the 2nd.'

'I am on holiday and won't be returning until the 7th.'

'Yes you will, Peckham,' came the curt reply.

'Now look,' he said with an anger he failed to disguise, 'I shall be with my wife's people in Surrey.   This is a long-standing arrangement which I can't alter.'

'This is not a matter open to negotiation. Our client could easily call on the Thursday or Friday and in that event you will be there so as to inform me.' The manager of the Atlantic First Commercial was about to persist in a fruitless argument as Hadfield drove home the significance of the manager's foolishness. 'Your current salary is £108,000 plus the car, a ridiculously cheap mortgage and other fringe benefits. I need not remind you that male divorcees who are unemployed are not ordinarily considered by the courts as suitable to have custody of their children. *You*, Mr Peckham,' he emphasised in a gravely voice, 'will be back at your desk on the 2nd. You have my number if our client rings, don't you?'

The question was not asked to confirm detail, it was spoken in order to confirm status and compliance.

Peckham took a frustrated breath. 'Yes,' he replied, knowing that he had little choice. The hollow sound returned. The conversation was at an end.

If Peckham was uneasy, so was Hadfield. He was a patient man but he would have preferred Dolan to withdraw the money before the snows came and schedules could so easily be affected. Once Dolan was out of the way and the cash safely deposited in his own bank, he could put his plans into action. His reconnaissance of the ground and his study of the maps and plans had satisfied him that a descent of sixty metres would be more than sufficient to trigger the detonators and cause two explosions in a confined space, with the inevitable result of a publicity-intensive operation to recover the nuclear material that would take nine to twelve months to complete.

***

For Chief Inspector Mark Faraday and MI5 agent Helen Cave, the previous few days had been taken up with a further review of the Permanent Operational Order for the three power stations, one at Oldbury, and the two stations at Hinkley Point. Cave liaised with the security service personnel deployed to those locations as she did discretely with the haven master at Avonmouth.

Detail upon detail had been obtained by Mark and fed by Cave into the computer. It was all double-checked as were the details of the owners of the two hundred and seventy-three boats moored in the city docks. Records at MI5 and MI6, Military Intelligence, the police National Criminal Intelligence Service and C4 of the Garda Siochana in Phoenix Park, were crossed checked with the Police National Computer at New Scotland Yard, SO13, the Severnside Central Criminal Intelligence Bureau, local District Intelligence Units, HM Customs & Excise and SB's Ports Units. Many of the leads appeared promising only to peter-out later.

During the previous week, Mark Faraday and Helen Cave developed a growing admiration for each other. However, Mark reminded himself from time to time that this admiration could very easily develop into affection and so he attempted to ensure that there remained a minor but distinct gulf between them. He assured himself that such a gulf was necessary because much of the responsibility was and would always be his. In any event, he knew that he was more comfortable making his own decisions and relying upon himself.   He had found it safer that way. Nevertheless, a respectful friendship developed and Mark was impressed with Cave's single-mindedness and commitment. She would doggedly pursue any lead, even the obscure and weak, spending hours pouring over the computer surrounded by coffee cups.

At least Mark could from time to time escape into the normal activities of district routine. In this regard, the Acting Chief Inspector, Bob Passmore, had excelled himself, taking much of the day-to-day burdens from his shoulders. Passmore, like Jane, never questioned his preoccupations.

Faraday saw Helen Cave stretched back in her chair and rub her eyes. 'I think we both need a complete break from this,' he said. 'You more than me, Helen. Look, I need to go up to the Tailor's Store at HQ today or tomorrow. Now's as good a time as any.' He looked at his watch. 'It's now twenty past two. We could both drive up there and stop off at the new marina on the way back.'

Helen Cave paused for a moment looking at the paperwork around her. 'OK,' she said as she took out a black make-up bag from her brief case. 'I just need a few minutes'. She raised and titled her head as she applied the lip balm and the lip gloss, then replaced them in the little black bag. Faraday remained in his chair, hands clasped under his chin, one elbow on the arm, unconsciously mimicking her posture. He realised that he was not just staring but examining the texture of her hair, the shape of her nose, the shadows created by her cheekbones and the sensuous curve of her mouth as she applied the mascara and eye liner. Her actions were not deliberately provocative, just confident and natural, as if Mark wouldn't mind her making up in his office at all. And he didn't.

Once the desk was cleared and the computer set to display the Audit Commission logo, Faraday spoke with his secretary and confirmed his commitments and appointments for the following day. The drive to force headquarters took them along the Portway and under the Clifton Suspension Bridge, onto the M5 and over the River Avon. As so often on a crisp November day, the sunlight was sharp and Faraday slipped on his dark glasses for the eleven mile journey. A familiar figure at Force HQ, Faraday was waved through the gates by a uniformed guard, but as always he acknowledged the man with a few words as he slowly drove over the speed humps.

Their time in the Tailor's Store was brief. Mark tried on his tunic and trousers in one of the changing rooms while Helen remained at the reception counter. She exchanged pleasantries across the counter with the chirpy staff, some at electric sewing machines, others with needle and thread, surrounded by little boxes containing different sized buttons, gleaming shoulder stars and crowns, and silver numerals. Behind these busy ladies was a large wall poster featuring UK, UN and NATO medals. The adjustments that had been made to Mark's tunic were perfect and they were able to leave with his new uniform, three white shirts in cellophane bags and a replacement pair of brown gloves. As they walked towards the car park they were seen by Sergeant Gordon Williams, the senior firearms instructor, who very clearly made a point of changing his direction of walk towards the chief inspector and the dark-haired young lady with the shapely legs wearing a dark grey business suit. Mark introduced Helen Cave. Equally clearly, Sergeant Williams was delighted to make her acquaintance.

'Is this your first visit, Miss Cave?'

'Yes it is.'

'Will you be coming here again?'

'Probably not,' she replied rather defensively, not wishing to be drawn into unnecessary conversations.

'Well, I'd better show you around now, hadn't I,' he said as he took her arm and led her towards the grey steel entrance doors under a canopy. The sergeant swiped his card and pressed some keys on the security pad. There was a distinctive click and he pulled the door open towards them. Inside the vestibule, the red sign outside the seventy metre long range was illuminated as Faraday and Cave followed the sergeant up a small flight of metal stairs, along a short corridor and through a door to the observation gallery. It was cool here and insulated from the range itself by a glazed partition running the whole width of the range. Below, a row of officers stood twenty metres from their targets, weapons held in extended hands, ear defenders in place, concentrating and ready to fire. The sergeant explained how officers were selected for the Basic Firearms Course and how they could then progress to the more specialised training as Faraday had done. As the officers on the range proceeded with their drills, the trio left the observation gallery and descended another flight of metal stairs to walk along a further corridor to the armoury.

On one of the armoury's walls was a vast collection of weapons that had been seized or handed into the police over the years. The sergeant removed one from the wall, a 1927 US Colt .38 *Detective Special* with its stubby little 2" barrel, and offered it to Helen. The MI5 agent made a pretence of examining the gun which Williams then exchanged for a formidable Colt .44 *Anaconda* with its 13" barrel. A Ruger *Security Six* was next followed by a Second World War service revolver made for the Royal Small Arms Factory at Enfield. She gauged the weight in her hand. It was a heavy weapon with a 5" barrel. As she turned it over, the sergeant pointed the word 'ALBION' stamped on the right hand side of the frame below the hammer confirming that this weapon had been produced by the Albion Motor Company. He broke the revolver open and pointed to the letters 'SSM' stamped upon the ratchet, the extractor and the other smaller parts, explaining that these parts of the mechanism had been manufactured by the Singer Sewing Machine Company.

'I don't suppose you have ever fired a gun, Helen?' he said.

She paused, rapidly considering what answer she should give, realising that the sergeant had probably noted the confident ease in which she handled the weapons he had given her.

'Only at university,' she replied.

'At university?'

'OTC,' she said casually, referring to the University Officer Training Corps.
'Maybe you would like to try our simulator,' Sergeant Williams said as he replaced the .38 Enfield back into its place on the wall. Then he goaded her, adding, 'All our visitors like to take the opportunity to use the simulator. Princess Anne always does when she visits us.' And, without waiting for a reply, walked through another door. 'It won't take a minute to boot-up the FOXS system.'

The FOXS system, the Firearms Operation Exercise Simulator, was, in reality a CD projector and panoramic screen, fed by a bank of CDs, about the size of side plates, linked to dummy, but authentic-looking, automatic pistols of the correct size and weight. A series of little lights flickered on the control panel of the hard-drive unit as Sergeant Williams pressed the keypads and the FOXS logo was projected onto the screen. Once the system was live, the sergeant removed two imitation automatics from a case and handed one to Helen Cave, retaining the other himself.

'The chief inspector is very familiar with the system, miss, practices twice a month. You've beaten the simulator every time, haven't you, sir?' he said with his back to both of them, not expecting an answer. 'But your luck will run out soon, sir. You can't beat the odds every time,' he mumbled as he made some final adjustments to the focus then cleared some chairs away from the front of the screen.

Turning around he spoke directly to Helen Cave. 'Nothing to worry about, miss. Some home computer games for the kids are more complicated. It's just like watching the TV, with the students in the position of the camera. If the camera moves forward, then that simulates you, the police student, moving forward. You will see on the screen witnesses, suspects and the bad guys, all of whom will probably be talking or shouting at each other or towards you at various stages as the scenario progresses. You do not have to vocally reply, the system anticipates your vocal responses for you.'

The sergeant made another adjustment at the control console as he continued to talk to Helen. 'I showed you the .357 magnum Ruger *Security Six*, often referred to as the *Speed Six*. That weapon became popular in the United States in the 1950s when the *High Noon*-type cowboy films depicting the quick-draw shoot-outs were the cinema rage. But what we teach here isn't just speed of reaction. What we teach is safety, accuracy and speed – in that order. I think the American firearms' schools encourage the policy of "slow down and hit".' He pressed a keypad and the screen cleared. He pressed another and after a very short delay the screen displayed a scene simulating an officer approaching a saloon car parked at the side of the road against a hedgerow. The scene was frozen with the bonnet of the car propped open and a man peering in at the engine. A second man was seated in the rear passenger seat. Both wore knitted woollen hats.

'Would you like to put your university's OTC skills to the test, miss?' the sergeant asked.

Helen Cave knew that it would have been prudent to have refused, but with the complimentary remarks made by the sergeant about Mark's skill in her mind, it was an invitation she could not refuse.
'I suppose so,' she replied as she took up her position between the white lines, legs slightly apart, her body perfectly silhouetted against the screen. Without comment and looking directly at the screen, she extended her right hand, palm upwards, and the sergeant gave her the imitation automatic.

'OK, miss. A call has been received from a reliable neighbour that men have been seen at a car, in an area that has been subject of numerous burglaries. The reliable witness believes he saw one of the men with a baseball bat. You are on lone patrol and approach the vehicle. Are you ready, miss?'

'Ready,' she replied crisply, all of her attention focused upon the screen.

Almost immediately the scene with the men wearing woollen hats was unfrozen.

The loudspeakers called out, 'OK, you at the bonnet. Stand away from the car.'

'It's OK, officer. Got a problem with the fan belt,' the man at the bonnet said, holding up a long spanner. As he did so, the passenger began to open the rear passenger door.

'You. You in the car,' called the voice from the loudspeakers. 'Step out of the car slowly with both hands gripping the top of the window.'

The passenger did exactly as he was told, and as he stood to his full height, the man at the bonnet leaned forward, grabbed a carbine and pointed it at the officer. Helen Cave instinctively crouched slightly as her right arm swung upwards and jabbed forward, squeezing the trigger and firing one shot. As she did so, a small, bright white disc appeared in the chest of the man at the bonnet. As the first man collapsed backwards out of sight behind the vehicle, the passenger dropped his right hand, pulled a revolver from his waist band and raised the gun towards Helen Cave. There was a blur as Helen's gun traversed to the left. She fired again and another little white disc glowed at the passenger's neck like a silver medallion. This second gunman was thrown backwards against the edge of the roof above the passenger door to rebound into the open door before crumbling to the floor. She lowered her weapon only to raise it rapidly again as a third gunman with a pump-action Remington suddenly bounded out through a gap in the hedge to the rear of the vehicle. She fired her weapon and a bright white disc appeared about six inches to the right of this gunman's chest. He fired his Remington. The screen froze and changed colour to a dark shade of pink.

'There you are, sergeant, I need to go back to university and practice a little harder.'

'I think you did very well indeed, miss. Don't you think so, sir?'

'An excellent performance, Helen,' Faraday said, then turned to the sergeant. 'Can you put up the sequential graphics, Gordon?'

'Of course,' the sergeant replied as he pressed the keypad and a series of fine, zig-zag white lines appeared. 'These lines indicate the movement of your weapon in the target zone and the figures along each line record the mille-seconds of each movement.' He moved towards the screen, a black figure against the bright screen, then pointed at the third gunman. 'You see here that you could have taken him out. You had the opportunity as your weapon moved across his chest. You should have fired then, but you hesitated and moved to the right slightly. The third man was unexpected and obviously unnerved you.'

'I didn't expect a third man,' Helen replied, then added, 'and I was worried that the first gunman would suddenly jump up again.'

'Even so, Helen, it was an excellent performance,' Faraday said. 'I'm really impressed.'

'Thank you, Mark,' she said as she handed the imitation weapon back to Sergeant Williams. 'And thank you, Gordon. It was kind of you to take the time to show me all of these interesting weapons and let me use the simulator. I really enjoyed it. Thank you very much.'

They left the simulation suite and walked along another grey corridor to the entrance door. The MI5 agent and Sergeant Williams shook hands and Faraday thanked him again.

'You're scheduled to come in for another practice session soon, aren't you, sir?' remarked Williams.

'Yes. Two weeks time Gordon.'

'Well, miss,' the sergeant said to Helen Cave, 'we'll see if his luck runs out then.'

Mark Faraday and Helen Cave walked towards the car park in silence. Faraday held the passenger door of his Volvo T5 open for her. She slid gracefully into the seat. Faraday walked around the car, opened the door and stepped inside. He started the engine but did not engage gear. He spoke instead.

'That really was a very impressive performance, Helen.'

'But not as impressive as your performance apparently. According to Sergeant Williams, you have a 100% success rate. Isn't that so?'

'Yes, it is,' he replied, 'but I have never fired my weapon in anger. I don't really know how I would perform in those circumstances.' They were quiet for a moment then he turned to her and asked, 'Have you fired your weapon in anger?'

'Yes,' she replied. 'I have. Four times.'

'And did you kill anyone?'

'Yes,' she replied again. 'Four times.'

'Back there on the simulator, you weren't fazed by the third gunman at all,' observed Faraday. 'You put on a very impressive *performance*, Helen, in which you deliberately missed the third man, didn't you?'

'Did I? How could you say such a thing?' she said as if shocked.

'Yes. Yes, you did. You deliberately missed. To have done otherwise would have demonstrated a skill not usually associated with a member of the Audit Commission.'

'Maybe you are right, but don't worry, Mark. If I do have to fire in anger, I won't miss.'

Faraday engaged first gear and drove slowly out of the car park, down the gradient to the main gates. Once through they made their way straight back to Bristol arriving back in his office at a quarter to five. Mark spoke with Jane for twenty minutes, reading some papers, signing others as the kettle boiled and Helen occupied herself at the computer in Mark's office. As Jane tidied her desk and left for the day, Mark took the cups of coffee into his office.

'On a job like this I would often get the feeling,' said Helen depressingly, 'that although I was getting nowhere, there was some crumb of a clue out there. But now I'm not even getting that. We're going over the same ground and we are coming up with the same results.'

'It's been a slog but it had to be done. Nothing's lost except a little time and we've plugged a few gaps, some embarrassing ones for us, but nothing that actually seems to help us. Why not change tact?' suggested Mark.

'OK, why not?' responded Helen, 'We've looked at it from potential targets' points of view and a police point of view. Let's put ourselves in his shoes.'

Cave pressed the keys 'C2' and moved her chair a little closer to his so that both could read the screen. They were close. She gently bit her lower lip as she realised that her breathing was becoming deeper. She pointed to the screen as a distraction, determined to concentrate upon her assignment. They both read for another twenty minutes and refreshed their memory only to reveal how little they really knew.

'I think I'll call it a day if you don't mind,' she said looking at her watch. 'I'll walk back to the hotel, it will clear my head of everything except him.' But she couldn't resist pressing 'B9' for a final update before she left.

There was nothing new except details of the entry that had been circulated that day by Scotland Yard. On page seven, under the category 'suspected', item 20 listed a suspect for three cases of fraud, reference number: MP(DR) 8806/396-430N. There was no photograph but an artist's impression. The text indicated that the suspect, Michael Beazley alias David Miller, had between 26th September and 30th October, opened a number of fictitious bank accounts in the Bristol area. He was described as being 5'11", proportionate build, 'IC1', hair light brown/sandy, extremely smart and well groomed. There was a caution added at the end of the entry: 'may be armed and should not be approached under any circumstances; sightings to be referred to OIC: DS Eccleston 071-230-1212 ext 684'.

'Well, our little make believe item reads quite authentically, let's hope someone spots our friend,' said Cave as they both began to clear their desks.

'Let's also hope that they do not tackle him,' added Faraday as Cave switched off her computer.

They descended the stairs to the foyer. As they reached the doors Faraday suggested, 'If you wait a moment I can easily give you a lift to your hotel.'

'No … No, thank you,' she replied, touching his arm for just a little too long, 'there's a few things I need to think through, Mark. I'll see you tomorrow.'

They left each other in the foyer; Cave to walk alone back along Redcliffe Bridge and to her hotel, and Faraday to his car.

At 7.40 p.m., the night shift arrived at office number 2 on the third floor. The day shift briefed the night shift, but there had been no developments and the last twelve hours had only been mildly more interesting than the previous twelve. Talk as usual hinged around the counter assistant with the brunette hair and a mind-boggling figure.

By 8.15pm., Norris, Charlton and Howard had settled into their routine of one of the three keeping observations on the bank for two hours at a time; coffee and tea making and the use of the toilets being restricted to change-over periods. There was also strict discipline exercised in respect of blackout procedures between 10.30pm. and 6am. During this time, no lights were allowed on at all except in the kitchenette and toilet – provided that the doors were shut. There was sufficient light coming from Corn Street to ensure that the three detectives didn't bump into furniture or lose their way to the toilets, but it wasn't bright enough to read by. However, from 8pm. to 10.30pm., the team had ample time to prepare the kitchenette for refreshment breaks, to check paperwork and the log, as well as read the evening papers.

At 6am. the blinds would still remain closed but the lights could be switched on again. It would attract no attention; the city was already alive with the semi-nocturnal people that most citizens never saw; the milkman, the fruit and vegetable market traders, hotel kitchen staff, the road sweepers, postal workers, bus crews and office cleaners. It would not be unusual to see office lights on at that time, it was common enough, and the police team were able to use the period between six and eight o'clock to freshen up and clean and clear ready for the day shift.

Like his colleague, Norris had changed from suit into sweatshirt, jeans and trainers. His sleeping bag was on the floor but for the moment he was seated in a comfortable swivel chair with legs crossed on a desk, reading the log and drinking coffee.

They worked surprisingly well as a team and that was mainly due to Charlton. He realised on the 24th that their fraud enquiry was now of secondary importance. He also realised that a sedentary fourteen years with the Fraud Squad did not really qualify him to take command of what was clearly now a Special Branch operation. At forty-eight years of age he could not be bothered with power struggles and conceded authority to Craig Howard of the 'Met'. They talked through each others' methods and agreed to share all tasks equally, the Met detective even agreeing to reduce the number of cigarettes he smoked. For three men cooped up in a few rooms, these arrangements and guidelines were essential.

Norris finished reading the log, got up and collected the cups, taking his turn to make more coffee. The two older men had grown quite fond of the younger man. Charlton was in any case naturally protective, but Norris had a restrained full-of-life cheerful enthusiasm that did not irritate the others. He did not speak a lot which was good, but would often ask the other two questions out of interest as well as to improve his own knowledge. The sergeant realised that the young constable would move up the promotion ladder in the future, outranking them both, but they did not resent this particularly as his personality and attitude were neither arrogant nor abrasive. Charlton and Howard were glad that he was on their team.

The younger detective returned to his chair and sipped the coffee as he began to read the latest hard copy of the intelligence reports. On the front page was the word 'confidential' and below that the coat of arms of the force.

He read each page closely and then came to Item 20 and the artist's impression of Michael Beazley alias David Miller.

Norris closed his eyes as if to close out the quiet talk of his colleagues. He had seen that face, or at least one similar before. Who was it? When? Where? The more he thought, the more faces came into his mind; faces of friends and neighbours, faces of those at the weightlifting club and The Old Duke public house, faces of defendants and witnesses. Faces. Faces. Some distinct, others vague.

As much as he worried over the artist's sketch during the night, he just couldn't remember and it troubled his professional pride until he left at just after 8am. As he quietly closed the heavy aluminium door it came to him. The sandy-haired, handsome, unsmiling man he had glimpsed moments before the door clanged shut the previous day. Top floor, office number 3, next door to their own.

He looked up but no lights shone this morning. He looked quickly around. He was not there. Detective Constable Norris walked past the Corn Exchange and stood in the entrance to All Saints Lane. It gave him a clear view of Corn Street and if the sandy-haired man walked from High Street, as he had the day before, he would not see the policeman unless he deliberately turned around to look.

Norris attracted little attention. He was dressed smartly as were many other young men who worked in the banks and insurance offices in this the old financial heart of the city, but by 9 o'clock the sandy-haired man had not appeared.

A window seat inside Cawardine's Coffee House, on this site in Corn Street since 1713, provided a reasonable vantage point, although Norris could not actually see the bronzed aluminium entrance door tucked just inside Exchange Avenue. By 11 o'clock and after four cups of coffee and enduring comments from the waiter about the problems of being stood up by girlfriends, one tired detective made his way home to a cold and empty bed.

Chapter 17

Friday 16th November.

Norfolk and Bristol, England.

ALONG THE north-east coast of Norfolk, the sea conducts a constant assault across the marshes to the west of Blakeney Point. The high pressure over Scandinavia, together with the low in the English Channel, results in bracing cold winds from the east. It can be a harsh, uninviting, wind-swept coast, yet possessing a compelling beauty.

Today it was cold and grey, but crystal clear with a gentle breeze, a place of solitude and privacy, ideal for bird-watching.

Here in Norfolk during the short winter days when much of nature's food is scarce, the county, together with its neighbour Suffolk, plays host to many thousands of wintering wildfowl and wading birds. One birdwatcher had walked for well over a half-mile on the undulating and slippery, sand-blown wooden boardwalk that snaked a path along the coast. Now he made his way between tall, spiky *marran grass*, delicate *sea lavender* and *thrift*, towards the brackish lagoons and salt marshes and the shingle spits beyond that are a feature of this coast.

The last two hours had been rewarding for him. He had had two sightings of the Glaucous Gull, a rare visitor from Greenland and Iceland. The more common dark-bellied Brent geese had already arrived from Artic Russia, flying in low, straggly formations; and the red bills of the Shelduck could be seen and the distinctive 'ak-ak-ak' of the female heard. Now he adjusted his Adlerblick 10x50 binoculars to bring into sharper resolution the handsome Ringed

Plover before returning his attention to the extremely alert 'sentinel of the marshes', the Redshank, whose hysterical volley of harsh piping notes warn of intruders.

As he re-adjusted his binoculars the burble of his cellular phone distracted him. He lowered his glasses and carefully extracted the phone from within his warm waxed jacket, but the noise, although muffled, and the movement, although slight, were sufficient to alert the large flock of Redshank.

'Yes,' he answered, pressing the earpiece close to his head and, facing out of the breeze, he sheltered behind a grass-topped dune.

'Mr Hancock?' asked the caller.

'Who is that?' Hadfield asked cautiously.

'This is Peckham.'

'What do you have to tell me?'

'Our client had visited us and has given notice that he wishes to close his account.' There was an awkward silence, then Peckham asked, 'Are you there?'

'Of course. Continue.'

'Oh. ... Ye'. ... Yes. Well, we require three clear days to arrange a withdrawal of that amount and so ... '

'How much?' Hadfield interrupted crisply.

'Um,' stuttered the manager who had not anticipated the question. 'It's … ah, £110,050 … in cash,' then added rapidly and enthusiastically, 'plus interest.'

'When will you hand over the cash?'

'The 21st or 22nd.'

'So you don't know which day?'

'Well,' said the flustered Peckham inadequately, 'one or the other.'

'I had hoped that you would have been more careful, more precise. That was a mistake, Mr Peckham. Therefore, remedies must follow.'

'Look, look, I got confused when my staff told me, I … '

He interrupted sharply, his voice slicing through the other man's stammerings like an axe. '*You* made a mistake and *I* do not like mistakes. Mistakes,' he emphasised, 'are expensive in terms of your future security and family stability. However,' he paused for effect, 'provided your handling of the concluding phase of your client's account is carried out properly, I may be prepared to overlook this error.'

'Thank you, Mr Hancock. Nothing can go wrong, sir.'

'Good. Let us hope for *your* sake that that will be so. Now listen carefully. Deal with this client as you would any other. Do nothing more. I shall contact you,' he said, although he knew that there would not be the need. 'Do you understand?'

'Yes, yes,' he said respectfully and willingly, repeating pathetically, 'Deal with this client as I would any other. Absolutely.'

Hadfield pressed the little button and returned the phone to his inside pocket.

Chapter 18

Wednesday 21st November.

Bristol, England.

MANY OF the lights had been switched off since 4.30pm., only to be switched back on again by the cleaners at the Atlantic First Commercial (Isle of Man) Bank. Gradually the staff had left their desks and now at twenty minutes past six, the manager himself could be clearly seen by Hadfield leaving his office. Moments later he emerged through the embossed plate glass doors into Corn Street, pulled his camel hair coat collar up about his neck and walked towards Wine Street.

Hadfield's Adlerblick glasses followed him as far as the contour of the road would allow, then he gently placed the binoculars into his briefcase. He neatly folded *The Times* and placed that too inside the case and moved to the kitchenette, but did not remove his surgical gloves to wash his cup and saucer, merely drying them delicately with the towel as the sink water disappeared down the drain. Methodically he unplugged the percolator then carefully emptied the old coffee into the pedal bin before finally checking the toilet and the main office. Satisfied, he placed his case on the small outer office desk and peeled off his gloves. These too were put into the case. He took his dark grey overcoat with neat velvet collar from the stand and when the buttons were secured, he admired and then smiled approvingly at his image in the long mirror.

A lesser professional would have been angry at the waste of a day and with Peckham who had not been able to stipulate which day Dolan would call to withdraw the NIRB's money. Hadfield mentally dismissed the day and this allowed his disciplined mind to fully concentrate on tomorrow – he was convinced that Thursday would be the day that the Irishman would call at the bank. True, Peckham could double-cross him but for what gain? None he reasoned. Hadfield had already tapped into Peckham's mind; he knew how he would act and react just as a consummate angler knows how to play his fish.

Hadfield pulled from his pocket a pair of fine, hand-stitched kid gloves. He put them on, turned out the light, opened the door and then carefully closed the door of office number 3 on exiting and made his way down the stairs into Corn Street.

Since his return from Norfolk he had not stayed at the Grand Hotel but in the Unicorn at Narrow Quay. He had also confirmed the purchase of the *Fairmile*. It would need a great deal of work to restore her to her former glory, but for Hadfield's purposes no restoration would be needed. The important aspects of this launch were a good sea-board and sound sea-keeping qualities. Although the hull was only constructed of two thin skins of mahogany lined with calico, she was hardy and her twin 650hp petrol engines were reliable and powerful enough to keep her on station in the River Severn.

As Hadfield left the building he did not turn towards the Grand Hotel which had been fully booked, but right along Exchange Avenue and across St Nicholas Street, down the broad and well-worn steps past the Market House Tavern to Baldwin Street. At the foot of these steps he bought the three star edition of the *Evening Post* which he neatly folded under his arm, then crossed over Baldwin Street and walked briskly towards the City Centre. The early evening commuter rush had come to an end but even so the pavements were busy with people, muffled against the cold, making their late way home or early way to restaurants, cinemas, clubs and bars. The roads too were not free from traffic, headlamp and driving lights. A multitude of red brake lights and orange indicators flashed and the grey wisps of exhaust smoke curled into the still, cold night air. This pattern was monotonously repeated the length of Baldwin Street.

At Telephone Avenue and Marsh Street, Hadfield took care to look right and then left before he stepped into the road. He had spotted the black man when he had bought his newspaper and had confirmed his suspicions at the junctions. By the time he had reached the City Centre there was one other possible; a white male, whom he suspected of being part of a Central Intelligence Agency team. Typical of Americans he thought, athletic, clean-cut and well-groomed.

Bristol City Centre is like an elongated Piccadilly Circus, over two hundred metres in length and comprising of Broad Quay, St Augustines Parade and Colston Avenue, in the middle of which are two long pedestrian islands with a long, cascading water feature and trees. There are also statues of Edmund Burke, Edward Colston and Neptune with his trident, as well as the Cenotaph. Flags of France, Germany, Holland, Portugal, Spain and Italy flutter from poles too. And now the Christmas lights.

Hadfield crossed over from Baldwin Street to the first of these islands and its illuminated water feature, turning right and crossing to the far side of the City Centre into Colston Avenue. For a few minutes he lost sight of the black man, but at the bus stop outside St Mary's-on-the-Quay, he sighted him near a cluster of trees.

The black man's pace was controlled but tiring. One moment he would be waiting patiently for Hadfield to appear or pass by and another anxiously trying to anticipate his next move or avoid the never ending evening traffic; at other times he would be sprinting to keep his elusive target in sight. Hadfield's pace was leisurely and natural, even restful in comparison.

The buildings and lighting, the bus shelters and trees, all conspired to shroud every part of this busy thoroughfare in a confusing mass of shadows and shades. There was present, every few yards, the potential to loose contact and as Hadfield neared St Bartholomew's Gate, his grey-coated figure disappeared up the quaint Christmas Steps.

The black man dodged the traffic and vaulted over a central reservation barrier with ease and gained the foot of the steps. Hadfield was already halfway up the Dickensian stone steps looking casually into the shops that sold hand-made boots and shoes, antique books, prints and maps, coins and stamps. Other shops provided watch repairs or offered the very best prices for gold and silver. It was an attractive setting with historic charm for such a deadly game as was being played out, illuminated by the dim light of Edwardian street lamps. The Steps were full of people, mainly young couples, some hand in hand or huddled at a shop window peering into the ill-lit interiors or examining menu cards and the cosy, inviting restaurants within.

At the top of Christmas Steps, Hadfield stopped to admire the beautiful medieval alms house and to read the stone carved plaque commemorating its founding in 1483 by John Foster. It was impossible not to be drawn to the illuminated ornate stained-glass windows of the adjoining Chapel of the Three Kings of Cologne, but for Hadfield, his admiration merely served to provide an opportunity to assess his position and to consider his options.

He was sure that his pursuer was below, near the second jewellery shop on the left. It was the only figure that had not moved. He could see no white companion either on the Steps nor up or down

Colston Street, or opposite into Lower Park Row. Maybe Hadfield had been wrong, maybe the black man was foolishly alone.

Hadfield waited a little longer, eyes never still, senses never at rest. Even now his pursuer's companion, if there was one, could be closing in. But he had seen enough and had analysed the black man's moves.

There was no apprehension, just calculation. Years of training had converted self-confidence into skilled superiority. Hadfield made his decision and turned right up Colston Street looking for the killing ground.

He passed Colston Yard and dismissed it. Even the American would be a fool to follow him there, his pursuer need only wait and trap him. Johnny Ball Lane, however, looked much more promising.

Opposite the main entrance to the Bristol Royal Infirmary, at the junction of Colston Street and Upper Maudlin Street, were grimy steps leading down an ill-lit lane. He waited long enough for the black man to see him dodge down the lane, increasing his pace across uneven and broken paving slabs, avoiding the litter banked in the corners, crushing under foot old mortar fallen from the high decaying walls. The lane turned sharp right, the lamp at this bend casting a weak light onto gaudy graffiti below.

The lane snaked on and down for the full length as far as the darkness allowed him to see. The stone wall to his left was at least three meters high and on the right, towering above was the windowless red brick expanse that was the rear of an old disused warehouse. This stretch of lane could not be overlooked even by the nearby commercial tower blocks of Greyfriars and Fromegate

House. Hadfield's eyes darted from side to side; if only he could find a place of concealment it would be perfect.

The black man meanwhile had waited near the graffiti and, when all was quiet, stepped cautiously out into the light which silhouetted him momentarily and indistinctly in its meagre glow. He knew this lane, another dark and shadowy seventy metres and it would turn abruptly left down a short flight of steps to Lewins Mead and back to the busy night-time heart of the city.

He sprinted on, alone and tense, searching the darkness, ducking and side-stepping the spiteful brambles that cascaded over the stone wall. Then Hadfield struck, aiming instinctively at the stomach.

The black man twisted to avoid the thrust but already the thin sharp blade was cutting through the outer coat, jacket, leather harness and shirt to jerk against the sternum and agonisingly scrape as it plunged deeper between the ribs.

Hadfield was calculating and strangely calm. He had not struck a clean killing blow and his face became taut as he tried to pull his knife free to strike again, but it would not pull clear, trapped between ribs and caught amongst the shoulder harness.

The black man shrieked as he clutched at Hadfield's wrists in a death grip, his eyes distended as if about to leap from their sockets. He shrieked uncontrollably again as the knife's point found the intercostal arteries and blood spurted into the middle lobe of the right lung. He began frothing at the corner of his mouth that opened and shut noiselessly only to shriek again hideously as they faced one another and danced a final, grotesque dance of death.

Hadfield swung his victim savagely and repeatedly against the rough stone wall, cruelly twisting and pushing the knife up and deeper as the black man's legs buckled and he slid jerkily down the wall still holding Hadfield's wrists, but now like a pleading child, his face unreal, his stare one of incomprehensible disbelief. For a final few seconds, the black man lay on the cold path, blood and froth bubbled from between his clenched teeth. Then, almost gently, his head rolled over his chest to the right and his arms slumped like a drunkard's to his side. He was quite still.

Hadfield checked the corpse as an attentive surgeon would but there was no pulse. Then he pulled off his blood-drenched right kid glove and pushed it into his blood splattered jacket pocket together with its mate. Calmly he went back to the old doorway recess and stooped to pick up his neatly rolled overcoat. With the overcoat on and buttoned to the neck, holding his briefcase, he was the image of the city executive again.

He walked further down the darkened lane to the head of the steps, then into Lewins Mead. He could not see clearly but he was confident that the bright amber streetlights would not identify any spots of blood that may have been on his trousers or shoes. Outside the Army Careers Office, he joined the bus stop queue. Thirteen routes used this stop, ideal thought Hadfield as he edged forward with the rest to board the bus to Filton, an anonymous face in an anonymous crowd.

He instinctively sat near the emergency exit with a clear view of the main door. He was quite controlled with a feeling of pleasant exertion, some relief, but only mild satisfaction. It would have been much more satisfying for him had the black man prove to have been a more formidable challenge.

Chapter 19

Thursday 22nd November.

Bristol, England.

THIS MORNING, Helen Cave had driven from her hotel and waited outside Faraday's district headquarters, then they had driven off together in her Rover 75 ZT, to be away from the station, away from people. It was now not an unusual practice, they had done this before a number of times in the previous few days, just to stroll and to talk over what had happened, what they knew and what they could only surmise.

They stood on the quayside of the old sand and gravel wharf. The sun was bright but gave little warmth to lessen the early morning chill, and the cold breeze that funnelled its way along the harbour was sharp, keeping their minds clear and fresh. It was good to get away, but Faraday had a meeting scheduled for ten and so at 9.30 they turned to walk back to Cave's car.

'The harbour master is always helpful,' Mark said.

'Yes, we should be able to patch into his registration computer by now. We're already linked into the Avonmouth coastguard, so we ought to have a pretty good idea of any craft that has been in or out of the city docks in the last month,' then added cheerfully, 'The bonus is that he'll keep it up-to-date for us.'

They reached the Rover and got in away from the cold. 'My only concern,' remarked Faraday, 'is that although Commander Legat is helpful, it will only work if he is given genuine details by owners. Boats and other smaller craft aren't registered like motor vehicles.'

'Right. OK,' Helen sighed. 'And a cabin cruiser or a sailing yacht will look like any other at night and Avonmouth will only record names that they are given. One could easily slip through. So, where do we go from here? There are no ships scheduled to use either Avonmouth, Royal Portbury or the city docks that have the slightest connection with nuclear warfare or the nuclear industry at all. All we know is that a terrorist has got hold of some small but powerful mines, some barometric-type detonators and that the target is a nuclear power station. At the moment all we can do is to try and second-guess the bastard.'

Cave began to reverse away, then turned onto the Hotwells Road.

'You know the area, Mark, if our friend is using a boat, maybe to attack the water inlets of the cooling system, do you think he would use Pill or Sharpness, somewhere like that, as his base?'

'No, I shouldn't have thought so. Too small. Every craft that moors would attract attention. By contrast, there are lots of boats in the city docks at this time of year, berthed for the winter, and on weekends there are still plenty of pleasure craft bobbing about. If our friend is going to use a boat, then the city docks would be his best bet.'

'Newport takes nuclear waste from Japan, doesn't it?' the MI5 agent said, thinking aloud.

Cave pulled the Rover into the kerbside at Hotwells and leant over, her elbow brushing Faraday's thigh, and opened the glove compartment. She pressed a few buttons on the information system that filled the compartment. Then a few more as the pale blue screen glowed. Within seconds information filled the screen.

'Yes,' said Cave as she read the information, remembering a briefing she had received at the end of last year. 'Purpose-built vessels do discharge at Newport, but nothing again until March it seems. I've seen these ships,' she said as she closed the glove compartment. 'The waste flasks are between fifty and one-hundred tonnes and are shipped down the line to a processing plant at Peterstone Wentlooge. They are importing more of this stuff now from Eastern Europe and it's either sent to Peterstone or Sellafield ….'

Mark's bleeper sounded. He switched it off and called the communication centre on the car phone.

'Chief Inspector Faraday, you bleeped me.' There was a pause as he digested the information. 'OK. I'm at Hotwells, ETA two minutes.' He turned to Cave. 'We might as well attend. Go straight on to the roundabout, exit at 1 o'clock, then straight onto the City Centre.'

'Problems?' Cave asked as she followed the heavier than usual traffic into the heart of the city.

'Oh, I'm sorry, there's no mystery,' he said as they sped towards the roundabout. 'A suspicious death at Johnny Ball Lane. The DI is there and one of the uniform inspectors, but they have asked the detective chief superintendent to attend as well. If he's attending then it should be something interesting.'

They past the Royal Hotel and into the City Centre and slow-moving traffic. Cave was able to edge the Rover forward then halted in stationary traffic near the Cenotaph. In the distance a crowd had gathered in Lewins Mead around a number of police cars and an ambulance.

'I'll get out,' said the policeman, 'and walk on. Catch me up and see if you can find a spot to park.'

As Faraday approached the crowd, Inspector Stacey was already walking smartly towards him. He gave Mark a perfect salute and spoke in his nasal voice.

'A Mr Wainswick found the body, sir. DI Davies is with him now. As you see, I've had everything taped off. If you walk immediately behind me sir, we won't disturb the crime scene.'

They went up the grey stone steps, then sharp right up a few more steps. The protruding legs could not be seen as Inspector Stacey droned on in a detached voice.

'Forensics and Dr MacDonald are en route, sir.'

The last few words were lost on the chief inspector. He stood quietly for a moment, his thoughts a mixture of deep sadness and acute anger. The black man was of course dead but his body, his face, did not seem at peace at all. The disturbed dust and litter gave evidence of the grim struggle that had taken place in this dreadful, ugly alley, as did the blood-soaked and ripped palms of the hands. The handle of the knife, trapped in the radio's shoulder harness, still protruded grotesquely from the trunk and blood had gradually seeped through the coat around it. Mark stood silently and numbed, then turned angrily upon the inspector.

'Don't you dare, *ever*, do that to me again. You could have warned me when I arrived. In fact, you *should* have warned me and *you* know it!'

'I didn't want to tell you in front of the men, sir.'

'Don't give me that crap,' and in a more level tone continued, 'You have the top of the lane sealed off?'

'Yes, sir.'

'Then your task is to ensure that this area remains sterile until more competent officers arrive.'

He looked again at the distorted form and then felt hidden tears sting his eyes. He had to get away, not out of fear or revulsion but because he knew he would be overwhelmed with emotion. He took several really deep breaths then walked back to the top of the steps and noticed for the first time that the young policemen and women who looked up at him were grim faced. Some had clearly been crying. He knew that emotions were contagious and he again felt tears beginning to fill his eyes. He would be useless to them if he lost control now - that would come later in his private moments. For now, he and these young officers shared a grief. Words were not necessary. They each knew.

Helen Cave walked towards him, her face etched with concern. 'What is it, Mark? Is everything alright?' she asked carefully.

'No … No, I'm afraid it isn't,' he replied in a strained voice. 'Someone has murdered one of my young constables … Constable Norris.'

***

Sean Dolan approached the ultra-modern counter across the deep beige carpet. The bank's interior was all bright, in stark contrast with the overcast and cold street. The grey-white marble walls reflected the light and made the rich wooden and steel-grey counter more prominent and the crisp blue-uniformed girls more distinct than their surroundings. Here at 12.40pm., there was orderly and calm activity behind the counter although the calmness was not mirrored in all of those seated in the comfortable clients' lounge. Two of the waiting customers were relaxed, one reading a newspaper, the other browsing through papers from a briefcase, but there was another who was uneasy, glancing nervously about, fiddling with his gloves.

At the counter, alongside the tall, silver Christmas tree, the pretty dark-haired girl with delicate freckles and a marvellous smile spoke first.

'Good afternoon, sir. Can Atlantic First Commercial help you?' asked Jackie Westlake.

'I was told to return today to close my account,' the Irishman said.

'May I have your withdrawal slip, sir, just for a moment.'

Sean Dolan pulled out his wallet from inside his coat and removed the account withdrawal slip.

'Is there going to be some trouble?' he asked in a distinctive Irish brogue.

'Of course not, sir, just confirmation of the arrangements.'

He handed her the slip which was taken with dainty fingers. It was placed into a horizontal aperture and the keys were pressed. Within seconds, the words 'Closure of Account Approved' appeared on the otherwise blank computer screen. As she returned the slip to Dolan, she spoke again.

'Everything has been arranged, sir. Mr Holland, our chief cashier, will attend to you in a moment. Would you care to wait in the lounge area to your left?'

'I'll be hoping it won't be taking long, miss?'

'Mr Holland is with another client now, sir, but he will only be a few more minutes. You might just have time for coffee. Would you care for one?'

'I think not, but thank you.'

Dolan selected one of the luxurious grey leather easy chairs with his back to a wall. He unbuttoned his coat and looked around at those seated with him. They all looked at him then lowered their eyes again. The rotund, bald-headed man was still fiddling with his gloves and the dark-haired man with a French onion seller's moustache, who had been standing at one of the telephone booths, had now joined them nervously biting his lips. The only female fascinated him. He had noticed her moments before standing near him at the counter, now she was seated opposite, clearly more fascinated by the sandy-haired man with blue eyes, reading his briefcase papers, than with him. Dolan was still thinking what a powerfully built lady she was when Miss Westlake approached.

'Mr Holland is free now, sir. Would you follow me please.'

Dolan's thoughts returned quickly to reality. His eyes darted about the interior of the building. This could be the springing of a trap by his former friends in the NIRB. He had thought of all the many ways it could be sprung.

Miss Westlake tapped on the door and walked in, keeping open the door for Dolan who stepped through, his eyes with lightening speed taking in the room, moving swiftly from the right, anti-clockwise, noting every detail including the high-mounted video cameras. Holland was alone but behind a screened pale oak counter upon which were two small computer terminals. The walls were of matching pale oak and carpet deep beige, but this did not disguise the formidable protection that it afforded to Mr Holland and the bank's assets. From counter top to ceiling, from wall to wall, were solid glazed panels able to withstand the impact from a .44 magnum. Below the reinforced counter was a cash transfer unit.

Mr Holland was a weedy, bespectacled man of about forty-five years with bony hands. 'Good afternoon, sir,' he said, smiling like an undertaker's assistant.

Dolan approached the counter, now off-guard. He had been briefed by his minders but he felt vulnerable, yet, he quickly realised that he was merely part of a banking process. Everything appeared normal and he relaxed just a little – but only a little.

In front of Holland was a computer screen and keyboard as there was in front of Dolan, except that the Irishman's was shielded so that only he could see his hands and the keyboard.

'If you would give me your withdrawal slip, sir, I have to insert it this side. Gets a little tricky if we leave it to our clients,' he said, pointing a bony finger towards a little slot. Dolan passed the slip forward and bony fingers inserted it into an aperture in the top of the keyboard. Mr Holland read the security details that only appeared on his screen, pressed a series of keys and waited. After about ten seconds both screens displayed 'Closure of Account Approved' and then 'Client to insert Personal Code now'.

'Using your keyboard, sir, would you kindly type in your personal code now.'

Dolan typed in the secret combination of digits.

There was a moment's delay, then the words 'Code Accepted' appeared on the screen. Almost immediately more text appeared, 'Withdrawal of £113,523 authorised in £50 notes, max. 30mm thick packs as requested'.

There was yet a further delay before the final text, 'At the conclusion of this transaction your account will be closed – thank you for your patronage'.

Dolan's eyes were fixed on the screen, transfixed by the figure of £113,523. He permitted himself a smile.

'Was there anything else, sir, before we conclude out business?' enquired Holland.

'No, just the money,' he replied with a tinge of anxiety in his voice.

'Of course,' Holland said, depressing a little button on the counter, 'we have it for you, sir, as requested, in bundles 30mm thick. It will be with us directly.'

There was a firm knock on a door behind Holland and two uniformed bank guards entered wheeling a wire mesh trolley containing the bank notes. The chief cashier checked the wire seals that secured the contents of the trolley, then clipped them off with a small pair of neat stainless steel cutters. One of the guards leaned into the trolley and removed the money from within, placing the bundles onto a table behind Holland. He then joined his uniformed colleague at the door.

'I see that you have no case, sir,' remarked Holland. 'May I enquire how you propose to transport the money?'

'I'll be carrying it in these,' said Dolan, pulling from his inside coat pocket two small rolls of plastic material. He removed the rubber bands, shook them and allowed them to unroll to reveal crumpled and flattened money pouches. 'Would you be kind enough to fill them up for me, Mr Holland?'

'Of course, sir. How very thoughtful of you, sir, if I may say so,' he said, 'but would you be wishing to check the cash?'

'Oh no. I'll not be doing that. I trust the bank,' said Dolan with a nervous chuckle.

'That is very gratifying to hear, of course. Thank you, sir. Would you in that case be good enough to place the money belts into the compartments in front of you when the door slides open?'

Dolan slipped the belts in as the door slid back slowly and then closed again. Soon, Holland's bony fingers were skilfully about his task, allowing Dolan to be free to observe the exit door and both guards.

The pouches were so compressed that the task was fiddly and took longer than Dolan had planned, but then it was finished with two little compartments unused. Dolan was relieved, he had not been sure that it would all fit in.

The filled belts were passed through the cash transfer unit. Dolan took off his overcoat and put it on the desk, then quickly removed his jacket and strapped around his waist the two belts containing £113,523.

Dolan stepped from the bank into Corn Street and walked briskly towards Clare Street. One of the gentlemen in the bank's lounge who had been reading documents from his case, also stepped through the door and as he did so, he adjusted the neat velvet collar on his dark grey overcoat.

By the time he had reached the end of Clare Street, Hadfield had noticed the two men. He could not afford to draw attention to himself so he stopped and looked discerningly at the expensive suites displayed in the shop window as one of Dolan's tails went by.

Dolan doubled-back once, then into a café in Baldwin Street, only to duck out through the rear entrance, where he was joined by one of his minders.

They quickened their pace and as they reached Queen Square, a silver-grey Saab 9000 pulled to a halt alongside Dolan and the other man, both of whom quite voluntarily stepped into the back seat, then drove off.

For a moment, Hadfield was angry, but with himself. This development was not an option he had considered.

***

At 10pm., Chief Inspector Faraday spoke to the night shift. He explained what had happened earlier that day and what action was now being taken. He told them that a date, the next Tuesday, the 27th, had already provisionally been fixed for the funeral. He cautioned them to be on their guard as they patrolled and explained the precautions that had been agreed by the chief constable.

'Whilst on patrol you will undoubtedly receive condolences from the public, you may also be subject to abuse. Some unthinking youths will no doubt make comments about PC Norris purely to provoke. You will at all time conduct yourselves with restraint. I do not want Carl's funeral marred or more sorrow caused to his mother by any unfortunate press reports.' He looked sternly at those seated in the briefing room, then added more soberly, 'Before you go out tonight on patrol, maybe we should think quietly for a few minutes of our friend Carl and remember him in our own way.' He did not ask them to stand but they did, their heads bowed until Faraday broke the silence. 'Thank you, Mr Hall,' he said to the inspector, and then to the other officers, 'Be careful tonight.' He was going to say more but during those silent moments he felt suppressed emotions swell up inside him. He turned quickly on his feet and left the room.

Snow, just a few flakes at first, gently tumbled down the windscreen as Mark drove from his district headquarters. The wipers and demisters quickly cleared the fine coating of snow and condensation.

A short while later he parked in an adjacent street and walked the short distance to the Marriott Hotel. He walked casually through reception and to the lifts. He pressed button '2'. The doors slid open and he stepped inside. The doors opened automatically again on the second floor. Faraday turned left and walked along the red carpeted corridors and stopped outside of Room 219. He tapped on the wooden door and it was almost immediately opened by Helen Cave. He walked into the lobby and turned as she locked the door. She stood there wearing a pale blue long-sleeved jersey top and bootcut denim jeans, the shadows created by a single down-lighter reminding Mark of her beauty. For a moment, Mark was unsure as to what to do, until Helen gently opened her arms. He walked to her and, as her arms encircled his body, his hands embraced her head in his neck. Faraday was able to stifle a sob but tears filled his eyes. She felt his heart beats and felt the tears on her neck, but said nothing. She simply held him, more tightly and completely still. She asked no questions, made no judgement, but there was understanding.

'I'm sorry,' he said finally as he eased himself free. She moved beside him and held his hand as they walked into the room. 'It's bloody silly really, all this stiff upper lip nonsense, but I've been on show all day and haven't had a minute alone.'

'Why did it happen?' she asked gently as they stood facing each other, hands clasped together.

'I don't know,' he replied.

'Was it robbery?' she asked, hoping to distract him by concentrating upon practicalities.

'No. Well … I don't think so. He was just doing some obs on a bank. The NIRB, the mines, the bank, they might all be connected. We just don't know at the moment. But it was a nasty stabbing, a cruel stabbing.'

'A drink?' she asked to distract his thoughts again.

'Yes. That would be nice,' he said, a smile returning to his face. 'Thank you. A small whisky and plenty of *American Dry*, if you have it.'

She poured him a *Grants* from two of those little bottles found in hotel fridges and handed it to him, but she didn't release her grip on the glass. Their fingers entwined as she looked into his eyes.

He realised, not for the first time, what an extraordinarily compelling woman she was.

'That looks suspiciously like a double whisky without *American*,' he said, 'and I will have to drive home soon.'

Helen Cave continued to hold him with her eyes as she softly said: 'I don't want you to drive anywhere tonight, Mark.' She relaxed her grip on the glass and both smiled smiles of acceptance. He placed the glass on the table by the brochures and guide books, then held her body again, but now his hands gently caressed the soft skin of her beautifully arched back, her slim waist and her muscular stomach. And, all the while, she held him captive with her eyes. As he stroked the ripples of her ribs, she raised her head a little more and moved her mouth to his. Their lips brushed, then explored each other, firstly, tentatively, then more passionately, then more intimately until there was nothing sacred or undiscovered.

Chapter 20

Friday 23rd November.

Bristol and Falmouth, England.

THERE IS always a serious air that pervades all murder enquiries, yet many officers also look upon them as a mental and professional challenge, an opportunity to excel, an opportunity for old teams to be reformed in which camaraderie and elitism can flourish again and, maybe, for old scores to be settled. To some extent there is also a terrible fascination akin to a pathologist craning over the dissecting table seeking the cause of death.

A murder investigation, of course, does not have to be repulsive or crude, it can be a dignified matter where unpleasantness can be reduced skilfully and where sorrow and pain can be minimised; where offenders can be arrested quickly and the public feel more secure; and evidence painstakingly sought, interpreted, collated and presented so as to stand firm against any onslaught from the sharpest legal brains in the land.

Investigating officers of all ranks are enthusiastic but naturally there are some murders where the determination and enthusiasm is at its highest peak. The enquiry into the murder of Constable Carl Norris was one such case.

Chief Inspector Faraday had sensed this throughout the two and a half hours he had spent in the computerised HOLMES unit, the hub of the enquiry. But there was also a sombreness today which would only partially recede after the 27th when the young officer was buried.

Faraday had sat in on the briefing by the detective chief superintendent. He was a short man with a ruddy complexion whose accent confirmed him as a native of the Forest of Dean. But he was no dim-witted country yokel as his precise and succinct briefing clearly illustrated, although he would often assume during interview the mantel of a bumpkin to ensnare an unwary and arrogant prisoner. However, Faraday felt uncomfortable because, although there was mention of the NIRB deposits in the Atlantic First Commercial, no reference was made to the theft of the mines and the possible presence of any sort of a terrorist team in the city. Faraday reassured himself without much conviction, that there was no direct connection and maybe any reference to it would only serve to confuse or betray other more sensitive enquiries.

At 12.10 he drove his Volvo from the underground car park at Area HQ, out into the daylight and crowded shopping centre, congested with throngs of pre-Christmas shoppers. It took him nearly twenty minutes to return to his own district headquarters at The Grove. It would have actually been quicker to have walked but he needed to be near his car and it was safer to carry the box of hard-copy statements in the car than under his arm. The last thing he wanted was to slip in the snow and scatter the papers far and wide.

When Faraday entered his office, Helen Cave was engrossed, peering at the computer screen.

'Hi. Found anything?' he said as he gently placed his hand on her shoulder and was about the kiss her on the head, but didn't.

'No, no updates,' she replied with a smile. 'I've already spoken to Camberwell and we can expect edited transcripts of Peckham's telephone calls to have been fed into this computer by mid-afternoon.'

'Is there likely to be anything there?'

'Talked to them a few moments ago, they think so,' she replied optimistically. 'They have been able to sift through a lot of commercial code and jargon and other junk. There's no doubt that a lot of dirty money is going in and out, shady stock dealings, tax fiddles, that sort of thing, but we'll find out more later … I hope.'

'Let's sit around the table and have a look through this lot,' said Mark, as he took the lid off the duplicating paper box containing the witness statements.

'You've got them then?'

'With a little help from a friend,' said Faraday tapping his nose with his forefinger, 'a chap called Keith Hunt. He and I were inspectors together on the same shifts but adjoining stations. I've got two copies of each,' he said as he handed the MI5 agent copies of the statements from the observation team. The sheaf of papers also contained the statements submitted in response to the e-mail requesting preliminary statements to be submitted to the murder investigators by any officer who may have had direct or indirect contact with Norris or any information, however apparently trivial, that might conceivably be of assistance to the enquiry.

Both worked on the statements until 6.20, their only interruptions being Jane with constant streams of coffee as well as mid-day sandwiches, two enquiries from the acting chief inspector and a call at 3.40 on the secure line to say that the transcripts were now 'on-line'. Mark himself had made numerous calls, a number to the area communications centre and the district intelligence unit, as well as one to Companies House, London.

'Let's just go through it again and see what we know and don't know, Helen,' the policeman said as he flicked over the pages in his shorthand notebook on his knee. All the entries were colour-coded with yellow, orange and green highlighter pens. Most of the entries had been crossed through and now only six were left.

'What we know is that Norris went to the communication centre and checked the keyholders' lists. This was on Tuesday the 13th at about 11.30am. – when he should have been in bed. He spoke to the sergeant in charge and passed the time of day with some of the controllers, but gave no explanation for his visit.'

'But he went straight to the indexes and apparently found the card he was looking for immediately. PC - who was it?' Cave said as she checked her pencilled list, 'Spence, thinks it was a pink one, so that would be commercial premises, but we don't know which one.'

'It's amazing that this local stuff hasn't been computerised yet. If it had, we'd know what Norris had been after,' said Mark as he scribbled a note. 'I'll give Hunt a call later but meanwhile we know that Carl next called at area intelligence, again with no explanation, and went through the nominal index database, apparently without success. He then returned to Comms and checked the electoral register. Spence asked if he could help but Norris said that he was going to check Companies House himself.'

'That seems to confirm the pink card,' Cave said. 'He assumed that he would find details of a company and keyholder's name and address quickly and when he didn't he hoped that intelligence would throw it up. Electoral register might mean something, but maybe a shot in the dark.'

'I think so, but we'll keep it on ice,' said the policeman, circling around the words on his pad followed by a large question mark. 'It's a bloody nuisance that Companies House has no record of his call.'

'Either he hadn't had time to make it or they've fouled up,' Helen replied.

Chief Inspector Faraday went to his desk and phoned an internal four-digit number.

'Frank, DCI Hunt please … I'll wait,' then turned again to Helen. 'The only change in pattern was on Wednesday morning before he went off duty. Norris used a shaver that morning, and did so up until the time of his death, yet, he hadn't done so prior to that Wednesday. Why? I don't shave before I go to bed!'

'I know,' replied Helen Cave in a sultry voice.

Faraday found himself smiling and it was only with a real effort that he was able to drag his thoughts back to the day's grim business. He doubted that anyone other than Helen Cave could have lightened his mood so effortlessly. He cleared his throat and Helen grinned at his discomfort.

'Shall I continue?' Faraday asked in a mocking rebuke and Helen inclined her head graciously. 'And, by the following Thursday … no, Friday,' he said as he double-checked his note pad, 'Charlton and Howard had noticed that Norris was taking full advantage of his breaks between observations to sleep. He was keeping obs somewhere but … ah, Keith,' he said as DCI Hunt took his call, 'any developments?' There was a pause as the DCI in charge of the Home Office Large/Major Enquiry computer unit, known universally as 'HOLMES', updated Faraday.

'Well, it's early days Keith,' said Faraday, 'could I suggest something, only a thought, but PC Norris went to the communications suite on the morning of the 13th and personally checked the manual keyholders' index, also the nominal index at district as well as the electoral register. It's a tall order, but can the keyholders' cards be fingerprinted?' There was a further pause then, 'OK, OK. Sorry, only a thought,' Faraday said apologetically as DCI Hunt confirmed that fingerprinting was already underway. 'I'll have to get up much earlier to catch you out, Keith. Anyway, keep in touch. Thanks.'

He replaced the receiver and returned to the coffee table. 'I'll have to be quicker than that, Helen. An action team seized all the cards at four this afternoon and are slowly printing every card.'

The little coffee table appeared cluttered and at the side of their chairs where more pieces of paper, but there was order in this apparent chaos as they methodically and painstakingly worked together. They checked through Norris' pocket book again and the observation team's log. Then they checked through the statements of DS Harper of the Met Special Branch, who had tailed Dolan and lost him in Queen Square.

It was just after 6.15 when Helen Cave went to Jane's office to pour more coffee. Mark sank lower into the easy chair and absentmindedly fingered through the photographs taken by the day-shift team.

'What still intrigues me,' said Helen as she re-entered the office with coffee, 'is why Norris starts his keyholder enquiries on the 13th. He was doing something between 8 and 11am., but what? What had happened to trigger his enquiries off?'

'He had four crime enquiries outstanding,' replied the policeman. 'There was a shoplifter, a GBH and two thefts from motor vehicles as well as some petty traffic stuff. They could be connected, but I very much doubt it. All have been checked out, and an action team is going back over his previous cases.'

'It may have been helpful if his sergeant had got in touch as soon as Norris failed to turn up on the 21st,' Cave observed as Faraday discarded another pile of photographs.

'He is scheduled to be interviewed again,' said Faraday, fingering more photographs. 'His story is that they all thought Norris was out with a girl and didn't want to drop him in the mire. If it's true, and there's no reason to … .'

'What have you seen?' asked Helen as Mark rose quickly from his seat and slid back the glass doors of his book case with a clatter. He pulled out the file containing the hard copy Intelligence Reports. He had only to thumb a few pages.

'Oh God. He's here. He's in the city,' said Faraday, as he found the entry on page seven.'

'What do you mean?' asked a puzzled Cave, as they huddled together.

Mark pointed to the artist's impression of Michael Beazley alias David Miller at Item 20, the suspect for the stolen mines and detonators, then held it alongside the photograph of Dolan taken as he left the Atlantic First Commercial on the 16th October. In the background, but perfectly clear, was Michael Beazley alias David Miller.

Helen Cave saw the anger in Mark's stony face as his eyes flashed between the photograph and the artist's impression.

'Let's think this through,' Helen said.

'OK. OK,' agreed Faraday sharply. 'I know it doesn't mean that he murdered Norris, but what other explanation is there?' He got up, still angry and walked to the window as Cave sat at the computer screen.

'Mark, let's see if the bank transcripts come up with anything,' she said quietly, trying to focus both their minds on the task in hand. 'It might confirm one way or another.'

Faraday pulled a chair nearer Cave who put her hand on his knee and gave it a gentle squeeze, then touched the keys and the screen was quickly filled with print.

'These transcripts are from the 24th October until the present time. And we should see,' she said as page upon page of script rapidly moved up the screen, 'that our guys will have highlighted what they believe may be connected with Dolan.'

'Hang on. What's that bit?' asked Faraday eagerly, his finger on the screen. They read the text. 'Our usual deposit Mr Peckham, will be made on Monday, not Tuesday. I assume there will be no difficulties?'

'It could be it, but our guys will only highlight if there appears to be a connection or pattern, and that includes voice prints.' She pressed the keys again as both were transfixed by the screen, their faces bathed in a ghostly pale-blue glow.

Four minutes later Helen was the first to speak.

'Here we are, the 25th,' she said as a Mr Hancock's conversation with Peckham was highlighted in yellow bold case. 'This looks more promising.'

Both read the text, revealing how a Mr Hancock had rung the bank at 10:55.

'Ah,' Faraday said as he continued to read the screen, 'the jolly old bank manager's been a naughty boy at the Lygon Arms with ... here it is, Miss Hopkins of Cornwallis Crescent.' He raised his hand, then continued. 'Hancock talks about a £200,000 deposit on the 1st and the withdrawal on the 16th, but we'll flag it up and press on,' he said as he made a further note on his pad.

Two minutes later they spotted the highlighted entry for 10.32am. on the 12th, when Hancock called the bank again.

'Nothing much there, just checking the Christmas holiday arrangements, but it is indicative of Hancock's approach and attention to detail,' commented Cave.

'Yes,' said Faraday, 'Peckham's jumpy. He's worried. That should help us when we have to shout in his ear.'

'Now the show's moving,' Helen said with a smile. 'The 16th and Peckham calls Hancock and he's being really cagey.'

'Dolan must have called at the bank between the 12th and the 16th, but our men didn't clock him,' said Mark checking the calendar. 'Peckham's so jittery, he must have rung this Hancock fellow as soon as he knew. I'll check through the logs again later.'

'Hancock says he will contact Peckham again,' said Helen Cave, but as more and more text moved up the screen, no further highlighted entries could be found.

'Well, where does that take us? I just can't work out the connection between Peckham, Hancock, Dolan and Norris, Beazley or Miller,' Faraday said as he picked up an empty cup and replaced it on the table.

'Give me a second,' said Helen, 'and I'll check the reference.' She moved the cursor, depressed a key and another field appeared. 'Here we are,' she said, 'Hancock's conversation is highlighted because his voice print is a possible match to calls made on the 6th February and 10th October to the NIRB, members of which are known to have visited the banks. There are some notes here,' she said as she continued to read the text, 'poor quality intercepts - only 60% positive.'

'Let me try and think this through,' Faraday said. 'I haven't a clue who Hancock is. He might be an opportunist but I doubt that very much, he wouldn't have picked up the details of the deposits and withdrawals on the 1st and the 16th by chance.'

'Observations alone would not have given him that information, nor the amounts,' Helen said.

'Then it must be someone in the bank. What about Miss Hopkins?' suggested Faraday.

'If it was Miss Hopkins, why had Hopkins and Hancock selected Dolan? Why not someone else with richer pickings?' said Helen Cave as she pressed the keys again and the text returned to the 25th October.

'Hancock didn't know the account number,' said Faraday. 'One would have assumed that if Dolan and Hopkins knew the contents of Dolan's account, then they would have known the number.'

'But Peckham didn't appear to on the 25th, and if Hancock did he wouldn't have made himself any more vulnerable if he had given the account number. On the other hand, he may have endangered Miss Hopkins if she was his accomplice,' countered Cave.

'But, if Miss Hopkins is a central figure in all this, why could she not phone Hancock as soon as Dolan is about to withdraw cash? Why does Hancock have to keep Peckham on the boil by ringing him from time to time?'

'Peckham can tell us that,' said Helen.

'Peckham can also tell us whose name appears on that banker's draft,' Faraday added.

'£84,950. What would that buy, Mark?'

'A very big car, a medium sized boat or a bloody small house.'

Chief Inspector Faraday borrowed a flip chart from the briefing room and this became the centre of their activities for another half-hour. Names, places and dates appeared. There were connections but no distinct pattern that gave any real explanation for the killing of Constable Norris. There were as many question marks as there were arrows, straight lines and dotted lines on the chart. The only extra details that had been added were replies to their enquiries from 'C' and 'F' Districts. Both Faraday and Cave now knew that Miss C Hopkins lived at 194b Cornwallis Crescent and the bank manager lived at number 3 The Cedars, as well as his elephone number.

The policeman focused on the flip charts. His mind usually quickly discerned patterns but he saw no pattern here. He broke the silence. 'Where do we go from here, Helen?'

'Our only real avenue at the moment is Peckham who might lead us to Dolan.'

'Completely agree,' he said, 'I propose to ring Mr Peckham and see if he's at home, then you and I will speak to him tonight. We've lost enough time already. Dolan was last seen at about 1.30 yesterday afternoon. He could be on the high seas now.'

'OK, let's do it,' Helen said, pleased, like Mark, to be getting out of that office with the prospect of securing a concrete lead.

Before they left the office, Mark called the bank manager's home. The phone was answered quickly and curtly by Peckham himself. Mark replaced the receiver without replying.

'He's there, Helen, let's move.'

The Volvo purred out onto The Grove and turned left into the light snow, then left again, across the narrow Princess Street swing bridge and into Wapping Road. They accelerated along Cumberland Road, past the old burnt-out prison gate towers destroyed in the riots of 1831, snow capping the old ramparts. It all looked very seasonal and romantic.

Faraday and Cave entered the Cumberland Basin fly-over system then drove straight onto the Long Ashton by-pass, accelerating past a fleet of road gritting lorries. As they left the yellow flashing lights in their rear-view mirrors, they continued to discuss and agree their tactics as they travelled. They knew they were quickly running out of time. They also knew very little, but what they did know should have the desired effect upon Peckham. He was vulnerable. All men were vulnerable and have something to loose, but Peckham could loose everything. That fact could work for or against Faraday and Cave, it could make him co-operative or hostile, informative or obstructive. They would have to be careful and be skilful.

The porch light of 3 The Cedars was on as were the other lights in the house. Mark rapped the brass lion's head doorknocker sharply twice and, after only a few moments, the rich cedar door was opened by an extremely attractive and sophisticated lady of about thirty-five years. Mark's immediate thought was what an idiot Peckham must be.

'Good evening, madam,' he said producing his warrant card. 'There's nothing for you to worry about but I am Chief Inspector Faraday. I'm wondering whether I could speak with your husband?'

'Oh,' was her only reply. She was uncertain whether to invite them both in or not when her husband came to the door.

'It's the police, dear,' she said, not looking at Faraday but at Cave who was standing behind the policeman, her back to him.

Peckham looked at his watch. 'A little late isn't it. Can't this wait?'

'Murder enquiries can seldom wait, Mr Peckham. May I step inside,' he replied as he entered the hall uninvited.

It was a beautiful house, exuding wealth and comfort.

'I can completely understand the confidentiality of clients' accounts,' Faraday said, 'but my colleague and I are investigating the murder of Constable Norris. I expect you've read about it?'

'Oh yes, the coloured chappy,' he said in an irritatingly patronising way. 'Can't see how I can help.'

'But I think you can help. Indeed, I *know* you can, Mr Peckham,' said the policeman who, although he smiled, the choice of words and diction were deliberately ponderous, cool and uncompromising. 'You see, I am *absolutely* sure that a client of your bank is directly involved in this particularly vicious murder.'

'My bank has many thousands of clients,' said Peckham unhelpfully.

'But *this* one is a Mr … a Mr Hancock,' Faraday said, looking directly at the point between Peckham's eyes.

The bank manager's supercilious and dismissive expression froze, Mark saw a vein on his forehead start to throb as the man's pulse rate raced and cheek twitched as Mark pressed on.

'May I have just a few minutes of your time, privately?'

'Of course, ah, chief inspector you said,' mumbled Peckham, who without looking at his wife walked away down the hall. 'My study is free.'

They entered a study, well furnished by 'G Plan'. Peckham quickly occupied the commanding seat behind the desk, his back to the bay window. Faraday did not sit down, nor did Cave who remained standing at the door she had closed.

'You place me in a delicate position, officers,' said the manager who had assumed that Helen Cave was a police officer and was now regaining some of his composure. 'I and my bank are always keen to assist the constabulary, of course, but there is the question of confidentiality and the Bankers Book Evidence Act. My other problem is that I can't off-hand recall anyone by the name of Hancock. There may be many."

'Think *carefully*, Mr Peckham,' Mark insisted and watched as Peckham made a pretence of racking his brains, although Mark was well aware that what Peckham was actually doing was trying to work out how much the police could possibly know.

'No,' he said as if the enquiries were meaningless to him. 'A Hancock certainly doesn't come immediately to mind. As I say, there may be many.'

'But only one who is *blackmailing* you.'

Peckham was shaken and his composure lapsed again. A weak smile appeared just for a second then disappeared. His little eyes flickered about the desk, then to his interrogator, then rested upon Helen, the expressionless, unsmiling and condemning stare of Helen Cave. He contrived a relaxed pose in his chair, elbows on the arms and fingers steepled.

'I'm not being blackmailed, chief inspector. I can't think for a moment why anyone should tell you that.'

'Are you sure?'

'Now look,' said Peckham angrily, his tongue moving nervously and involuntarily between his lips. 'I don't think I have to take this you know. I think you'd better leave.'

'Mr Peckham,' continued Faraday, 'why have you given confidential details of one of your bank's clients to Mr Hancock?' There was no denial but a weak attempt to maintain an assured and aloof air.

'And why should I do that?' he said with a nervous chuckle as if the question was preposterous and of no importance.

'*Because*,' said the policeman slowly, 'you wish to keep your illicit liaison with the beautiful Miss Hopkins of 194b Cornwallis Crescent a secret.'

The corner of Peckham's mouth twitched as he tried to remember how often he had visited her flat and how many of those intoxicatingly exotic visits would be known to Faraday. He leaned forward across his desk and threw down a last desperate challenge.

'I shall *deny it*,' he hissed.

'As you wish,' Faraday replied curtly. 'You obviously think that it would be so much safer to deal with the bank's internal investigators than ourselves.'

'I have a responsibility to all my staff,' he blustered. 'As I am sure you will know, there are always domestic and welfare matters that require any manager's attention.'

Faraday could sense how high Peckham's stress levels were as he began to rationalise his behaviour, to admit yet deny. Now was the time for Faraday to press home his advantage, to bombard Peckham with facts and to create more fears; to give him little time to think and lie, and also, to provide him with an escape.

'*Where?*' At the Lygon Arms?" he asked almost casually, then continued more sharply. 'There are numerous avenues of enquiry that I can pursue vigorously in respect of murder, Mr Peckham. As you know, there is considerable media interest in the United Kingdom's first murder of a black police officer, and I am hoping that you can assist me in one very small matter to such an extent that I shall not be forced to approach your directors or drag you as a hostile witness before the Crown Court. Both are undignified procedures.'

Peckham's mind raced. He thought of Miss Hopkins, the seductive Miss Clare Hopkins; he thought of his wife in the public gallery of some future court; the bedroom at 194b Cornwallis Crescent; only 'one very small matter'; his wariness of Cave and the passion at the Lygon Arms. Thoughts of Miss Hopkins again filled his mind, only to be replaced by the shocked faces of his children.

'Let me help you, Mr Peckham,' said Faraday. 'There is only one piece of a very large puzzle that I don't have just at the moment. Your bank issued a man named Dolan with a banker's draft on the 16th October. I merely want you to tell me to whom the draft was made,' adding reasonably, 'That is all we require.'

'I could obtain the details for you tomorrow.'

'No,' said Faraday uncompromisingly, 'it would be so much tidier for me if we take you to your bank now and you provide me with the details there. I am sure you will be able to put your hands on the details within minutes. That will then conclude our association. I need trouble you, your family and your bank no further. You could be back here in your own home by, say nine-thirty.'

'How can I be sure that this is the last I shall hear of this?' asked Peckham, looking at his watch, obviously eager to take advantage of the offer.

'Because it is logical, Mr Peckham. I am only interested in arresting a killer and you can help me do that. Your friendships are a matter for you, they are of no importance to me at all, nor,' he added menacingly, 'need they be to anyone else.'

Faraday could imagine the thoughts that were no doubt racing through Peckham's mind at that moment; if he co-operated his liaison with Miss Hopkins could continue, his job and home would still be secure and he would be doing a public duty in assisting the police in bringing a murderer to book.

'Alright, chief inspector, let's get it over and done with.'

They re-entered the hall. Mrs Peckham was still there, waiting, anxious and uncertain.

'Going to the office, dear. I should be back by ... ?' he said jauntily, looking towards Faraday.

'About 09.30, sir. It's very kind of you to put yourself out like this at such short notice,' smiled the policeman, then added, 'we can all go in my car, Mr Peckham.'

Faraday and Cave deliberately did not speak to Peckham on the way back to the bank but spoke inconsequentially between themselves. When they arrived at the bank, Peckham went straight to the chief cashier's office. The banker's draft records would be there. It was easy to find - £84,950 made out to a 'R.J. Hagley & Sons (Falmouth) Ltd'.

'There you are. My side of the bargain as promised. Now, if you don't mind,' he said, a cockiness returning to his manner, 'you can take me home.'

'Be patient, Mr Peckham. Just a few minutes longer,' said the chief inspector. 'I have only one call to make.' He picked up the telephone and dialled out.

'Chief Inspector Faraday. Who is that please?' There was a pause. 'Bert, get in touch with the Falmouth police now, I think their comms centre is at Camborne. I want the keyholder's name, address and phone number for R.J. Hagley and Sons in Falmouth. I don't know the address. And ask them what line of business Hagley is in. I'll hold.'

It took only a few minutes for the reply. Faraday jotted down the details and replaced the receiver.

'We can take you home now, Mr Peckham.' It was 8.51pm.

***

Hadfield had parked his rental in Greenbank Road and walked up towards Beacon Street, then climbed on into Bassett Street and the approach to Beacon Cottages. The wind here, overlooking the Penryn River, was cutting, his ears soon burning with the cold whilst his body was snug within his Goretex zoot suit.

After forty minutes, he had reconnoitred thoroughly, and continued to wait patiently.

At twenty to eleven, he walked across to the red-painted post box, his hood pulled up, and made a pretence of considering the collection times, at the same time studying the cottage. The curtains were drawn in the lounge and a dull light shone from the landing into the small bedroom immediately above the front door. The curtains of this small room were not drawn, nor were those in the larger rear bedroom. He recalled his visit on the 17th October and surmised that Dolan would probably be using the rear bedroom with potential access from the flat roof over the modern bathroom and toilet extension. That could be useful, he thought, as he walked towards the cottage, wisps of snow dancing in the street lights only to dissolve on his face.

As he approached the cottage, the front door opened. No lights shone out, and Hadfield could only just distinguish a figure as it pushed past the overgrown shrubs and bushes and approached the old garden gate, disturbing the snow as he went.

The man, coat buttoned to his neck, turned into the terrace and up the slight rise of Glasney Road. Hadfield followed. They walked on in the snow, but Hadfield constantly kept his man in his sights until two hundred metres later he mounted the few wide steps to the fish and chip bar. Hadfield walked by and crossed the road into the lane alongside the lock-up garages and waited in their shadow. It would not be complicated, he only had to count to provide the answer to his most critical question.

As he waited a racy little Peugeot stopped outside the bar and two, young, noisy couples got out, laughing their way up the steps. The owner of the bar took notice of these young people but his lone customer did not. Sloppy thought Hadfield.

The owner passed over to his customer the wrapped portions of fish and chips. The man unwrapped the portions to add more salt and vinegar, then re-wrapped the parcels and placed them into a plastic carrier bag.

Hadfield counted. Three parcels, three targets.

Hadfield disappeared down the pitch-black lane as his quarry lit a Silk Cut cigarette. Still smoking he trudged his way back to the cottage, pushed open the rickety garden gate and made his way towards the front door, searching for the key in his coat pocket. He had sensed something but had not understood what, by which time he felt the ice-cold contours of the Nexus silencer grind into the side of his throat.

'Do not speak,' said Hadfield, slowly and deliberately, 'Just open the front door and you have a chance to live. Fuck up and you're dead.'

The man opened the front door and they both entered the small, outer hallway. The man opened the inner, glazed door.

'Is that you?' said a voice from the kitchen.

Hadfield twisted the gun painfully into the man's neck and applied pressure to the man's left shoulder joint. Hadfield could smell the man's fear.

'Yeh.'

'The plates are warm and the lagers are cold,' said a cheery voice from the kitchen beyond.

As Hadfield appeared in the doorway, the man balancing the lager cans on the warm plates, froze in front of the crackling fire. Dolan, seated on the couch, looked round, stunned and confused.

If I squeeze the trigger,' said Hadfield as he continued to jab the menacing silencer of his SIG 9mm semi-automatic into the man's throat, 'I shall blow your sloppy friend's head inside out. Then, I shall kill you.' With hardly a pause he continued. 'You on the couch, you must be Dolan. Silly man. Did you really think these shits intended for you to keep your money? They intend to kill you.' He kept staring at the man with the plates. 'No reply. You at least know that what I'm saying is true.'

Before he could answer, Hadfield barked an order. 'Put the plates on the floor in front of you, now.'

The man stooped and placed the plates and cans carefully on the floor.

'Turn around,' said Hadfield to the plate man as he sunk his fingers more deeply into the collector of fish and chips' shoulder.

As he did so, Hadfield could see in the mirror over the fireplace, the frightened expression on his otherwise pleasant face.

'Now,' he said to the plate man, 'put your right hand behind your head and slowly take off your belt with your left hand and unbutton your flies.'

As the trousers slipped down his legs, Hadfield snapped another order. 'OK, Dolan. This is your only chance to stay alive and remain rich. My score with these shits is your only opportunity. Tie his hands behind his back with the belt.'

Dolan, still not master of events, had little time to consider, his thoughts only of living, of the money and a hatred of the English. He quickly rose from the couch and tied the hands of the plate man with the belt, so tightly that his captive winced.

Hadfield fixed his eyes upon Dolan. 'Step back two paces,' he ordered. When Dolan had done so there was another uncompromising order. 'Now, three paces to your left.' Dolan did as he was told - precisely as he was told. 'Now you,' he said to the collector of fish and chips, 'move forward to the left two paces and drop the bag.' Encouraged by a further sharp metallic jab in the throat, the collector of fish and chips obediently shuffled the required two paces and dropped the plastic carrier bag onto the carpet, the wrapped parcels of hot fish and chips spilling over his shoes. 'Now,' snapped Hadfield, 'put your hands on your head.'

He did so, instantly.

'Step over to the fire,' he said menacingly, then snapped, 'don't turn around', adding in a quieter tone, 'now, leave your right hand on your head and with your left hand, take off your belt and unfasten your flies.' The collector of fish and chips did as he was told, his trousers slowly falling around his ankles. 'Now,' Hadfield barked, 'put both arms behind your back.' He did so almost instantly. 'OK, Dolan, same again. Tie his arms, but at the elbows this time.'

Dolan responded quickly and when the task was completed, Hadfield told both men, the collector of fish and chips and the older, plate man, to turn and face him. They were frightened as they waited to obey the next instruction from this sandy-haired man standing before them holding the powerful pistol in his right hand with the ugly 8" long silencer cradled in the crook of his left elbow. Then Hadfield spoke again, rather like an unfeeling chairman addressing a board of directors about the closure of an ailing factory.

'Well, Mr Dolan. I want to thank you for your assistance and support here, but your usefulness to me is now at an end.' He pointed the gun towards Dolan and fired one shot. There was a soft dumph as the 9mm round, travelling at 350m per second, slammed into its target.

Dolan's chest seemed to spontaneously erupt and the shirt instantly changed colour, a bright crimson red, as Dolan collapsed, like a puppet whose strings had suddenly been cut.

Dolan's companions looked at each other, shocked by the casual ending of a life as Hadfield looked around the cottage. These frightened men had made up beds on the two settees and one in the arm chair. Fires now roared in both grates.

'Where's the money?' he asked in a slow and cool, matter-of-fact way.

'I … in, in the bag, th … the beige bag,' said the collector of fish and chips eagerly, nodding towards a number of holdalls on the couch.

Hadfield moved towards the couch, leaned forwards without taking his eyes of his captives and unzipped the bag with one hand. His fingers explored the interior until he grasped, then pulled out the money belt. He flicked open the first pouch and ran his finger across the notes. He gently lowered the money belt over the back of the couch, then plunged his hand back into the beige bag.

'What is this for?' he asked coldly, pulling out an ACE Cleaning Company boiler suit.

Both men looked at each other. The collector of fish and chips clearly the subordinate.

'It's a boiler suit,' said the plate man.

Hadfield tipped up the holdall onto the wooden table and quickly searched through the contents, pushing each item aside with the silencer of his gun. He stopped, then held up an identity card.

'What is this?'

'It's an ID card, that's all,' said the collector of fish and chips.

'Just an ID card? Come, come,' said Hadfield as if questioning a child, 'it's an ID card for a nuclear power station, which allows, I'm sorry, *allowed*, your friend Dolan entry. What were your intentions?'

'Look,' said the plate man, 'we're just small fry, people higher up are dealing with this.'

Hadfield ignored this useless comment and began to search through the pockets of a jacket on the back of an upright chair. As always he was thorough. He pulled out a wallet from an inner pocket and discarded the jacket on the floor. He examined the contents, then moved the upright chair forward a little.

'Sit down,' he said reasonably, and the collector of fish and chips sat obediently in the chair, still shocked and confused, his back to Hadfield but facing plate man. Hadfield then removed a hank of olive-coloured paracord from his pocket.

'It's quite alright,' he said soothingly as the man became more agitated. 'It won't hurt. I'm just making sure you can't run away.' He tied the cord around the belt, then through the wooden uprights, around the man's trunk a number of times, securing him firmly to the chair. Then he examined the contents of the wallet more closely.

'I see that you're from MI6,' he said to the plate man as he turned the government ID card over in his fingers. 'Well, that *is* interesting. I thought that it was MI5's job to look after *internal* security affairs. Please tell me what you are doing here and what part you had intended the late Mr Dolan to play?'

'Look, mister,' said the plate man, still standing in his underpants, his trousers around his ankles and hands tied behind his back. 'You've got the money, leave it at that.'

'I have *some* of the money of course, but I am more interested in your intentions, why MI6 was involved with Dolan and your intentions for him. Please tell me, or I shall kill your friend.'

'We can't tell you anything, buster.'

Hadfield remained standing behind the collector of fish and chips tied to the wooden chair. His captive did not see nor comprehend what was happening at first, then gasped desperately like a drowning fish, trying grimly to tear with his teeth at the clear plastic bag that had been pulled quickly over his head. He struggled hopelessly and rocked back and forth in the chair, but Hadfield steadied the dying man's exertions almost gently.

His colleague stood there transfixed and terrified, whilst the fires continued to crackle and the aroma of fish and chips still hung in the air. But now there was a new aroma, the acrid smell of a dying man's urine.

The struggles of the collector of fish and chips gradually weakened, he twitched for one final time then his head seemed to virtually drift backwards to hang silently over his chair.

'I think we understand each other now and you will want to fully co-operate with me, won't you?' said Hadfield and, without waiting for a reply, continued, 'Please sit in the armchair behind you, whilst I sit here on the couch.'

Plate man responded robotically and sat awkwardly back into the armchair starring blankly at a very dead collector of fish and chips. His eyes darted nervously towards Hadfield as the smiling killer spoke again.

'I think you will agree, we have much to talk about.'

Chapter 21

Saturday 24th November.

Cornwall, England.

HELEN CAVE'S metallic Tempest Grey Rover 75 was a spiteful and powerful blur as it sped, Xenon headlamps, long-range driving lights and fog lamps blazing, cutting through the swirling wet darkness and along the undulating A30, deeper across the remote and bleak, boulder-strewn Bodmin Moor,

Chief Inspector Faraday had assumed that the MI5 agent would have called up a helicopter to fly them from Filton or Lulsgate to the Royal Naval Air Station at Culdrose only twelve miles from Falmouth, but Cave wanted her Rover, equipped as it was, to take on the role of a mini forward Tac HQ. It would also provide her with personal mobility and independence of action. No such vehicle was available near Falmouth, no helicopter had been immediately to hand and the weather had already closed in. There would be no help from those men and women of MI5's A4 Branch, universally known as 'The Watchers'. They were on their own.

Faraday also knew that, without debate or agreement, authority had passed to Cave. The policeman's authority of course extended throughout England and Wales irrespective of local police force boundaries, but Cave was now in the driver's seat in more ways than one. She was driving a security service's car with security service communications, into a situation unfamiliar to a policeman, to confront a known NIRB terrorist and very likely a devious, cunning thief and traitor, who was probably also a cold and sadistic killer.

Faraday had quickly recognised the slight and subtle changes, with Cave now in her element. There was an eagerness about the agent now, an assured tenseness mirrored in her firm yet sensitive control of the powerful 2.5 litre car that topped 130 mph on the M5 motorway between Bristol and Exeter, and was now nudging 90 as they passed the black outline of the Jamaica Inn on the windswept Bodmin Moor. It was 12.02am.

Faraday was enjoying the experience as he compared the Rover's V6 engine's effortless performance and tenacious road holding with that of his 240bhp five-cylinder Volvo T5. Faraday tried to discern the comparative qualities of each vehicle. Both were impressive performers, but what impressed him most was Helen Cave who, with apparently effortless skill, steered her vehicle through the rain that turned to blustery sleet as the dark night wore on.

The vehicle's standard equipment was good but what had fascinated the policeman were the security service additions. There was the auxiliary radio fitted into the boot with a handset concealed under the passenger footwell. In the glove compartment was a laptop-style computer screen and keyboard. Part of this system automatically and continuously searched the air-waves, isolating and locking on to the regular and routine transmissions of the local police, garage recovery vehicles and the gas, electricity and other utilities. The standard GPS navigation system had been replaced by the government's destination, route and tracker system, providing up-to-date information on twelve scales of Ordnance Survey maps, potential routes and destination ETAs, as well as allowing automatic vehicle tracking by MI5 headquarters in the event of emergencies.

To the casual observer, the vehicle looked to be no more than the typical property of a company executive, however, a fax machine had been installed behind the rear centre armrest and the 'Spyglass' thermal imager, the 'Dark Invader' image intensifier and the orthodox binoculars tucked neatly under the deep front passenger footwell and the array of weapons in the boot, including the Remington 870 pump-action shotgun, would not be seen. Nor would the two Heckler & Koch MP5K machine pistols concealed in the roof lining behind what appeared to be the access to a non-existent sunroof.

The high-speed journey had been surprisingly restful for Faraday. The vehicle was extremely comfortable and stable in the capable hands of Cave, whom he found even more intriguing, intoxicating even. Gone was her formal business suit, instead, Helen Cave wore a grey polo-neck jumper under a black, shockcord-waisted rain jacket and jeans. They looked good together, a natural pair with Mark in black T-shirt under a grey, heavyweight sweat top. Both wore *Nike* trainers.

Since passing Exeter, Faraday and Cave had talked almost continuously, to some extent through a mixture of nervous anticipation and excitement, but mainly about themselves. They found each other easy companions. They first spoke of university, Helen of her BA in Political History from Manchester and an MSc in Computer Studies from Canterbury; Mark of his MSc in Leadership Studies from Cardiff. She spoke of her gap year in Italy, the terrorist attack in Bologna and how and why she had volunteered to help in the city's casualty rest centre. She explained how, when she returned to England to undertake her masters, she had been approached by the university's net ball coach who had introduced her to recruiters from MI5. For Mark, his attraction to the 'blue light' services was almost inevitable given his late father's long career in the fire brigade.

A conversation that had started for both of them as purely a factual recollection of chronological events punctuated with light-hearted remarks, developed into the unconscious sharing of more private and sensitive memories. For Mark, it was the loss and absence of parents and the failure of his marriage. For her, it was the loss of her husband in a helicopter crash whilst serving with the Army Air Corp. For both, these recollections became too personal and, as if reading each other's mind, they gently squeezed each other's hand followed by silence.

Then they had sped on across the bleak moor until Mark's thoughts turned to Hancock and the silence was broken.

'In many ways Hancock and Peckham are not dissimilar,' said Mark breaking the silence. 'Peckham likes playing with lots of money. I bet he's up to all the tricks in the book, wheeling and dealing. He needs the stimulation. He gets that from the job, his Porsche and Miss Hopkins. If what we suspect about Hancock is true, then the only difference between them is that Hancock is mad.'

'He's not necessarily mad,' Cave responded, the revs climbing as she dropped from fifth to fourth gear. 'Extreme, yes, but to him I suspect that this is all part of another stimulating business deal.'

'I can understand someone who requires stimulation, we all do, but Hancock, he's in a different league.'

'But not any more inexplicable than being a Formula One racing driver, a stunt man or an army bomb disposal engineer,' suggested Helen, her eyes flitting from the road ahead to the rear view mirror. Cave had spotted the other car too.

'We make him sound so bloody normal. And if he is normal, he'll be difficult to … ' said Faraday, his comments interrupted by the automatic interception of a police transmission.

'Charlie Two Zero Eight to Whisky Hotel.'

'Go ahead Charlie Two Zero Eight.'

'Charlie Two Zero Eight, location A30, three miles south of Temple New Bridge and now in pursuit of a grey Rover 75.'

The pursuing police vehicle continued to give the index number of Cave's car and requesting a PNC check, as both Cave and Faraday noted the pursuing car in their rear-view mirrors.

'It's a small Ford I think, Helen,' said Faraday looking to the rear, 'it's your call.'

'We could outrun him but we might land up in a squelchy ditch, or they could. Wouldn't do anything for inter-service co-operation,' she said with a beaming smile. 'If we don't stop it might draw too much attention to us, and result in lots of silly paperwork,' observed Cave as she dropped her speed in direct response to the pursuing police vehicle switching on its blue lights.

The Rover pulled off the road onto the rough lay-by.

'Say nothing, sir, if you don't mind,' said Cave, for the first time giving Faraday a direct order yet calling him 'sir' as the constable in white cap and reflective yellow jacket approached the driver's door. Cave had already lowered the window down and the ruddy-faced policeman, his waterproofs already wet and water dripping down his cheeks, spoke first.

'You're in a hurry, madam, driving far too fast on a night like this. I'll be seeing your driver's licence if you please?'

'I'm sorry to have caused you inconvenience, officer. May I ask you ... ,' said Cave, but she was interrupted by her own in-car radio picking up the police transmission.

'This is Whisky Hotel to Charlie Two Zero Eight.'

'Go ahead, Two Zero Eight,' replied the policeman's colleague in the Ford as Cave and the very wet traffic constable looked at each other.

'Yes, Charlie Two Zero Eight. PNC has this number blocked.'

'Wait one, Whisky Hotel,' replied Charlie Two Zero Eight.

'Are you two the police?' asked the now very wet policeman.

'Not exactly, but we are on the same side,' Cave said as the other policeman approached the car.

'Jack, the number's one of they queer 'uns,' blurted out his much younger colleague.

'Just a minute,' said the first constable, uncertain of what to do as his colleague tried to peer in through the window, curious to have sight of those within.

'May I ask you,' said Cave formally, 'to contact your HQ and merely say "Green Sunlight". They will understand. We are on a little exercise, but we are behind schedule and it *is* important.'

Jack gave instructions to his younger colleague who scurried back to the patrol car.

'Get into the back, officer, if you like,' Helen suggested. 'It's far too wet and cold outside.' It was a request difficult to refuse.

The constable stepped gratefully into the rear of the warm car as Cave touched the impulse button and her window slid closed. Within seconds all three occupants could clearly hear the police radio transmissions.

'Charlie Two Zero Eight to Whisky Hotel, re. our PNC check on the Rover, the occupants have told us to tell you "Green Sunlight". Does this mean anything to you?'

'Wait one, Two Zero Eight,' came the reply, but the wait was much less than one minute, and the reply was much more urgent.

'Charlie Two Zero Eight, this is Inspector Craven. Back off now. Allow the vehicle to proceed, and that means now. Confirm.'

'Roger, sir, Charlie Two Zero Eight.'

'Well, I'll be getting out then folks,' said the policeman, stepping back out into the driving sleet. 'We all best be on our separate ways.'

'Thank you, officer,' Helen said, then added genuinely, 'I'm sorry if we troubled you.'

The Rover rolled off the glistening and noisy gravel onto the road again, gently increasing speed along the dual-carriageway that skirts the town of Bodmin to the south.

At the end of the dual-carriageway is Innis Downs and a track leading to the hamlet of Innis itself. Helen pulled up this track away from and completely out of sight of the main road. 'Stay there,' she said touching his thigh. 'I won't be a moment,' and stepping out into the sleet, quickly went to the boot. Faraday remained in the car as she tampered with the front and rear of the vehicle then returned to the boot again.

'What were you up to?' Mark asked Helen as she returned to the driver's seat, her jacket soaking wet.

'Just changing the number plates. All sorts of people could have picked up those transmissions and some inquisitive policeman may later draw attention to us by poking about.'

'Stop a second,' Faraday said as he searched in his pocket for a handkerchief. He leaned towards her, as she did to him, so that he could wipe the rain from her brow, then her nose and upper lip.

'It has your initials embroidered on it, Mark. That's nice,' she observed as she fingered the corner, then took it from his hand and tucked the handkerchief into her jacket before engaging reverse gear. As she turned around in her seat to obtain a clear view to the rear, Mark kissed her gently on the lips. 'Don't distract me,' she said softly, then kissed him again slowly. 'Later,' she purred before reversing the Rover onto the main road.

'I didn't realise you had another set of plates,' Faraday said as if to help him concentrate again.

Oh, I haven't,' said Cave deviously, 'I have another three.'

They passed through the cold and slumbering Indian Queens and onto the A39 towards Tresillian, reaching the cathedral city of

Truro by 12.26. Eleven uneventful minutes later they were on the outskirts of Falmouth.

Faraday's earlier telephone call from the bank to the Falmouth police had established that the keyholders for Hagley's estate agency were the two sons, one of whom lived at Mabe Burnthouse and the other at Penryn. Helen Cave concluded that the shop premises of R.J. Hagley and Sons of Killigrew Street, Falmouth, would be unoccupied and, that as the estate agents never dealt with ready cash, the alarm system, if any, would be cheap and easy to by-pass.

The Rover pulled to a halt inconspicuously alongside an AA telephone and Cave and Faraday both got out of the car into the dirty grey slush and biting cold wind and changed seats. Cave opened the glove compartment and pressed a key, then another to bring to high resolution a digitised map of Falmouth onto the screen in the central Black Oak fascia above the gear stick. Then the reference numbers were tapped in and Killigrew Street appeared in the exact centre of the screen.

'If we drive off down here to this junction and turn left and left again, you could drop me there,' said Cave, her beautiful finger following the road network.

The policeman drove the car to Berkeley Vale and drew into the kerb.

'I can guess what you are going to do, Helen.'

'It's better you don't know,' she said as she pressed further keys and a local authority planning department's plan of Hagley and Sons' premises appeared in response, confirming the policeman's suspicions.

'It's now 00:47. I'll need twenty minutes. Listen to your watch. If you hear, let's say, two bleeps like this,' she said, pressing with her index finger one of the little buttons on the side of her watch, 'then go straight back to Bristol. You know who to contact. Otherwise, see you at the top of this road by the park in twenty minutes.'

'OK. So *our* transmissions won't be detected, but what if I pick up any police transmission?'

'No problem,' she said, inserting the small skin-coloured receiver into her ear, 'I'll pick them up as well,' and stepped out into the cold, driving sleet again.

'Be careful, Helen,' said Faraday, but she was gone.

Mark drove down Dracaena Avenue into Falmouth Road, past the yacht marina and into the all-night petrol station. He got out and made a pretence of checking the tyres, constantly fingering his unfamiliar ear-piece. He was uneasy. This was not what he had been taught to do. His thoughts were confused. He thought of President Nixon and the Watergate scandal. He thought of Constable Norris in that grim alley. He thought of Helen Cave trapped in the estate agents, the alarm bell ringing and the building surrounded by police cars and dog handlers. Even if he did race back to Bristol, even the most half-baked detective investigating the burglary would at least query Mark's enquiry with the Falmouth police.

Helen looked at her Seiko. She was in the building and on schedule. She walked from the manager's office with the details of 3 Beacon Cottages firmly in her mind and returned to the small staff room-cum-kitchen at the rear. She had wiped up her wet trainer prints on the tiled floor with paper kitchen roll, as she had on the ceramic tiles of the window sill. She checked the kitchen again then stepped up on to the sink, then the sill, pushed open the unlocked aluminium-framed window and out into the dark, sheltered alleyway. The agent leaned back through the window, wiped the sill again, picked up the flowerpots from the draining board and placed them back onto the sill, then closed the window. Stepping onto a sloping downpipe, she leaned through the transom window and secured the main window lock with an Allen key. She could not of course secure the transom that she had earlier sprung open, but she was sure that Hagley's staff would attribute it being open to carelessness. There would be no reason for them to suspect otherwise.

She checked her watch again. Four minutes to go. Most of the alleyway was wet with thawing slush and the snow had remained only in the corners, packed up against the walls and the rubbish sacks. By stepping carefully, no footprints were evident, just as if she had walked along the bed of a stream.

'Sorry to be late,' Helen said as she opened the passenger door and glided into the seat, 'but only by one minute. Dolan's place is close by. Straight down the road if you don't mind and turn right at the bottom.' She looked at Faraday with a huge smile. 'It's OK, I checked the map on the manager's wall,' then touched his thigh and said more seriously, 'Thank you for worrying, Mark. I knew you wouldn't abandon me.'

Faraday was too relieved to say anything.

They drove less than a mile to Frobisher Terrace.

'It's number three,' said Cave, checking the digitised map, 'just up behind us. I'll want another twenty, maybe thirty minutes. If you pick me up again at Symonds Hill.'

'Helen, Dolan and Hancock could both be there. We ought to get some back-up, even if it means waiting.'

'Look,' she said without rancour, 'I'm not suicidal, Mark. I don't believe that they will be there anyway. All I want to do is check the location so that I have a better idea of how to get in and out when we have to, and to help us decide what type of back-up we will need.' She smiled that smile again. 'You worry too much, Mark. In any case, I want to see you again. So, trust me.'

Helen Cave got out of the car, but not before she had kissed him on the cheek.

'Listen to your watch,' she said, 'and if I press the button twice, then just call the local police and tell them to get to number three as quickly as they can, but tell them to be well armed.'

She closed the door and she was lost again, enveloped in the swirling sleet.

In typical English fashion there were only two Beacon Cottages, numbers one and three, situated in the fork in the road, perched on a congested hillside of muddled houses, looking down towards the Greenbank Hotel and over the river to the village of Flushing. The gates to the front gardens of both cottages faced onto the fork of the junction where Bassett Street divides into Polwheveral and Langton Terraces. Number one was built flush with Polwheveral to the left, but, because the hill sloped down to the right, number three was raised up so that when Cave walked up Bassett Street towards the cottages and along Langton Terrace to the right, all there was to her left was a solid retaining wall reaching upwards to join the windowless side of the cottage.

The rear garden was long and narrow, only about twenty metres in length and could be reached by way of well-worn steps and another rickety gate. It had once been a neat and well-stocked kitchen garden with potatoes, cabbage, leeks and runner beans, turnips and cauliflower, but was now unkempt, the plants spreading in search of light and soil or overwhelming or strangling their neighbour. It was ideal.

Helen Cave saw no lights as she approached the front of the cottage and nor here at the rear either. The privet hedge between the two cottages was dense although not tall, but, because the garden sloped the street lights in Polwheveral Terrace cast a black shadow across the garden in front of her. It was therefore easy for her to crouch and move undetected up to the rear of the cottage, stepping around the mounds of dripping snow that perched on top of the overgrown and dying plants, into the snow-free dips.

At 1.31am., Helen approached the Rover in Symonds Hill, a wide grin on her face. Faraday, in utter relief, returned the smile.

'If we move off now and go around the corner and stop, I can check if my little bug's working,' she said, clearly pleased with herself. Mark stopped the Rover a little way round the corner. Helen opened the glove compartment and depressed the keys to the security service's channel. Almost immediately a faint but rapid pinging sound could be heard in the speakers.

'That tells us that it's working,' she said.

'Is anyone there?' asked an impatient Faraday.

'If there is then this little baby will tell us. It was easy to get to the back door. No signs of life but I've stuck a bug onto the frosted window of the toilet on the ground floor. There are no downpipes other than those from the roof guttering, so I'm pretty sure it's the only toilet in the place, which seems to be all part of a new ground floor toilet and bathroom extension. If they're in there, when they use the toilet we'll hear it. It will sound like the Niagara Falls,' she said laughing. Then they both laughed, the laughter of relief, then he kissed her upon her temple.

Helen Cave turned and kissed him, very gently. She gave him that special smile as she pressed her forefinger to his lips, then dialled out on the cellnet phone.

'This is Delta One Seven Alpha,' she said. 'I believe the square and round packages may have been delivered to ... ,' she paused momentarily as she checked the unique codified reference pin-pointing within eight feet the location of 3 Beacon Cottage, ... '0510.0227. We have posted a letter and await a response. Have you any news of our other deliveries?'

'Affirmative, Delta One Seven Alpha, two parcels en route for early morning delivery, ETA 2½ hours.'

'We'll wait at Papa Two Two. Thank you.'

Cave slipped the mobile into her jacket pocket and looked at Faraday. 'Some of my colleagues will be with us just after four. I think we can risk trying to get some rest and also something to eat,' she said, 'there should be a dockside café around here somewhere.'

***

Two teams had arrived at half past four and were now gathered in a rather dull, grey-painted room overlooking the dockside cranes. The action team's leader, Mike Jackman, had been briefed by Cave.

From this room they were able to monitor, as they ate their bacon sandwiches and talked, any activities from within Beacon Cottage, but there was none.

At 07.45, Cave put down another mug of steaming tea and addressed the remaining members of the team. She had washed and tidied her hair, but she and the policeman both looked tired and drawn.

'Well, we've kicked this around and we are fast approaching the time when we'll have to take a look-see,' she said with easy authority. 'There doesn't appear to be any movement within and Andrew's team have not detected anyone else keeping obs on the cottage or any other bugs. That doesn't mean there aren't any.' This remark brought knowing nods from the others. 'Colin has worked his way up the street posting his double-glazing leaflets and we now know that the cottage has an old, well-worn Yale at the front and the new back door is even easier. We have the green light from 907 who have informed the local chief constable.' She turned to the maps and plans clipped to a board. 'As discussed, Colin and I will take the rear; David and Bob in support in Langton Terrace here. You, Ron, will take the front with Mike; Tony and Steve as support in the van.' She turned to the policeman and said a little formally, 'I suspect you would like to come along, Mark. Would you care to go with Tony and Steve?'

'Of course,' Mark replied simply.

'You are most welcome but can I ask you to remain in the van at all times unless I call you,' she said politely but in such a way that Faraday was reminded of the likely risks of his getting in the way.

'I shan't get in the way.'

'Everyone happy?' she asked looking at each member in turn. There were eager nods in reply. 'Let's get Colin on the air. It's now 07:52. Simultaneously front and rear at 08:55.'

At 08.49am, the grey-liveried British Telecom Sherpa van parked in Bassett Street. Ron got out of the driver's seat and stood by the van looking up and down the road, seemingly checking a work sheet with Mike who had joined him from the front passenger seat. They both went to the rear of the van and collected their tool kits and closed the doors. They did not lock them. Tony, Steve and Chief Inspector Faraday remained inside as Ron and Mike strode up the road towards the cottage.

At 8.51, an old brown-coloured Bedford van pulled into the kerb at Langton Terrace adjacent to the steps leading to the rear of Beacon Cottage. The van was rusty and battered, the engine smooth and well-tuned, the words 'Bateman and Sons, General Maintenance' had mostly peeled off the sides. Helen and Colin, wearing overalls and grimy baseball caps, likewise opened the rear doors of this vehicle, removed the tool bags of their trade and walked up the soggy garden path to the rear of the cottage.

At 08.54, Ron was at the front door and pretended to press the front door bell whilst inserting a master key. The door silently opened to his turn. He pushed the door ajar and mimicked a conversation with an unseen occupant and then he and Mike were in, crouching in the hallway, their FN 9mm pistols grasped in both hands, tense, listening, sensing their surroundings. They were motionless, covering the hall, lounge door and staircase as they heard Helen and Colin forcing the rear glazed door, the screws of the cheap bolt springing out and glass rattling noisily in the frame as the door swung open against the wall.

Helen and Colin moved swiftly in well co-ordinated silence, one checking the toilet, the other covering; one checking the shower unit, the other covering. They entered the lounge. For a moment their rhythm checked as they saw two bodies, one crumpled on the floor, the other grotesquely seated in the chair against the dying embers of the fire. They moved swiftly, covering, checking; covering, checking, and cleared the lounge.

As they entered the hall they donned their CT-12 respirators, an almost indiscernible acknowledgement to Ron and Mike as they hit the stairs, Colin first to the dog-leg landing, then Helen, mounting the stairs to pass her colleague who had already lobbed the gas grenade onto the upper landing, the incapacitating fumes drifting like skeletal hands through the bedroom doors.

As Mike took the stairs to the dog-leg, Colin bounded to the upper landing and, as they did so, the under-stairs cupboard door latch quivered in response to their heavy movements on the stairs, then the cupboard door swung open and a bound body fell out backwards onto the floor to roll and face Ron's trained gun.

Once the top floor was declared clear came the task of checking the bodies. Faraday remained in the hallway as Colin, Ron, Tony, Steve and Helen assembled in the lounge. They began the gruesome task. As Helen began allocating tasks, she saw Mark staring at her. He smiled and nodded, thankful that she was safe and, just for a second, she winked at him and smiled that smile again.

They photographed every room, from all possible angles, plans were drawn then the task of identification commenced.

Dolan was quickly recognised, all clothing stripped, bagged and tagged, as were the contents of his pockets. Then the corpse itself was bagged and contorted so as to fit inside the packing cases, brought in from the old Bedford van and identical to those used during any domestic re-locations.

Once photographed, the plastic bag was pulled from the face of the collector of fish and chips and the paracord cut so as to release him from the wooden chair. The teams worked expertly and quickly, noting, photographing, stripping, noting, photographing and bagging.

'This will interest you, Helen,' said Colin, holding up the MI6 ID card for inspection. Cave and Faraday read the authorisation.

'Do you know this guy from Z Department?' Faraday asked.

'Peter Bridgeman. No,' she responded with a frown, 'but Z Department is the one attached to the Department of Trade and Industry.'

Undeterred by this development, the methodical process continued, bodies were stripped, items logged, then all placed into packing cases. The body in the hallway, however, could not be identified with certainty; the shot in the left ear had removed the right-hand side of the face but from the identity card discarded under the stairs it could be assumed to be that of Michael Preston of MI6 (Z).

Gradually the teams returned to their vans and drove back to the dull, grey-painted room overlooking the dockside cranes, their presence replaced at number 3 Beacon Cottage by 'after care' services, those people responsible for clearance, cleansing and restoration work.

Chapter 22

Monday 26th November.

Bristol, England.

CHIEF INSPECTOR Mark Faraday's Sandstone-coloured Volvo cruised along the meandering Coombe Lane, past the university's sports ground and the up-market detached homes. As the road levelled out he picked up speed, the fallen autumn leaves swirling around behind his car clearly visible as he checked his mirrors again before slowing to a stop immediately opposite the dismal entrance. When the on-coming traffic had passed, Mark pulled across the road and drove through the open, black wrought-iron gates and drew to a halt outside the lodge keeper's house. He checked the notice board, white letters neatly painted on a black background: 'Gates will be closed at 4.30pm. daily'.

A few people were walking along the neat avenues amongst the trees, couples and small groups, mostly heads bowed in thought. The miniature traffic lights, hidden discretely in the nearby tree, had been switched off, but tomorrow these little lights would regulate the hearses, each mourning family allocated their twenty minutes, if they were lucky, maybe a little longer. But, as the year drew to a close and the colder weather took its toll, twenty minutes for each funeral was all that could be allocated at this municipal crematorium.

Whilst twenty minutes would have to suffice for most, Faraday had at least been able to arrange for the funeral of Carl Norris to take place immediately before the lunchtime break. As a result, mourners at the previous funeral would have time to disperse before the arrival of Constable Norris' cortege and it would allow the police the freedom to mount a discreet parade without causing inconvenience to others.

In the cold afternoon sun, he drove slowly along the silver birch-lined driveway of Canford Cemetery, as the Chief Constable's car would the next day as it led the hearse to the crematorium chapel. He was unable to see Sergeant Bullock at the far end of the drive, but he knew he would be there, out of view, with the six constables. He drove slowly on, past a tiny old lady muffled against the chilly air seated alone on a bench deep in private thought. Ninety metres on and he reached the red brick crematorium chapel. He did not stop but continued on a further fifty metres to the old granite chapel at the edge of the cemetery. As he parked the Volvo, a very large Sergeant Bullock strode smartly forward, as one would have expected of a former Coldstream Guardsman.

Bullock opened Mark's car door and threw up a perfect salute. Mark liked Sergeant Bullock, he was reliable and it was reassuring to see a friendly face. He smiled to himself as he looked at the young officers and thought of their rehearsal for Carl Norris' funeral. That was the irony of it all. After such a short life, an even shorter time to say good-bye.

'Good afternoon, sir. Everyone present and correct,' the sergeant said and then looking towards a sombre-looking civilian added, 'You know Mr Scrivens, sir, the undertaker.'

Scrivens moved forward. 'Good afternoon, Chief Inspector. A sad occasion indeed, sir.'

They shook hands as Faraday replied: 'It's very kind of you to allow us the opportunity to practice, Mr Scrivens. Thank God we don't have the need to do this dreadful business very often.'

'That is the least that Scrivens, Copeland and Peach can do, sir,' he replied, head bobbing up and down. 'Always willing to assist the constabulary in any way.'

Faraday turned to Bullock. 'They look pretty downcast, Jim,' he said.

'They are a bit, sir. We've been practising in the gym with one of those long benches, but now they're here … well, they'll be alright, once they get into it.'

They checked their watches and discussed the time which allowed them forty minutes, so the rehearsal started immediately, the sergeant reproaching one of the young constables. 'No white gloves, no white gloves! What do you mean reporting for duty here with no white gloves?'

'Left them in my locker, Sergeant,' the young constable replied.

'Oh, left them in my locker did you,' he said in mock amazement. 'I see. So this practice is going to take place in your locker, is it? The next thing is you'll be wearing carpet slippers!' The sergeant paused, and leaning forward stared at each anxious constable in turn. 'Is anyone wearing slippers?' he questioned in a grave but humorous tone.

'No, Sergeant,' they replied in unison and grinning. Ice broken a little thought Faraday.

Bullock directed the constables to the rear of the beautifully polished black hearse as Scrivens whispered to Faraday from behind a gloved hand. 'The coffin is weighted, sir. The appropriate weight of course'.

'That was thoughtful of you Mr Scrivens', Faraday said turning to the assembled constables. 'OK, gentlemen, your attention please.' He waited until they were quiet. 'Today is not a test. Nor is today a time for sadness because your job is not to be sad. Your job is to get a long heavy box up some steps, through a narrow door and into a building without tripping over or dropping it and to do exactly the same on the way out. If we allow emotions to take over, we all foul up. OK?' They all nodded as Faraday continued. 'Coffins were not designed for your comfort. Coffins are heavy and have sharp edges that become sharper with every step you take. Coffins dig into your shoulders, so Sergeant Bullock will provide you with little pads to go between your shirt and your tunic. What you are now going to do is practice taking the coffin out of the hearse, placing it on your shoulders, turning and getting it up over a few steps. In this case, three,' he said pointing to the old chapel door, 'but tomorrow at the crematorium chapel, there will only be two. So, tomorrow it will be easier. You must look upon this as an exercise, nothing more, nothing less, maybe like the leadership exercises you did as recruits, you know, getting the barrels across a river. If you start thinking about who is in the coffin, how he got there, you will make mistakes. Mistakes are not what Mrs Norris wants and, tomorrow, Mrs Norris is my *only* concern. We get one shot at this; we can't ask the priest to stop whilst we have another go. Do we understand where *your* focus *has* to be?'

'Yes, sir,' they all replied, then the dry runs began.

Sergeant Bullock was in his element sorting the constables into position to receive the coffin from the hearse, then lift it upon their shoulders.

Faraday stepped away, allowing the constables to fumble, then struggle with the strange weight and shape. He walked amongst the graves for a while, the graves of the Warners and Huntleys, the

Hudsons and Mellors. He glanced up to see the coffin bearers trudge forward to execute the right turn. The Warner's headstone told the story of an infant lost, the Huntley's of a wife re-united with her husband, the Hudsons of a family once again gathered together after so many years apart. He looked back towards the old chapel; the bearer party was beginning to move more confidently as they rehearsed each stage, Bullock patiently directing his little team, whilst Scrivens stood impassively. The tricky part would be carrying the coffin draped in the Union flag, but Faraday need not have worried. Bullock handled it with his usual flair. At one stage the constables rather unceremoniously bundled the coffin back into the gapping rear of the hearse, glad to have some relief from the weight, and let it roll forward until hitting the stops with a loud bump. They all looked at each other sheepishly, sharing the blame, awaiting censure, but Bullock ignored their clumsiness.

'Have any of you tried to lift your grandmother's dinning room table with the table cloth still on it?' the sergeant asked.

'No, Sergeant,' they replied, some with grin, some with grimaces.

'Well, after this little lot, you will be well qualified to do just that,' he said. 'So, get back into your positions and 'urry up.'

They rehearsed each stage, out of the hearse, up the steps, through the door, into the chapel. Then they rehearsed again. At last they were able to perform their role reasonably well. It wasn't faultless, but it would have to do. Faraday and Bullock nodded at each other as the constables lowered the coffin from their shoulders and slid it forward into the hearse – more gently this time.

Sergeant Bullock took care of the Union flag and Scrivens closed down the polished rear door. Faraday thanked them all for their efforts and reassured them.

'Excellent, all of you,' he told them. 'Well done. Now, tomorrow, the important thing to remember is – do ... not ... rush. No one is in a hurry. Sergeant Bullock will be with you. If any of you have a problem tomorrow when you are carrying the coffin, all you have to do is quietly say one word – "sergeant" and Sergeant Bullock will call you to a halt. Once everyone is ready we will just carry on. But, from what I have seen, you will be fine. Well done.' He asked the sergeant if he had any final remark, which Faraday knew he would have.

'Right,' the sergeant said, turning his attention towards the young constables. 'When you get home tonight, you will all need to do lots and lots of practice. You will need to practice in your hallways or, in your case, Baker, your locker.' The constables all began to chuckle. 'Quiet ... and what you will be practising is slow marching. You will all practice so that Mrs Bullock and me will be able to hear your shoe laces creak when we're sat up in bed drinking our 'ot chocolate. Right, I'll see you tomorrow at eleven o'clock sharp, at Central, under the canopy. Any questions?' They had none.

As Faraday drove along the empty tree-lined driveway behind the police crew-bus towards the wrought-iron entrance gates he checked the time: 4.36pm. He apologised to the man at the gate holding a heavy chain and padlock, but the man didn't seem to hear as he dragged the heavy gates closed.

Pulling out into Canford Lane and re-joining the stream of traffic, Mark soon slowed to almost a crawl, then stopped, just one car amongst hundreds in the city's gridlock. There were always inevitable delays from about four o'clock onwards, but today the traffic seemed to be much slower and much heavier than usual. The inboard police radio soon provided the answer for the delay – one non-injury RTA involving three vehicles and a bus on the White Tree roundabout at the junction of Westbury Road and North View. Although Mark was only about a mile from his apartment, an accident at that location, on one of the city's main commuter routes, would mean a frustrating delay. He called Helen on her mobile. She answered in his kitchen.

'Hi,' replied Mark. 'Have you found everything?'

'Yep,' she replied cheerfully. 'But one item's missing. I've checked the bedroom, but no, still missing.'

'What's missing?' he asked, bemused.

'You are,' she replied in that slow, sultry voice.

'Sorry, I'm not thinking,' he said and, still not thinking. 'There's been a bit of an accident.'

Helen's tone changed immediately as she anxiously asked, 'Are you OK?'

'Sorry, sorry,' he quickly answered apologetically. 'I'm fine. Accident ahead and there's a bit of a hold up in the traffic. I'm fine. I'll see you in about thirty minutes I should think.'

'Don't hurry, Mark. You know I'll be here,' she said, then rang off.

It was already dark and in the emptiness of his car he began to lose himself in thoughts that were filled by the sound of her voice and how she spoke, what she said and how she smiled. He realised that he found her an extraordinarily attractive woman, but he also realised that his feelings for her were deeply emotional and not merely an understandable sexual attraction. He had known her for exactly three weeks and now found himself thinking of her continuously.

Faraday was jolted back to reality when the motorist behind Faraday sounded his horn and he realised that the commuter traffic was beginning to move again. He waved an apology as he edged forward. The traffic was moving now, slowly but at least moving. Soon he was able to cross into Great Brockridge and eventually through the narrow un-surfaced Hollymead Lane and on towards Avon View.

As he entered his apartment, the slight aroma of orange, onion and garlic brought a smile to his face. Then Helen Cave appeared in the hallway. She was dressed in a light and dark blue horizontally stripped slash neck sweater which exposed her beautifully neck and a denim mini skirt which showed off her long shapely legs. He realised now what he had known from their first meeting - she would always be impossible to resist.

'Give me one minute,' she said as she disappeared into the kitchen.

He followed her. The creamy carrot and orange soap was simmering and the rump steaks were waiting to be placed into the heated frying pan. Helen adjusted the controls of the Bosch hot plate as he ran his hands around her waist and kissed her neck. She closed her eyes and arched her back as he kissed her neck once again. She turned and gently nibbled his lower lip, their tongues tasting each other.

'Lay … the … table,' she said slowly as they both reluctantly broke away.

She had already prepared the couscous and tomato salad and so Mark laid the table, two places, one candle. He dimmed the lights, stacked a selection of CDs in the player and opened a bottle of Australian Cabernet Sauvignon.

They sat against the French windows and ate their soap and little milk rolls, overlooking the bend in the river below. Their conversation was light and easy as the CD 'Pure Piano' played 'What Does it Mean?'

The soup finished, Helen returned to the kitchen and Mark followed with the dishes. As they waited the twelve minutes for the steaks to cook, they took an almost innocent pleasure in each others' company. When the steaks were cooked she added the oyster, garlic and onion relish and, as they ate, a Phil Collins' CD played: 'Another Day in Paradise', 'Against all Odds', 'In the Air Tonight' and 'Take me Home'.

They sipped the last of the wine as the CD played the track: 'One More Night' and their conversation lessened as they listened to the words. There was a moment's silence when the track finished. 'I need more that just one more night, Mark,' she murmured.

Chapter 23

Tuesday 27th November.

Bristol and London, England.

TODAY CANFORD Cemetery would be different. The coffin would not be empty, nor would the pews. Officers would crowd in the aisles and around the doors once the service had begun. There would be inconsolable grief, there would be tears and there would be anger.

'OK?' asked Mark as he peered into the DCI's office.

'Two minutes,' replied the overburdened detective surrounded by case files.

'We'll be out the front,' said Faraday, as he walked off down the corridor with Helen Cave.

As Mark's car turned onto the road from the station garage, DCI Wills was already on the pavement clipping on a black tie. As he got into the car he acknowledged Helen seated in the rear, severe in a black suit and hat.

'Sorry, Mark,' said the detective, 'we're not too late are we?'

'No, I'm just agitated that's all. I'll be fine once we are there and I know everything organisationally is spot on,' he replied. 'How did it go this morning at Clevedon?'

'We've closed down the scene. Nothing more to do there but the PM's thrown the spanner in the works.'

'What do you mean, I thought this was a straight forward accidental death?'

'Not now it isn't,' replied Wills. 'What we thought was an old drunken man falling into the sea is now probably the murder of an old man. No sea water in the lungs.'

'No heart attack before he entered the water?' asked Mark as they drove up Park Street.

'No heart attack before he fell in. No. The doc says he was suffocated. There are marks on him where he's probably been in the boot of a car, then pulled out, something like that.'

'Is this one ours?' asked Faraday.

'Sorry, this one's ours, Mark. He lived in the "Sally Ann" at St Werburghs and washed ashore near Clevedon,' he replied, referring to the little, rather quaint Victorian town on the Severn Estuary coast a few miles south of Bristol. 'Nothing on him, but fingerprints confirm him as Arthur Palmer. Had a few pre cons for fighting and drunkenness. The Salvation Army rang in to report him missing.'

'Since when?'

'Saturday night. Sad really,' said the DCI who was still fiddling with the black clip-on tie, 'after all he went through in World War Two. We might never have found him of course, usually bodies are swept completely away, but you know what the currents are like, they swirl about. Left him tangled up in the supports of Clevedon Pier.'

'What could he have been doing there?'

'Dunno. No reason for him to be there. I had assumed he'd been drinking and fell in at Clevedon, or further down, or even across on the Welsh coast, but no. From enquiries it is clear that he always kept to pubs around the city docks, it's where he spent his days, wandering about, talking to the boat owners. Harmless old bugger apparently.'

'Couldn't he have fallen into the city docks and been taken out to sea when the lock gates open?' Helen Cave suggested.

'If he did, it would be the first time,' replied the DCI, then added quickly: 'Sorry, that was rude. What I meant to say was that bodies usually drift ashore on the twisting river bank a long time before they reach the sea. Those that have reached the sea have done so after weeks, bobbing about, drifting onto the banks to float off unseen later on. But carried down to the sea in a couple of days, I doubt it.'

'Any relatives?' asked Faraday.

'No.'

'You said he did something during the war?' Faraday prompted.

'Yes. Bit of a hero apparently. He was in the raid on St Nazaire. 1942. Awarded the Distinguished Conduct Medal. Corporal or sergeant,' the DCI said, then checking his pocketbook corrected himself, 'No, a corporal in the Somerset Light Infantry attached to 2 Commando.'

That's when HMS *Campbeltown* rammed the lock gates and the Germans couldn't use the docks for the rest of the war,' Mark recalled.

'The gates weren't repaired for another forty years,' said Helen.

'What was his involvement?' Faraday asked.

'Not too sure,' the detective replied. 'But there were some photos in his room, with his war-time mates, and with his boat, a civvy boat, pressed into service. He had a model of it in a glass case. A *Fairmile,* a beautiful thing, just right for cruising about in when I retire. But in 1942 it was different. According to the hostel's warden, there were dozens of those sorts of boats that went in with the *Campbeltown*, all bristling with guns, attacking targets, landing commandos. Made Jerry hop about a bit.'

The two police officers and the MI5 agent arrived and parked in Canford Lane. All three walked through the gates into the cemetery, the detective in dark lounge suit and Faraday in uniform greatcoat. Helen Cave had dressed sombrely, but even so, she attracted immediate attention in her black double-breasted, full-length cashmere coat with military-styled collar buttoned high at the neck. She wore a very plain black Spanish *Cordobes* hat that gave her a commanding elegance. Acting Chief Inspector Passmore and Inspector Eastfield were already there as were others, assembled as discreetly as possible so as not to cause possible offence or disturb the tranquillity of the funerals of others.

Mark left the arrangements to Eastfield, taking the opportunity to speak to members of Norris' shift, exchanging conversation with a councillor and a member of the Police Authority, acknowledging the presence of representatives of the local fire brigade and ambulance service. More and more uniformed officers appeared and he did not at first see Superintendent Wynne-Thomas and Inspector Stacey, standing together. When he did, he went smartly up to them. There was an exchange of salutes but there was a coldness about them both.

'Good afternoon, sir,' said Mark.

'Where do you want me to stand?' asked Wynne-Thomas gruffly.

'You will find that there is a place for you near the main doors. As the motorcyclists approach, Mr Eastfield will call everyone to attention. You should remain at the salute as the hearse approaches and the coffin taken out. The chief will lead the coffin in; the family will follow immediately behind. You should then make your way to a seat reserved for you in the fourth row on the right.'

'So, everything's in order then?' he said with a malevolent sneer.

Mark's thoughts were on the funeral arrangements and the short service to come and so did not notice the malice in his voice.

'I believe so, sir.'

'You might believe everything is well in hand, Faraday, but I don't, not when one of my men is killed due to your incompetence. He was far too young, too inexperienced, to have been put on observation duties of that kind. If I had been here, I would never have sanctioned it,' said the Welshman.

'Well, you weren't here. And I don't think this is an appropriate time or the place to discuss it,' said Mark saluting. 'If you will excuse me.'

Mark was thankful when the service had ended and he drove back to the station with Cave and Wills. It was difficult to be removed from the emotion, the sadness and grief. It was heartbreaking to see Mrs Norris. At first there had been a resigned sadness and composure, but as the service progressed and the priest, then the chief constable, said their words, her mother's pride was replaced by an almost silent and numbed expressionless weeping that seemed not to end. Mark knew enough to know that all her adult life had been devoted to her family. It had not been easy, particularly since her husband's death. Then shortly after there were riots and public enquiries, but her Christian faith had strengthened her. She had not wanted her son to join the police, she knew it would not be an easy road for him, but Carl was determined and she had been equally determined to support her son. When the bands had played and the flags had fluttered at his recruit passing-out parade, she had been so proud. One black face. Now her life was empty, an emptiness only to be filled by lonely sorrow.

They drove back to The Grove. Even the gregarious Peter Wills was quiet.

Jane had anticipated their return and had laid out coffee for three, but Faraday and Cave drank alone, a subdued Wills returning to his office as soon as they had parked.

Whilst Helen played absentmindedly with the computer, Faraday fiddled distractedly with papers on his desk, moving one file to a little heap, only to move it on to another. It was difficult to concentrate on anything.

Helen, of course, was not so intimately affected by the funeral, but it was impossible not to be moved by the service, and out of concern for Mark she too remained quiet. She knew how he was hurting and so she hurt too. She pressed the keys and scanned the screen almost robotically, mesmerised by the constant stream of details of vessels entering or leaving the city docks and Royal Edward, Avonmouth or Royal Portbury docks. The details were greater than she had imagined, mostly light pleasure craft on weekend excursions, just for a few pleasant hours and a few more nautical miles in the owner's log.

She depressed a cursor bank key and the boat's name reappeared again.

'She was observed at 21:04, passing the Avonmouth signal station on return passage to the city docks,' mumbled Helen Cave to herself as she turned to grab a pad. She depressed the cursor again, then again and stopped.

'There she is, leaving Avonmouth at 10:13 on passage to Lundy,' she muttered again, then cross-referenced with the register.

'Mark, I think we have something here.'

Faraday got up from behind his desk with little enthusiasm. 'What is it?' he asked.

'Come and have a look-see,' she said, sitting back in her chair, still trying to comprehend the significance of what she had read.

She pushed the screen around slightly so that Mark could see more clearly.

'This vessel here,' she said, pointing to the screen, 'the *Gay Dawn*, goes out from Bristol just after 10 o'clock on Saturday morning, en route to Lundy Island. That evening,' she continued, as data ran up the screen, 'at 21:04, she returns.'

'Yes, go on,' Faraday said, 'I'm not sure I'm with you.'

'Well, we think the old war hero was killed during the Saturday don't we?'

'Saturday or early Sunday,' he replied, 'they haven't been able to be more precise.'

'What vessel did your DCI say that the old man had served upon?'
'I think it was a *Fairchild* or something like that.'

'No. No, it was a *Fairmile*, Mark. I'm sure he said it was a *Fairmile*,' she said, her face determined as she scanned the screen. 'And the *Gay Dawn* is a *Fairmile*.'

'Are you sure?'

'Yes,' replied Helen as she pressed more keys. 'It is confirmed with the harbour master's register of vessels moored in the city docks.'

The screen had rapidly filled with lists of vessels. *Gay Dawn* was highlighted, and alongside the entry appeared: '*Fairmile* motor launch, former "B" class boat of the 28th Motor Launch Flotilla, Coastal Forces, decommissioned 1944; 112' by 19'6"; two 650hp Hall-Scott petrol engines, max speed 18 knots. Owner: Andrew Harvey Leach, Dymchurch, Kent.'

Faraday's stomach tensed, a strange all-consuming apprehension seized him, something that had never occurred in his life before, as if he was in close communion with an evil beyond his control.

'Why should anyone want to suffocate an old man who lived in a Salvation Army hostel,' pondered Faraday, 'then take him out to sea? There were no apparent injuries consistent with a struggle or a brawl. He wasn't mugged.'

'This may just be coincidence, but it's worth looking into, Mark,' said Cave. 'On the other hand, it may be nothing. After all he was just another old drunk.'

'He wasn't born a drunk, Helen,' snapped Faraday.

'I didn't mean it like that, Mark,' she said genuinely. 'I'm sorry. Of course, there may be a connection.'

Faraday walked to the window and looked out across the harbour. 'No, it's me who should be sorry, Helen. I didn't mean to snap at you.'

She was already beside him. He felt her fingers entwine with his. He turned to face her and kissed her on her lips. 'I'm sorry,' she said. 'I don't want anything to come between us.'

'Nothing will come between us,' he said and they kissed again. For a few more moments they looked out upon the harbour scene, the inky-blue water lazily slapping against the bobbing craft, Mark deep in thought. Then he spoke again: 'If the old man had been involved in a fight, if he had been mugged, the likelihood is that his assailants would have just left him were he was. Maybe I'm imagining things but this old man was suffocated, not straggled, not beaten, not stabbed. He was suffocated. He was taken out to sea, or at least driven fifteen miles to Clevedon. No, it doesn't take a great detective to speculate within acceptable accuracy about what happened,' Mark continued. 'Suppose the old man, seeing the *Fairmile* which held such strong memories for him, clambers abroad, an old man reliving those exciting and dangerous days of 1942, his dreamings disturbed by Hancock returning from Falmouth. By then he's seen too much. Maybe Hancock offered him a cup of tea, the old man accepting, grateful to reminisce with a kindred spirit, then Hancock put a coat or something tightly over the poor sod's head, took him out to sea and dumped him overboard into the Severn. With the second highest tidal range in the world, he shouldn't have been found for weeks.'

'Maybe murdered with a plastic bag like O'Brien and the MI6 agent,' Helen said. 'According to the records, *Gay Dawn* is still berthed in the marina just below the SS *Great Britain*.'

'We want reliable teams for observations on her, the whole length of the river, and the coast,' the policeman said decisively. 'Get *your* people or the military, Helen. Get them to do it. As soon as they can.'

***

The MI6 man, Colin Sutton, strode across the entrance salon, leaving behind the bitter, evening cold. As normal, he ignored the doorman, entered The Colours and made his way to his usual place in the corner of the drawing room of Blacketts, gesturing to a footman for attention. As he reached the leather Chesterfield, Brigadier Midford silently approached from the library and faced Sutton.

'It's quite alright,' said Midford to the footman who was now standing obediently at the Chesterfield, 'Mr Sutton will not be needing a drink, he will be leaving directly to have a jolly time with us.'

Panic gripped Sutton, whose immediate instinct was to run. He turned and was about to go but saw an ominous figure silhouetted in the doorway wearing a trench coat. He stopped and turned on the soldier.

'This is my club. You are not a member. What in the devil do you think you're doing here?'

'More to the point, old boy, it's what you've been doing that is of interest to me. You know who I am, as you do Colonel Sullivan over there in the doorway. You will come with us.'

'You can't arrest me. You have no jurisdiction at all,' blustered Sutton.

'Don't be an ass,' Midford replied calmly, 'you know how we work. At the moment this is an internal matter, so, we need no powers of arrest, no warrant, we just need *you*. Now,' he continued as he leaned forward and spoke more sharply in Sutton's left ear, 'walk with me in a dignified manner to the black Rover that's parked outside, or a rather large and brutish staff sergeant will bounce you painfully down the bloody stairs.'

The journey lasted for just over an hour and a half. No secret was made of where they were going. Sutton could guess. He asked questions but received no reply. The only voice was his.

'You can be holier than thou if you like,' he said, 'but you know something had to be done. There were greater stakes involved, our continuing and profitable relationship with the United States, the global benefits. If I hadn't taken the initiative, just think what could have happened.'

They did not answer his questions nor respond to his remarks. Sutton fell silent, preoccupied with his imaginings of what lay ahead as the car sped on through the black winter's night.

The Rover had been expected and did not reduce its speed as it rumbled across the narrow stone bridge and passed under the granite archway that was the entrance to the barracks, skirting the guard house, kitchens and maintenance sheds. It drove on alongside the perimeter fence, past the officers' mess and onto the rain-swept causeway to the distant and isolated blockhouse.

Staff Sergeant Collins drove into the very small courtyard and expertly parked the car adjacent to the main entrance door. He stepped out into the howling wind and sound of the pounding North Sea. He thumped on the wooden door and at the same time opened the rear door of the car. Simultaneously, one half of the blockhouse door opened to admit its latest guests.

The air was cold and dank within, the granite walls grim grey. The only illumination was provided by light bulbs encased in wire mesh, dangling from their own power line, trailing from the entrance, down through a further archway, to a lower level, which, in times past had been the gun room for the old cannons, the yawning gun ports now bricked up against the winter seas.

Sutton followed the staff sergeant, through another doorway into a wooden floored corridor, well lit by orthodox ceiling lights, but still austere, a corridor of grey painted walls and brown heartless doors.

In front of him doors opened and closed, footsteps marched on, then they entered a room, empty save for one chair and one trestle table. Sutton turned to protest, but to his astonishment Brigadier Midford and Colonel Sullivan had been replaced by two equally po-faced corporals. The staff sergeant spoke. 'Be a good sir and empty out your pockets. Place everything on the table.'

'I demand to speak to your superiors,' Sutton said angrily.

'Do you now,' said the staff sergeant, breathing stale breath into Sutton's face. 'Well, no one can 'ear you down 'ere. No one, except me and the corporals.'

Once Colin Sutton had emptied out his pockets and his tie, braces and shoe laces had been removed, he was left alone. As the door slammed shut he called after them.

'They'll have to carry through my plans,' he shouted, then added with a sneer, 'they have no choice, the smug bastards. And they know it.'

Chapter 24

Thursday 29th November & Friday 30th November.

London & Bristol, England.

COLONEL RICHARD Sullivan of Military Intelligence and David Reed of MI5 looked out from the fourth floor window and down upon a sunlit Horse Guards Parade. Sullivan smoothed his moustache with his knuckles, deep in thought, as his eyes followed Helen Cave who was walking towards St James's Park. As she approached the grey Rover parked alongside the Guards' Memorial, a tall man got out of the front passenger seat. They spoke for a few moments, then both got into the car and drove away.

Sullivan turned from the large, tall window with his companion and resumed his favourite place in front of the fire, retrieving his half-finished cup of coffee.

'Tall chap must have been Faraday, I suppose,' the colonel said. 'Yes, think you must be right,' replied David Reed.

'Seems to have worked out better than we had hoped,' Sullivan continued. 'At least we know where Hancock is. Pity we don't know if he's still got the mines and things with him or whether he's already planted them. Still,' he said as if consoling himself, 'we know where he is.' Then added in a self-congratulatory tone, 'Tremendous advance since last week, and all down to Cave and Faraday. Very pleased with their work.'

He returned the cup and saucer to the small occasional table.

'We were very lucky, Richard,' said Reed. 'If Sutton's foolish initiative hadn't have been discovered, the security services would have looked worse than complete blunderers. Sutton is bloody fortunate to have been transferred and given that South American posting.'

'I'm not too sure that Ecuador will prove to be an attractive posting for him, David,' replied the colonel with an ill-disguised spiteful chuckle.

'The trouble is,' reflected Sullivan, 'Sutton's little scheme with the Americans wasn't too bad. Lacked refinement of course, but still basically sound. Anyway, not to worry, we still have a little time left to develop his scheme. We'll have to arrange for the cleaning company's clothes and the identification card to be conveniently discovered at Beacon Cottage once this Hancock business is out of the way. Then Special Facilities Branch can get Dolan out of the fridge and arrange for him to be killed all over again in a shoot-out somewhere.'

'Northern Ireland would be best, don't you think?' mused Reed.

'Yes, yes, I think so,' Sullivan replied reflectively. 'Yes, Ireland it is. Best all round, much neater,' he said, clearly pleased with himself. 'The security service would been seen to have succeeded yet again, and the nuclear people will be able to use the Dolan drama as an excuse to reduce output, which is apparently all that is required to stop it all going bang. At least it will provide the Americans with breathing space so that they can dream up a cure. I don't think that should be beyond them. More importantly of course, they will owe us a favour and, at the same time, we keep our finger in the nuclear pie. DTi and British industry should be pleased too.'

'And the chief inspector?' asked Reed.

'Yes, he could so easily be a problem. He's not one of us of course, and the police have this inconvenient inclination to be honest most of the time.' Sullivan remained silent for a moment, considering options, then continued. 'Faraday could always reveal that MI6 were tied-in with Irish terrorists. The DTi's involvement could be surmised of course, and when Dolan pops up again, that policeman will know the true background. On the other hand, the amorous chief inspector has provided us with a rather attractive lever in the form of the alluring Miss Cave.'

There were smiles of mutual congratulation.

'As you said, Richard, very neat and tidy.'

'Absolutely,' replied Sullivan abruptly with a Machiavellian grin. Then dismissing the matter altogether continued: 'Medallion of pork today, I think. Come on David, Miss Cave has already made us late for lunch.'

***

Between 2.30pm. and 5pm., numerous non-descript and quite orthodox looking vehicles passed along St Andrews Road and turned to enter through the gates of the former fertiliser factory.

The site had been vacant for fourteen months and had now taken on a depressing, decayed air with a lazy door swinging back and forth; broken windows abutting the road, smashed by passing youths, and sodden paper and other litter trapped by the wind against the chain linked perimeter fence or tangled in the barbed wire above.

Behind the grime and neglect and 'TO LET' signs, the buildings deeper inside the site were vast and sound. The hanger-like corrugated building, once used to store the raw materials, now gave shelter to a van, two removal lorries, an emergency generator, a catering unit, three grey Rover saloons, a white Volvo police staff car and five dark green 4.6 litre Range Rovers. The dilapidated work's canteen had been rigged for communal feeding; the drying plant was stacked with camp beds and bivi bags; and the board room, denuded of its rosewood conference table, was equipped with trestle tables and transformed into the briefing room. Even the old accounts department was given a new and temporary lease of life as a communication centre, manned jointly by a seven-man team of Special Branch, MI5, Royal Signals and 264 Signals personnel, and linked to an array of communication dishes and antennae bristling form the top of the site's thirty metre high concrete water buffer-tank tower.

Immediately adjacent to the communication centre was a command centre. It was here that the decisions by the security services of the United Kingdom to pre-empt Hadfield's actions, or to act in response to them, would be taken.

If Faraday felt a little superfluous, Frank Simmons, the Deputy Chief Constable certainly did, although Mark at least was able to wander about with Helen, seeing how everything was being set up. But both he and Helen were tired. They were dressed casually in tracks suits, Mark's underneath his navy zip sweat top with hood, Helen's under her hoodless, charcoal-grey track top. Both had started at 5.15am. and now they had to remain for the briefing.

In the middle of the old conference room was a group of ten trestle tables in two rows of five, upon which were large and detailed maps of the city docks and the surrounding coast. Sitting in a horseshoe-shape well back from but around this map, in chairs separated from each other by desks upon which were papers and pens, ashtrays and coffee cups, were members of the ESG, the Executive Sub-Group. Seated were Brigadier Peter Midford of Military Intelligence, Captain James Cleeve of Naval Intelligence, Andrew Longhorn of GCHQ's 'J' Division, Major Timothy Coates of the Special Boat Service and Major Paul Matthews of the 22nd Special Air Service Regiment.

As usual, Chief Superintendent Packham of the Anti-Terrorist Branch, standing at the opening in the horseshoe against a backdrop of portable screens hung with further maps and photographs, had delivered a succinct brief which, whilst clear, remained an anti-climax. The deputy chief constable joined Packham who was rearranging some papers, and guided him to a more discreet corner of the room, whilst brushing off the dust he had collected on his dark blue pin-striped double-breasted suit.

'Thanks for that, Charles. A very useful briefing,' he said.

'Glad to have been of help, sir. There remains of course, plenty of gaps unfortunately.'

'Could be worse; we at least know what he looks like,' the DCC said, pointing towards the artist sketch and photographs. 'And we know the names he has used, although they are false.'

'I had hoped that we might have been able to identify Hancock by now,' said the chief superintendent. 'He has to eat and sleep, but we've discreetly checked hotels, ships' chandlers, boat and sailing clubs, car hire companies, but Hancock's name doesn't crop up.'

'Nor Leach?'

'No, he doesn't exist. Complete blank with our enquiries in Kent. But these enquiries were always likely to have been shots in the dark and the results are not unexpected. We know we are up against a professional who is unlikely to be casual and careless. Yet, he's human, and human beings make mistakes, caused by tiredness, familiarity, weakness and so on. That said, we should have got closer to him by now.'

'I wonder whether you are being too complacent and too cautious, Charles,' the Deputy remarked. 'Show the bloody photos to the media and be damned.'

'Orders from the Joint Intelligence Committee prohibits that I'm afraid. At least we think we know where he is, thus the reason for calling in the army's Long-Term Surveillance Unit.'

'But they have to come over from Ulster and can't be deployed until this evening. In any case, we're not absolutely sure he's on board that bloody boat and, even if he is, we still don't know what he's up to, do we?' said an exasperated Simmons. 'He's apparently left the city docks and gone into a God-forsaken little creek. What's it called?'

Just above Stup Pill, sir. Here it is,' Packham said, pointing at a tiny inlet on the Ordnance Survey map, 'Dyer's Rhine.'

We've got a madman loose with explosives, intending to blow up a nuclear power station, and the sum total of all our efforts is that we believes he's on a boat near Stup Pill,' commented a frustrated DCC. 'Who ever dreamt up a daft name like that? It could only be the English. No wonder the French can't understand us and the Americans think we're quaint. Now the bloody tide's gone out and this nutter's stuck in the mud.'

'If it is him, then I don't believe it would be an error on his part. He's taken the ground there like many sailors have done before moving on.'

'But why?' he snapped.

'We have considered a whole range of options,' replied Packham calmly. 'We have assumed his boat is fully fuelled, so he could go anywhere along the South Wales' coast or all the way down to Land's End. That puts him easily in range of a number of nuclear power stations and, as I said a little earlier, he could possibly use the mines in some way against the sea water inlets that provide the coolant by taking advantage of the tides we get here. The thirteen-odd metre rise and fall could trigger them off, but the boffins haven't quite worked out for what purpose yet.'

'Could he be waiting for an accomplice?'

'He could of course, but we believe he's alone. The only voices our long-range kit and intercepts have picked up so far are domestic radio transmissions and the shipping and weather bulletins.'

'But if push comes to shove,' asked a pessimistic Simmons, 'you are confident that we can take him out before he is able to attack a nuclear station?'

'That in many ways would be the easy bit. The problem remains that we have no idea what he may have already done with the mines or what he intends to do with them,' the chief superintendent said as he took a few paces towards the maps. 'The tide will be in shortly, so he could be on the move then. HMS *Puncher* is here, near Lavernock Point, well out of his radar range. Special Boat Service craft,' said Packham, stabbing his finger at the map as he visualised the 55 knots stealth FTCs, 'are here, here and here, and four, four-man patrols of one of the SAS's Sabre Squadrons are strategically deployed so as to cover the approaches to the power stations.'

The deputy slumped frustratedly onto a canvas camp chair.

'This all looks very good, Charles,' he said gesturing around the room, 'but the bottom line is that we haven't really a bloody clue. We're just guessing. The mines could already be in place and Hancock, or whatever he calls himself, could detonate them remotely.'

'True, but I think we have made some progress and narrowed it down a bit but, as you say, the mines could already be planted and Hancock could set them off later in the New Year. Faraday and Cave,' he continued, 'have a view that it won't be a power station.'

'Why not?' he asked, turning in his little chair and scowling towards the policeman and MI5 agent.

'They think that a power station isn't a soft target at all and it's no secret that the Atomic Energy Authority police are one of the few UK forces that are armed. Cave and Faraday have worked closely together and their hunch is that a power station is just too obvious and too risky for the NIRB or anyone else to attack.'

'I'll be a lot happier when Faraday works a lot less closely with *Miss* Cave and a lot more closely with *me*. It's a bloody scandal that whilst we are full members of the Executive Sub-Group, the police are not members of the Joint Intelligence Committee, but are *invited* along when it suits. Now I have a chief inspector who probably knows more about his bloody operation that I do.'

The deputy chief saw Faraday look at his watch, then check the time against the newly installed wall clock, bright and clean against a grubby, pale-green wall. Simmons checked his own watch. It was 9.20pm. as Mark Faraday and Helen walked towards the door.

'You're not going off yet are you Faraday?' he called.

'Only popping out for a few minutes, sir.'

'No further than five minutes away, Faraday. The tide's on the turn and I want you back here by 10.30 at the latest.'

Faraday and Cave went down the staircase, paint already peeling from the walls. 'What's on your mind, Mark?' she asked.

'We are sat around doing nothing, Helen. I mean, there is nothing to do but wait.' He paused as he reflected, then continued, 'It's the detonators that are bugging me. I just can't see how or why they are going to be used against a power station. If you want to blow up a power station then just plant the bomb and detonate it by means of your mobile. It is much more likely to be something to do with the tides or shipping, so I thought we may as well call in on the chief of the Port of Bristol police. He's been told that "an exercise" is in progress involving elements of the SOCA and local Crime Squads. A courtesy call can't do any harm.'

They walked across the cold factory yard into the former storage building. It was like a great hollow cavern, every footstep echoing and strange shadows cast by the auxiliary lighting, old conveyor belts and hoppers. They used the MI5 car, Mark at the wheel, and drove out over the weighbridge, right into St Andrews Road and, after a short distance, right again through the main entrance to the docks at St Andrews Gate. Mark pulled the car to a halt at the barrier and identified himself to the dock's policeman who waved him through.

The docks' police station was situated a little beyond the main entrance gates to the port. Chief Inspector Chris Bowles was still in his office but, as Faraday and Cave mounted the external stairway to the front door, he was there to greet them, forewarned by the officer at the gate.

'Your lads are on the ball, Chris.'

'Better than jungle drums here, Mark. Come on in, tea's brewing,' he said as he invited them both into his office, the walls of which were adorned with plaques and framed photographs of ships.

'Let me introduce you to a colleague of mine. This is Helen Cave,' Mark said.

'Well, Helen,' replied Chief Inspector Bowles, 'I thought the jungle drums were exaggerating, but they described you perfectly.'

***

Hadfield washed the soup dish and spoon in the galley sink as he waited for the hot milk to boil. He allowed the dish to drain for a few moments then dried it with the tea towel and neatly stowed it away. He poured the hot milk into two small stainless steel thermos flasks and fitted them into the webbing pouches. He checked methodically the equipment he had laid out upon the table, from the one-man storm-proof sleeping bag that he would need during the five hours until the tide turned and brought him back, to the 'brass button' compass and green and brown camouflage sticks.

He was completely prepared, in perfect control of himself – what he would describe as restrained elation. He had mentally absorbed the tide times and Admiralty charts, now he set the detonators for the equivalent of thirty-eight meters below the Ordnance Datum, approximately one mile past the sea wall pumping station. He would prime the mines themselves later, once he had come ashore.

Within *Gay Dawn* there was almost silence, disturbed only by the hum of the radar screen and the slight rubbing squeak as the radar rotated above where Hadfield rested. There were other sounds, the gurgles as rivulets of water made their way across the coastal mud towards the distant ripple of the sea and the squelching below the keel as the light wind moved the *Gay Dawn*. He studied his chronometer, laid his head upon the bunk, and closed his eyes as if asleep.

***

Faraday knew that Home Office police forces often looked down upon the small private forces, but, if his senior officers were not prepared to discuss the operation with Bowles then, from a practical point of view, it was prudent for him to do so. Not, of course, to reveal the exact details, more to emphasise the importance and sensitivity of the 'exercise'. But that was not the only reason for speaking with Chief Inspector Bowles. Faraday knew that the police and security services were uncertain as to Hancock's target, and it was a reasonable assumption that if mines were involved then the port's police might be able to help. Bowles, Cave and Faraday examined the port map and shipping schedules set out on a large table against a window which gave them an aerial and panoramic view of the West Wharf towards the Swash Channel beyond. But this examination took Faraday and Cave no further forward at all.

'I'm not going to embarrass you, Mark. You and I have been friends for too long, way back when you were with the Drug Squad. But I suspect that this "exercise" is actually an operation. If it involves a ship, then it might help if I knew the vessel's last port of call or its cargo or country of registration,' said Bowles, fingering his beard.

'OK, OK,' Faraday conceded. 'I suspect it would be carrying nuclear weapons, nuclear waste, something like that.'

Bowles didn't seemed to be shocked at this revelation. 'We have warships on courtesy calls. Officially, none carries nuclear weapons,' he said, 'but the navy wouldn't tell me if they did. Anyway, no naval ships are due here until next July, and the one that is on station off Lavernock Point,' he said with a wry nautical grin. 'is P291 - HMS *Puncher*. She doesn't carry nuclear anything, but she's very fast, very manoeuvrable and very nasty I shouldn't wonder if anyone was minded to take her on. *Puncher* is, of course, just the sort of vessel for intercepting a shipment of arms. I suppose any vessel could be carrying small amounts of nuclear material and we wouldn't know.'

'You've sparked something off in my mind, Chris,' Faraday said. 'What about nuclear subs, they are going up and down the Irish Sea all the time?'

'You're grasping at straws, Mark. Subs like that never come up the Severn.'

'What about that naval auxiliary that got lost carrying nuclear weapons or something?'

'She was the *Throsk* from Portsmouth, but that was Ca can assure you nothing like that comes anywhere near

'Nuclear waste goes to Newport though,' Faraday said casually.

'Yes, there are five or six ships, specially designed for that work, but they never call here.'

'What if such a ship developed a convenient engine fault, would it not conveniently limp into this port?' suggested Cave.

'Yes, that does happen,' Bowles replied, 'but it just won't happen at the moment with any ship carrying nuclear waste because, since the fiasco with Japan and Greenpeace, no nuclear waste ships are scheduled to berth at Newport until next March at the earliest.'

Faraday looked out through the window and across the docks, just like a small city, he thought, a thousand lights illuminating roads and ships at berth, piers and jetties, elevated conveyors and shunting rail tracks. 'Oh well,' said Faraday, 'I suppose nuclear weapons or waste could be stolen by terrorists, but if nothing like that is shipped through here, then you Chris are unlikely to be the target.'

'But it is,' Chris Bowles said.

'You said that ships never called here,' said a startled Faraday.

'Ships don't, but nuclear waste does.'

'I don't understand,' Faraday said.

'It comes by train in fifty-tonne yellow flasks from Europe en route to the reprocessing plant at Peterstone Wentlooge.'

'ut why should these trains go through your port,' Helen Cave
~d, 'it's not on a direct line?'

'No it's not, Helen, but we have some inconspicuous sidings alongside the river, and as nuclear and chemical trains are prohibited from passing through the River Severn rail tunnel when other trains are on the lines, they have to wait. They wait there, that's all.'

'Oh shit,' said Faraday, his mind racing. 'Let me borrow your phone, Chris.'

Faraday snatched the phone, before Bowles could answer and dialled the Communications Centre at his Force Headquarters.

'Surely,' questioned Faraday as he waited for his call to be answered, 'they could just hold up the train for a short while, why put them into your sidings?'

'There's a lot of passenger and goods traffic you know,' Bowles said, 'and there's more of these flasks coming now from Eastern Europe. The wagons can't be ...'

'This is Chief Inspector Faraday, dig out the Permanent Operational Order on the Severn Tunnel please. Clearance Code 4299,' he said, then turning to Bowles. 'I'm sorry, you were saying?'

Anyway, the wagons will be moving out tomorrow morning at about 5.30.'

Faraday held up his hand to silence Bowles as he spoke to the policeman on the other end of the phone. 'Excellent,' said Faraday. 'Now turn to the back, I think it should be there, a map of the tunnel location and a plan of the tunnel itself.' Faraday drummed his fingers on the desk as he waited, mouthing silently come on, come on'. 'Good,' said Faraday as the officer found the plan. 'Now, tell me, officer, the tunnel is what, four miles long?' checked Faraday.

At the other end of the line the constable thumbed through the document with infuriating slowness until he found the paragraph specifying the length of the Severn rail tunnel as 4 miles and 638 yards in length.

'OK, just over four. Now, does it show how deep down the tunnel goes?'

The constable referred to the scale plans again and became a little confused with the detail.

'Don't worry if you don't understand what it means, just tell me how deep?'

'It's in feet, sir,' said the officer.

'That's OK. Just tell me how many feet,' persisted Faraday calmly.

'It says "154 feet below the Ordnance Datum",' he replied.

'Thank you, officer. I understand that,' said Faraday, then added as casually as he could, 'That was all, just a query. Thank you.' He replaced the received and turned hurriedly to Bowles.

'The sidings, Chris, show me exactly the ones you mean?'

The chief of the ports' police went to the wall map and pointed out the sidings, which ran virtually parallel to the coast, but were obscured inland by warehousing and the massive oil-tank farms.

'Where is … ' said Faraday, then turning to Helen Cave continued, 'what was it called, Stup Pill?'

'Dyer's Rhine,' corrected Cave, 'somewhere near Stup Pill.'

'Just here,' the port's policeman said, pointing to the chart.

'And this?' probed Faraday.

'It's a very narrow service path, Mark. You can't get a vehicle along there. You will need to go out of the docks and drive for a little over four miles and park up here,' he said, tapping the chart, indicating an area overshadowed by old slag heaps.

'Bless you, Chris,' Faraday said through clenched teeth, then added, 'I must ask you to say nothing, Chris. Please take no action.'

As Faraday reached the bottom of the stairs, he turned and looked up at his bearded friend, 'Alert no one, there's no time and I don't want anyone frightened off.'

Faraday drove the Rover to St Andrews Gate, then sharp left along St Andrews Road. He ignored the 40 mph speed limit as he pressed the accelerator pedal to the floor and sped along the 1.2 miles of perfectly straight, but slightly undulating, road. Little traffic was on the road and he had already reached 90 mph as he approached the red traffic signals at the entrance to St George's Industrial Estate to his left. He moved a little further to the right. He could not see any tell-tale lights merging from the left, although an approaching car angrily flashed its headlights at Faraday but he maintained his 'silent approach' - no blues and twos - nor did he slacken his speed as he hammered across the junction.

Meanwhile, Cave sat at his side, head up and alert, checked their firearms in the dark - one round in each chamber.

At the junction of St Andrews Road with Kings Weston Lane, the traffic lights were at green. The Rover's speed was now 102 but, once through the lights, Faraday slowed as they approached the un-manned railway level-crossing, rumbling over the rails, the 17" radials loosing some of their adhesion. But Faraday, in complete control, maintained his speed as the road wound its way to the left then accelerated to take the gentle right bend at 81, dropping his speed to 44 as he negotiated the off-set Cabot Park industrial estate roundabout, entering at six o'clock and exiting at ten, to dip headlights and reduce speed again as they approached the hump-back bridge which crossed over the local freight rail line.

Faraday and Cave were now motoring parallel to the Severn Estuary and the main railway line to the left, beyond which they could clearly see the illuminated Second Severn Crossing Bridge, the pattern of the road bridge's wire ropes appearing like the bright white sails of great phantom boats in the night. But Faraday wasn't distracted. He would need all of his advanced driving skills as he took the next right-hand curve at 77 and, responding to the slight drift, approached the first of two insane ninety-degree left-hand bends. He reduced speed to 26 mph and dropped into second gear to accelerate away, the MacPherson struts, Z-axle suspension and gas-filled dampers taking the immense strain as gravity battle to overcome the surge of power as Faraday accelerated forward again, only to break harshly to meet the next ninety-degree left-hand bend, the ventilated brakes sucking in cool air onto the red hot disks. They approached the next right-hand curve, the camber favouring Faraday as he accelerated rapidly away, now once again parallel to the railway line and the dark unseen coast, his mind, partly on the road, partly on visions of what failure might bring. He imagined the mouth of the Severn rai tunnel belching thick acrid clouds of smoke which would be blown or simply drift in the prevailing winds towards Bristol and Gloucestershire and the Midlands to kill thousands insidiously for years to come. He imagined those innocent people hearing the explosion, opening their windows and doors and staring out into the night, breathing the cold night air and, in so doing, condemning themselves to a slow and hideous death.

Ever alert, Cave spoke for the first time, merely saying, 'Ahead. Left, left at 500.'

'Roger that,' Faraday said as the slag heaps, dark masses against an angry sky, loomed ahead. He reduced speed to stop silently in a grubby lay-by. To their left was a heavy, three-barred aluminium gate, behind which were large granite boulders. In front of the gate was a mass of discarded rubbish. She handed Mark his firearm and then both climbed out of the car, closing the doors silently behind them. They began to pick their way through heaps of sodden old clothes and shoes, burst black plastic bags of cans and bottles, passed old fridges, chests of drawers and a rusty pram to carefully climb through the gate. Skirting the slag heaps, Faraday and Cave made their way alongside a network of thick overgrown raspberry brambles, like dense barbed wire in a 'no-man's land', then crossed a narrow field leading up to an embankment below which, on the far side, was the railway line.

It took Faraday and Cave nearly twenty minutes to reach a point from where they could peer down onto the railway line and the seven nuclear flasks cradled on their wagons, beyond which were the main sea defences. They waited, but there was no movement that they could detect. They could see nothing other than the light of a red signal and the yellow-coloured nuclear flasks scarcely illuminated by a series of dim, track-side lights. Both wondered silently whether his instincts had been right and if they would be in time.

'Up for it?' asked Faraday with an unseen smile.

'Of course,' replied Helen Cave. They pressed on.

***

Hadfield checked his course with the compass in the starglow, two luminous dots, indicating the north, as he counted off the paddle strokes, calculating time and distance, the flooding tide propelling him forward. Nearer and nearer, the navigation buoy and the glow from the red railway signal beyond confirming his course.

Eight hundred metres to go. More strokes, leaning forward, driving down, pulling back, checking the white froth then using the tide race, as the black over-cliff looming up against the moonless night. Then he was there, the canoe grounding roughly on the shingle and mud.

He smelt and saw the sewage overflow protruding from just below the top of the sea defences, like a great gun supported on two spindly metal legs with large concrete boots. He sprang nimbly from his canoe and pulled it further up the bank, securing it by a length of cord to one of the metal legs, then made his way along the rising waterline and darted into a dark gully, climbing upwards in the blackness towards the wire fence on top of the sea defences.

He crouched in front of a concrete fence post amongst the grass, stars his only company. In the darkness he felt again for each of the small mines fixed to his webbing belt. Reassured, he waited listening, then peered forward and there below, about eighty metres away, he could see the eerie yellow-ribbed nuclear flasks only fractionally illuminated by some evenly spaced track-side safety lights. From out at sea the flasks would not be visible, and their presence inland was obscured from public view by an embankment. There were seven flasks, one to each wagon. The wagons were low and long, and the yellow flasks looked quite small in comparison.   The track was deserted; there was no locomotive attached to the wagons, nor where there any rolling stock on the other three tracks.   From his slightly elevated position, Hadfield had a very clear and commanding view of the sidings.

As he looked out across the darkness, he subconsciously ran his fingers over the mines once more. He felt them there – cold and smooth, small but powerful – waiting to play their final part in his plan. After all the careful planning, the stage was now set. He was ready. It was just a matter of crossing the eighty metres of rough ground, then priming the mines and attaching them to the flasks. Confident, he rose up and easily stepped over the fence. As he did so he silhouetted himself against the starry sky and the illuminated bridge behind.

He heard people to his right, but he was not alarmed. He thrust his right hand into his underarm holster and withdrew his SIG semi-automatic. Hadfield was fast, as fast as Faraday who drew his Glock 17. The SIG and the Glock both fired a 9mm round at an identical muzzle velocity. Pistols jerked and two 9mm rounds sped through the air towards their targets at 350m per second, one round hitting the sternum and causing the rib cage to disintegrate, the other round penetrating the right ventricle, destroying the pulmonary veins taking arterial blood to the heart.   Both shots were fatal.

In the otherwise still night, the noise was deafening. Then there was utter silence. Helen Cave looked at Mark Faraday. He was standing there, as she was, slightly crouched, both aiming their fired weapons at were Hadfield had been thrown backwards towards the sea, his hand still gripping the butt of his unfired 9mm pistol. He was hanging there, suspended by his left ankle ensnared in the wire of the fence, his dark crimson blood oozing over the mines strapped to his waist and dripping unseen onto the grass and the dark grey mud below.

Chapter 25

Wednesday 19th December.

Buckingham Palace, London, England.

BRIGADIER PETER Midford and Deputy Assistant Commissioner John Bennett stood a little apart from the others waiting in the left-hand wing of the Picture Gallery. They waited before being called to receive their CBEs from their Queen and talked quietly as the Household Division played a selection from Gilbert and Sullivan. Amongst those assembled in the right-hand wing, waiting to receive either gallantry awards or Membership of the Most Excellent Order of the British Empire, was Superintendent Mark Faraday.

'Just seen Faraday,' said Bennett. 'He seems pleased with his MBE.'

'Yes. Very pleased for him too. A good chap,' replied the Brigadier who glanced about so as to ensure they were not overheard. Satisfied, he continued. 'I don't suppose that it's worked out too badly after all.'

'Are there any loose end?' asked the policeman.

'Always loose ends, John, but none that should cause embarrassment.'

'Rather nice for Charles Packham, of course,' said Bennett.

'Yes. What was the full title?' asked the Brigadier.

'Overseas Police Adviser and Inspector-General of Police, Dependent Territories. Rather grand, don't you think?'

'Yes it is,' remarked Midford, 'and it's always jolly useful, of course. If difficult questions are to be asked about him in the House, the Home Secretary can say that it's all a matter for the Foreign and Commonwealth Office and they in turn can say it's really a matter for the Home Office. That sort of prevarication can go on for years. Very useful.'

'And Sutton?' enquired Bennett.

'Rather odd that. Only been in Quito a few weeks, then gets himself mixed up with some Ecuadorian drug runners,' replied the brigadier in a matter-of-fact tone. 'I always felt that Sutton had a tendency to be a bit of a Walter Mitty you know. Silly chap. Never pays. Keep to the script and it will be alright. Deviate and you end up like he did - dead in a dusty roadside gutter.'

'And the whole business has allowed us legitimately to review security at all nuclear power stations,' observed the policeman.

'Only a prudent and responsible thing to do,' the brigadier replied reasonably.

'And of course, it has necessitated a reduction of output capacity at a time when a few teething problems cropped up,' said Bennett with a smile.

'Precisely,' replied the brigadier.

'And Helen Cave?' Bennett asked.

'Oh yes, the lovely Miss Cave,' the Brigadier said with a twinkle in his eye. 'She did a splendid job of course and, as part of her development, has been posted to the FBI Academy at Quantico out of the way. She wasn't too keen to go by all accounts, but she will be there for a year or two I shouldn't wonder. Bright girl. Will go far.' Midford paused for a moment as the Lord Steward approached, then observed: 'I think we're on, John.'

As both men walked into the Ballroom to meet their sovereign, he added with the twinkle still in his eye: 'Had a sneaking suspicion that maybe Cave and Faraday were getting a little too close, but I was probably wrong.'

'Oh, I'm sure you were, Peter,' replied the policeman with a knowing smile. 'Best not to probe.'

******

The Mark Faraday Collection continues…

The second **Mark Faraday Collection** crime novel

Heartless murder and ruthless self interest

DIE Back

by Richard Allen

WHEN SUPERINTENDENT Mark Faraday defies orders and begins to investigate the disappearance of a local lorry driver, a top secret US and UK intelligence operation, designed to destroy the poppy fields of Afghanistan, is unwittingly undermined.

As Faraday is drawn deeper into the secret world of intelligence, he confronts his own senior officers and foreign law enforcement agencies, cynical self-interest and murder.

From the splendour of the House of Lords and the beauty of the Venetian palazzos to the vastness of the deserts of Western Australia, Mark Faraday relentlessly pursues his investigation, haunted by the murder of one colleague and mesmerised by the beauty of another.

Available as eBook or paperback direct from
www.amazon.com or www.amazon.co.uk

The third *Mark Faraday Collection* crime novel

Treachery casts a long and deadly shadow

Darker than DEATH

by Richard Allen

THE DEATH OF A RESPECTED BRISTOL ARTIST is written-off as the unfortunate consequences of an apparently bungled burglary by an unknown opportunist. But at police headquarters, Superintendent Mark Faraday is not so easily convinced.

As Faraday, with DCI Kay Yin, investigate the death, he begins to uncover a web of betrayal and dishonesty that stretches from the battlefields of the Great War and an abattoir in the small Belgian village of Boesinghe in November 1914 to the very heart of present-day British government and the headquarters of the United Nations in New York, oblivious to the betrayal and dishonesty that stalks him with his own headquarters, where loyalty by many is fleeting and deceit by some corrupting.

Available as eBook or paperback direct from
www.amazon.com or www.amazon.co.uk

Printed in Poland
by Amazon Fulfillment
Poland Sp. z o.o., Wrocław